# Of Birds Crying

# Of Birds Crying
## by Minako Ōba

TRANSLATED BY

MICHIKO N. WILSON & MICHAEL K. WILSON

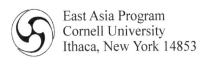

East Asia Program
Cornell University
Ithaca, New York 14853

The Cornell East Asia Series is published by the Cornell University East Asia Program (distinct from Cornell University Press). We publish books on a variety of scholarly topics relating to East Asia as a service to the academic community and the general public. Standing Orders, which provide for automatic notification and invoicing of each title in the series upon publication, are accepted.

   Address submission inquiries to CEAS Editorial Board, East Asia Program, Cornell University, 140 Uris Hall, Ithaca New York 14853-7601.

The *shikishi* calligraphy on the cover is a gift from Minako Ōba to Michiko Wilson.

Number 160 in the Cornell East Asia Series.
New Japanese Horizon Series Editors:
Michiko Wilson/Gustav Heldt/Doug Merwin
Copyright English language translations ©2011 by Michiko N. Wilson and Michael K. Wilson. All rights reserved.
ISSN: 1050-2955
ISBN: 978-1-933947-30-3 hardcover
ISBN: 978-1-933947-60-0 paperback
Library of Congress Control Number: 2011935437
25 24 22 22 21 20 19 18 17 16 15 14 13 12 11       9 8 7 6 5 4 3 2 1

*This translation is for*

*Mary B. McKinley, Mary McConnell,*
*Chieko L. Mulhearn, Becky Thomas,*
*and*
*Edith B. Turner*

# Acknowledgments

I would first like to express my appreciation to Toshio Ōba and Junko Kojima who provided information on some of the obscure expressions and place names that I encountered in the original text; Tomoko Kimura who kept an eye on Japanese newspaper articles by and about Ms. Ōba; Sonja Arntzen for translating the famous classical poems from the *Sankashū* as well as *Tales of Ise* (except the one on page 101); Zjaleh Hajibashi and Robert Hueckstedt for their encouragement; novelist Kenny Marotta who looked over the early drafts and Conan Carey for his resourceful comments and suggestions. I am grateful to Doug Merwin, Gus Heldt, Yōko Arai and Kayoko Hisano for their unwavering support and friendship, especially during the last stages of this project. Gus Heldt kindly made sure that the information on Japan's classical literature in the glossary is accurate. I am also grateful to the two anonymous readers for their comments and the managing editor of Cornell East Asia Series, Mai Shaikhanuar-Cota, who has ensured the safe delivery of this project after a long gestation. I want to thank the University of Virginia's College of Arts and Sciences and the Office of the Vice President for Research and Graduate Studies, which partially funded the publication of this translation. Also, this project would not have been possible without the gracious permission granted by Yū Tani. Finally, Michael K. Wilson shared the arduous yet enlightening translation process of "carrying over" the novel from one language to another.

# Introduction

Minako Ōba (1930–2007), one of the finest writers of modern Japanese literature, published over thirty novels, numerous short stories, literary biographies, essays, and a collection of poetry. Major literary awards given to her work include the Akutagawa and Gunzō prizes (given to new writers), the Joryū Bungaku (Women's Literature), the Tanizaki Junichiro, the Noma Bungei, the Kawabata Yasunari (twice), the Yomiuri Bungaku, and the Murasaki Shikibu Bungaku prizes. A true poet at heart, a painter, and a brilliant cultural critic, she was also the translator of many classical works, most notably the tenth-century masterpiece *The Pillow Book*, which she recast into modern Japanese for the young readers. She also translated children's stories by American writers: "Morris's Disappearing Bag: A Christmas Story" and "Stanley and Rhoda" by Rosemary Wells; "Grandfather and I" by Helen Buckley; "The Story of Noah's Ark" by Elmer Boyd Smith, as well as a nonfiction work, *A Rap on Race,* by James Baldwin and Margaret Mead.

*Of Birds Crying* (Naku tori no, 1985), the recipient of the Noma Bungei Prize, is loosely based on the author's own life, recounting six months in the lives of Yurie Mama and her husband Shōzō. She is a well-established middle-aged novelist and a free spirit; Shōzō has retired early from the life of a "salaryman" (salaried white-collar employee) in order to relish new experiences as a househusband, full-time secretary, cook, and dependent of his wife. Their only child, a daughter Chie, born overseas, has long since left the nest. Although their intellectual interests are poles apart—Shōzō was trained as a chemist—their interactions with each other, often in the form of absurdist repartee, reveal how these differences add spice to life and keep boredom at bay. The main plot of Yurie's unconventional marriage dovetails with three subplots: the stories surrounding her cousin Mizuki, married to a German; her controversial uncle Shigeru, his wife Fukiko and Mizuki's extraordinary mother Fū; and Yurie's Chinese-American friend Lynn Ann and her husband Henry. A fine intermeshing of diverse characters and a probing of the complex workings of their minds reveals the sophistication of Ōba the raconteur at her best.

A tapestry of extraordinary moments expands and interconnects via interior monologues and dialogues ranging from the humorous and farcical to the somber and meditative. Acutely perceptive social and cross-cultural commentaries fill the narrator's voice and the characters' lively conversations. Long-forgotten incidents come back to life, triggered by the sight of an ancient tree, the name of a flower, or the crying of a bird, and memories spawn tales within tales. Despite the fact that the characters' motives for their actions defy prediction, all of these seemingly disparate elements are woven into a coherent whole, a reflection of the interdependency of humanity and nature in its wholeness that is one of the many underlying threads of the story. It is no accident that the names of the three main female characters are taken from nature: Yuri(e) (lily, a nickname used by her close friends), Mizuki (dogwood), and Fuki(ko) (butterbur, a plant whose stalks are considered a delicacy in traditional Japanese cuisine).

Ōba's interests in humanism, clear-eyed realism, anti-romanticism and anti-sentimentalism, were shaped by the most real and surreal event of the twentieth century, the dropping of the atomic bomb on Hiroshima. Forever seared into the mind of the fifteen-year-old Ōba, mobilized along with her schoolmates to provide assistance in the aftermath of the bombing, was the ghastly sight of survivors, barely alive, escaping the scorched air of the leveled city. Out of the ashes of this macabre scene came the spirit of a trickster-artist, not unlike that of Kenzaburo Ōe, a power to penetrate racial, cultural, and gender barriers with her impacable gaze on humankind. Her literary imagination, intellectual acuity, and cross-cultural insight, which enable her to see men and women, society, nature, and the world in their interconnected wholeness have rarely been equaled in modern Japanese literature.

Ōba also draws upon the images of her decidedly unconventional family members and their idiosyncratic lifestyle to create a world imbured with a sense of daringness and free-spirited thinking. Many episodes, real or passed down by word of mouth, in the lives of her progressive-minded grandparents, self-confident, self-assertive aunts, and idiosyncratic parents—whose adoration for each other was scandalous to say the least by prewar Japanese standards—gave the young Ōba not only a voice and a choice to pursue a different life but also an emotional shield against the totalitarian propaganda of the imperial regime under Emperor Hirohito. Inoculated, as it were, against this emperor-centered ideology, she chose to attend one of the most progressive academic institutions in postwar Japan, Tsuda Women's College, and received a four-year liberal arts education, an experience she cherished for the rest of her life. The education provided her respite, affirmation, and an intellectual grounding that would sustain her creatively and spiritually for years to come.

Her marriage to Toshio Ōba in 1955 had also a fortuitous consequence. He was stationed between 1959 and 1971 in the small Alaskan town of Sitka, then famous for its salmon and lumber. This totally unexpected move to a faraway land, a drastic measure by 1950s standards, became a launching pad for Ōba's writing career. The change in habitat also placed her in the vanguard of expatriate housewives during Japan's economic boom (1965–1990). Considering its monolingual culture that left Japanese ill-prepared for assignments in the English-speaking world, most would have considered this move across the Pacific Ocean undue hardship, but to Ōba it came quite naturally—it even felt foreordained. In her own mind, she was following in the footsteps of the founder of her alma mater, Umeko Tsuda (1864–1929). Tsuda, aged six, was the youngest of the five girls who had been sent to the United States as part of the Meiji (1868–1912) government's self-modernization program. She had been away from home for eleven years; Ōba's American odyssey was of exactly the same duration that enabled her to observe Japan literally with an outsider's eye and to hone her cross-cultural perspectives on Japan and the United States.

A life overseas also awakened her long-dormant wanderlust. She crisscrossed the North American continent many times over with her husband and took graduate painting courses and English and American literature classes at the University of Wisconsin and the University of Washington. It was during her eighth year in Sitka that she sat down and wrote the award-winning "The Three Crabs" (Sanbiki no kani, 1967), the first story she ever submitted to a Japanese literary magazine. It became an overnight sensation and won the coveted Akutagawa Prize for best debut short story, garnering praise from the selection committee for its gritty and unsentimental portrayal of a Japanese housewife living abroad, torn between her role as a *shufu* (housewife) and a need to find her own identity.

In 1979 she returned to the United States as a writer-in-residence at the University of Oregon and in the following year participated in the International Writers' Seminar at the invitation of the University of Iowa. In 1987 she became one of the first two women to serve on the Akutagawa Prize Committee, thus ending almost three quarters of a century of all-male membership. She gave a special address at the Rutgers Conference on Japanese Women Writers held at the university in April 1993. She graciously extended her stay to give a public lecture on *The Pillow Book* and other classical works written by Japanese women at the invitation of the University of Virginia's East Asian Center and the Center's long-time benefactors, Jamie and Mary McConnell.

Ōba's works of fiction and nonfiction have been published in *The Collected Works of Ōba Minako* (10 volumes, Kōdansha, 1991). A new twenty-five–volume Nihon Keizai Shimbunsha edition that contains Ōba's complete works is now available. Some of her recent works include: *Kaoru ki no uta—haha to musume no ōfuku shokan* (The Poetry of a Fragrant Tree: Correspondence Between Mother and Daughter, Chūōkōronsha, 1992, a collection of letters); *Nihyaku-nen* (Two Hundred Years, Kōdansha, 1993, a work of fiction); *Yawarakai feminizumu e* (Toward a Pliant Feminism, Seidosha, 1993, a collection of interviews with other female artists and writers); *Mukashi onna ga ita* (Once There Was a Woman, 1994, Shinchōsha, another fictional work); *Motte no hoka* (Out of the Question, Chūōkōronsha, 1995, a collection of short stories); *Kumo o oi* (Chasing the Clouds, 2001, a collection of essays); and the aforementioned *Ōba Minako no Makura no sōshi* (Ōba Minako's The Pillow Book, 2001).

Paralyzed since 1996 by a stroke, Ōba continued to write, dictating her works to her husband. The autobiographical *Tanoshimi no hibi* (Days of Joy, 1999) captures her surrealistic experience as an invalid whose consciousness, in her words, "seems to float in a dream." Ōba's long productive career ended on May 24, 2007, when she died of heart failure. Her unfinished posthumous work, *Shichiriko* (Lake Shichiri), was published by Kōdansha in 2007. More than several of her works have been translated into English, French, German, Russian, as well as Hebrew.

Michiko Niikuni Wilson
Charlottesville

# Of Birds Crying
## by Minako Ōba

# *1* ⁓

YOU SHOULD BE CAREFUL what you say because it might come true.

MIZUKI WAS BUSY PUTTERING around in the cottage garden halfway up Mount Hiei when the telephone rang. The call was from Yurie Mama.

"I was beginning to think you weren't home and was about to hang up—Thank goodness I didn't. I'm in Hikone."

Mizuki was again drawn to the tone and pitch of Yurie's voice, so much like late mother Fū's. The simple knowledge that their likeness as first cousins was nothing extraordinary seemed to hold some mysterious power over Mizuki.

She could not help thinking that she and Yurie had been bonded by karma even before they were born. Or Yurie might be the very stranger with a weird voice who had phoned her repeatedly ever since she and Karl had begun living at Hiei half a year ago. Or perhaps, they had been lifelong friends, drawn and bound to each other by a mysterious, invisible thread. Mizuki, being an only child, sought in Fū's much younger cousin something akin to an elder sister. However, because Yurie is somewhat scatterbrained, I shall always think of her as my little sister, Mizuki said to herself.

Mizuki had started on a translation of one of Yurie's novels without any prospect of a contract to publish it. Since Mizuki had come to Japan with Karl on sabbatical, the two cousins had kept in touch with each other, talking of either Mizuki going to Tokyo or Yurie coming to Kyoto. Now this telephone call from Hikone—at last the time for a reunion.

Week after week Mizuki had endured her cousin's ramblings, which were scarcely more than a series of monologues, half hallucinatory and half fantasy. The cloying and persistent dark shadow that had always hovered around her seemed now to materialize into something almost tangible, as it slowly edged toward her.

"Shōzō's with me. I wonder if we can come over."

"Oh my, I'm delighted. Actually, I'd love you to stay with us tonight. We talk about you all the time. It's our ritual, you know, like a daily cup of tea or bowl of soup. Karl wants to meet you, too."

Seeing Shōzō in the flesh gave Mizuki a shock. Yurie's likeness to Fū notwithstanding, Shōzō, who had no blood ties with Mizuki's late father, was his spitting image. The way he stayed in the background, muttering to himself with his head lowered ever so slightly, nodding with an enigmatic smile on his face while Yurie rattled on, projected both a serenity and implacability that made it difficult to tell whether he was being courageous or cowardly.

"Can your husband speak Japanese? His God-awful German 'R' on the phone jars my ears." Yurie did not waste a moment. "Daily conversations are okay, but with you and Shōzō, we'll probably have to stick to English," said Mizuki,

It had been twenty years since the Mamas came to visit Mizuki during one of their trips across the United States; she had still been in graduate school, debating whether she should marry Karl.

"My goodness, you've put on weight, Yuri, you're looking more and more like my mother."

"I know. We were often mistaken for sisters. She suddenly gained weight after Seiichiro died, but her height saved her. I'll probably end up looking like a Bodhidharma doll. This guy calls me piggycat," said Yurie, thrusting her chin at Shōzō and sneering. "What does that mean?"

Mizuki thought she had gotten used to Yurie's way of talking on the phone, but hearing the actual voice and having the person right in front of her threw her off completely.

Shōzō coughed—ahem, ahem, stretching out his neck, as if he had a scratchy throat. This is how he hides his embarrassment, Mizuki mused.

"Come on," said Yurie in the challenging tone of a math teacher, poking his side with her index finger, "What's on your mind? Be clear—crystal clear." Quickly she added, "He always makes fun of me."

"Put a pig and a cat together," said Shōzō innocently, "and what do you get—something outlandish and comical. I do respect you, you know, whether you realize it or not."

"You mean you want to flatter her," said Mizuki, who was quick to read the look on his face, while simultaneously trying to understand Yurie's thought processes, which were by now quite familiar to her through Yurie's voice on the phone, and the writings she had read so far.

The iron rule in married couples' disputes is not to take sides. But for diplomacy's sake, you need to ignore the rule and glue yourself like a bat to one side or the other in order to keep them in good humor. In general, it's best to side with your own gender. If you followed your instincts, you'd be tempted to empathize with the opposite sex, but it is often the case that you have to go against your nature just to maintain order in the universe.

"In her case, clarity becomes a very sensitive issue," Shōzō continued in a level voice. "She hates it if I say something that's clearly meant to flatter her. The best thing is to play it safe by throwing together all sorts of ambiguities, then increase the complexity to the point where she won't know what you're talking about."

Compared to Yurie's incomprehensible, argumentative style, Shōzō's was quite easy to follow. He spoke each word slowly, pausing frequently.

"It must be tough, having a novelist wife," said Mizuki casually, trying not to set Yurie off.

"If things are too vague, that won't please her either," he said with his usual long-drawn-out sigh. "She always scolds me, 'Don't speak to me like someone in a coma.' You know, I'm really impressed that you'd even bother to translate her work."

"Her writing digs up my past. Dead parents, people I used to know, and everybody I've ever met, like earthworms crawling out of the dirt one after the other," responded Mizuki, choosing words carefully to compliment her. Yurie was all smiles.

Prior to Yurie and Shōzō's visit, her youngest sister Momoe had shown up at the mountain, bragging and complaining about her in the same breath. In the end, it was difficult to tell what Momoe really meant to say.

"Yuri's lost a marble or two, you know. Be aware and don't take her too seriously. It's gotten to Shōzō as well. They're no longer young lovebirds, but the way they're glued to each other all year round, trailing each other around—I call them goldfish turds. Shōzō just listens with a straight face, hypnotized by his wife's egotistical ramblings. I really wonder sometimes. I'm not one to interfere with domestic squabbles, so I just shrug my shoulders. But after all, I'm a blood relative. Once in a while I want to talk to her in private, right? I find it oppressive that Shōzō tags along all the time, like a goldfish turd.

"You'll absolutely exhaust yourself if you show the slightest concern for her. And if I sort of play indifferent to please the two, she berates me. 'You dwell on other people's business too much and it wears us out. You're really dense.' And if I don't: 'You're impetuous and dull-witted,'" she says.

"I was born after Kiku, my middle sister. Being the youngest, the psychological damage is rather limited, but I do pity her. It's all Yuri's fault. It's my opinion that Kiku, dominated by Yuri's egotistical chatter, has lost out every time. Parents aren't very rational, so they tend to leave things alone even when the older sibling says something totally outrageous. It certainly doesn't pay to be the youngest. Well, Yuri's excuse in all this is that she's got to take care of her two little sisters to protect them from outside enemies. I'll tell you one thing, though: she can be so mean—but then be so sickeningly sweet and gentle. You're either taken in or willingly accept her as is; she certainly knows how to make you feel good in an all-round way.

"When she's upfront, you've got to be the same. She may get pretty hotheaded, but later on she cools off and takes it all back. I would say that's her one redeeming quality." So ended Momoe's candid commentary on her big sister.

MIZUKI WAS MULLING OVER this long drawn-out assessment when Yurie spoke up right after Shōzō had stepped out to go to the restroom as if she had read Mizuki's mind, "I'm sorry I've brought him with me."

"He wants to be with you all the time. Are you a sorceress with a stag, or is Shōzō a wizard with a doe? Which is it, I wonder?" Mizuki laughed. Yurie, looking rather pleased, shrugged her shoulders.

"He could have left us alone but it just doesn't occur to him," she said haughtily. "Today's typical. He once had a crush on your mother, although he was a nobody in her eyes. When he was so eager to meet the daughter of the woman he had his eyes on, I couldn't possibly say to him: 'You can't come with me.'

"I wouldn't have brought him here if you were a man. It'd be fun for me to make him jealous, but I guess his imagination isn't like mine because he shows no interest in men. No use trying to make him jealous; he's one of those happy guys who only shows an interest in women he likes.

"Men and women are bonded together, and why look at one without the other? I feel less stressed with Shōzō around than being by myself in the presence of a man accompanied by a woman. He likes women, so no woman will ever think ill of him. That helps deflect female hostility toward me. That's also why, to borrow Momoe's expression, we end up being goldfish turds. Besides, he drives for me."

"What a comfortable life," said Mizuki dryly.

"Far from it. I've got to work like a slave." All of a sudden, Yurie was fuming.

Mizuki went blank. Dealing with married couples is risky, she said to herself. I'm sure Yurie will launch into a verbal machine-gunning of Shōzō any minute now, just like I've endured many times during those long telephone calls. If that happens, I'll just grunt—Uhhh … —and refuse to go along with her.

"He left a company that paid him well," continued Yurie in resignation, "and insisted: 'Feed me, I'll be your gigolo.' I was really flabbergasted."

Mizuki feigned total indifference. Yurie seemed rather composed in spite of the sudden venomous outburst.

"If I don't have the guts to throw him out, there's nothing I can do but give in."

"You have a point there. Why not think of him as an unpaid chauffeur?" Mizuki's tone was as monotonous as someone reading straight from a script.

"You must really despise me. You're saying: It serves you right," said Yurie, hanging her head. Was she doing this on purpose, or was it natural? Mizuki couldn't tell.

At that instant, Shōzō reappeared and commented, "Autumn leaves are so pretty, the color patterns of a brocade."

On her high school summer vacation more than twenty years ago, Mizuki had stayed at their house in the United States. With a young daughter to take care of, Yurie the student-wife read books into the wee hours, and was still in bed every morning when Shōzō went to work. Well, no wonder—this is what you get, Mizuki said to herself as she carefully observed the pair.

"Shōzō, Yuri writes anything she damn well pleases, doesn't she?" taunted Mizuki.

"It seems she writes things that really infuriate men. When her husband isn't upset, why should they be?"

"They're probably furious about you, too. Like husband, like wife, they'd say," said Mizuki, trying to bait him. She wanted to see him a bit ruffled, but he merely nodded his agreement, completely unperturbed.

"I guess so. You may be right. Seiichiro was just like that," he said, bringing up the subject of her father.

"The female protagonists in Yuri's stories do what they damn well please with men," she tried again, this time gravely.

"It seems my counterparts are either cuckolded or bovine; also quack doctors, incompetent scholars—sometimes retirement-age company men kicked upstairs."

"Oh dear, you mean you like all that stuff she writes?"

"Maybe so. You never have a dull moment hanging around a woman like Yuri."

She was silenced, unable to think of a retort.

"Seiichirō was like that, too, I hear," he said.

The subject bounced right back to her father.

"Don't you agree with me? He was crazy about Fū. Rumor has it, though, he hit her from time to time."

"All right, all right." Astounded, she just stared at him, because something Yurie had once said came back to her—"He hit me."

"Shōzō also hit me," said Yurie as if on cue, almost bragging about it. "My cheekbone must have a crack in it. When it's cold, it still hurts." She placed her hand gingerly on her left cheek to catch his attention.

"It's so annoying that novelists exaggerate things," he countered. "That's just the way I've been trained over thirty years, and no wonder very few things faze me. I guess this confirms Newton's law of energy conservation. I've let her do whatever she wanted to do, so I've got to do the same for myself. I think it's about time for me to get out of the salt mine. After all, if I get too old, my body won't do what I tell it to, and I couldn't live the way I want.

"On a weekday I once strolled around the city in broad daylight and found the whole world to be quite different. I saw women happily playing tennis, or reading history books—or whatever else they were reading in the library at the time. This was while we men were fiddling around with boring papers, and kowtowing to clients we had no desire to meet. I recognized that there's an entirely different world out there. It really made me think.

"When I watched young kindergarten teachers with children in the park, I felt something uncanny about the way the women were going about life as it comes, calmly and at the speed of life. Well, that's fine. All we men are really doing is hanging on to bits and pieces of an incomprehensible world, tightening a screw here, pushing a thumb tack there. While we think to ourselves that we are debating national and world policy of the utmost importance, there's a different world out there where women can watch children grow. That's not a bad deal, either. Well, since our daughter Chie is already married, there's no harm in us doing nothing, taking it easy."

Yurie shrugged her shoulders, casting him a contemptuous look.

"I told you. He really knows how to manipulate me," she said. "I was talking about the time when you gave me a black eye. Don't change the subject. When I told my mother about that, she got even angrier than me—I'm the one who got the beating—and said, Your father never raised a hand to me. How can you live with a man like that?"

Something's wrong with where this conversation is going, thought Mizuki. Her head was spinning.

"Why did he hit you?" she asked slowly.

"I don't remember," said Yurie resolutely. "I must have said something really nasty. When he gets excited, he can't get a word out."

God only knew whether she was defending him, or belittling him.

"Now I remember. I couldn't before, because I didn't want to remember. I badmouthed his mother."

Shōzō was looking down, stealing glances at his wife; there was a frightened look in his eyes—he was not so eloquent now. Mizuki almost burst out laughing, but judged that silence was best, so as not to encourage Yurie to diverge into one of her weird tangents.

"His mother was just like me," said Yurie. "That's why I bad-mouthed her. Lo and behold, he got so angry that his mouth froze up. His teeth began to chatter, and that's when he hit me."

"I got it!" Mizuki blurted out. "You've been trained so well by your mother, who was just like Yuri, and that's why you can put up with her, Shōzō."

"It's just that nothing surprises me. It's been this way since I was born," he said with perfect composure.

"How brave of you to hit her."

"I just lost my equilibrium. No logic to it."

"No logic, hmm," parroted Mizuki, rather impressed. Male and female relationships are just not logical.

"Everybody in the world thinks I'm a bad wife. I'm always to blame," protested Yurie. "Shōzō's always the good guy. You must be kidding me. I lose out every time. He comes from a long line of weasels. He plays the silent and composed type and does what he damn well pleases. I'm always taken in by that, and work like a slave."

"But you said Shōzō's mother was just like you," Mizuki reminded her.

"You're supposed to be translating my work, and you don't even understand the nature of contradictions? Contradictions are the stuff of humanity; they're in every Greek tragedy." Yurie narrowed her eyes and stared at Mizuki.

Shōzō's face unexpectedly broke into a smile, and he resumed his discourse on Yurie as if nothing had happened. Mizuki shut her eyes in resignation.

"You could say that Yurie Mama's writing is successful in introducing good-for-nothing female protagonists—or good-for-nothing men, for that matter. It's safe to say that a man has this instinctive urge to sow his seed in every woman in the world. He craves provocation, so it would be funny not to have a woman around who wants to provoke him. A man or woman, it doesn't matter which—if one side does all the taking, the energy builds up until it results in an explosion, inviting a gender backlash.

"Our generation gets flak from all sides. Men have oppressed women in this and that, blah, blah, blah. It's all men's fault: utility poles are too high, *daikon* radishes are priced too high, babies cry, women are stupid. Even women's weaknesses are all men's fault. It's men who start wars and lose them, make A-bombs and use them.

"Of course, what we want to say is that all these things wouldn't have happened if women didn't give birth in the first place—but since men started this destructive process and were born of women, they keep quiet.

"Watching a man let himself be wrapped around a woman's little finger isn't what bugs men; it's the other way around. How could a woman let herself be manipulated by such a good-for-nothing man? There are two possibilities for why a man doesn't openly cheer on a woman who refuses to play by the rules. One: he's worried that other women who act otherwise may resent him. Two: those of his own sex might ostracize him. But I tend to think that he secretly applauds the woman who is no man's toy."

Mizuki was totally confused. Is he putting his wife on a pedestal or just being assertive? This may be what Yurie means by his cunning, crafty nature. Mizuki was on guard. Suppose this were the only type of man around, she said to herself, how disconcerting life would be.

All of a sudden Yurie began to fume. "See, I told you. He's so good at justifying himself and I am always to blame. I'm supposed to believe he worships me. He never gives me a break."

"Well, it's your life," said Mizuki tersely, jerking her head away in exasperation. Yurie immediately changed the subject.

"Doesn't Mizuki favor her father? More to the point," she said suggestively, "she doesn't look much like Fū." Now playing the perfect coquette, she sidled up to Shōzō. I look more like Fū, therefore, more attractive, she probably wanted to say. Mizuki knew right away her comment was aimed at Mizuki's dislike of Fū.

"Your mother was extremely popular with men. All I could do was watch her flaunting her charms. If you observe someone like that long enough, isn't it possible you become a bit like her? Personality-wise, that is."

"You get so fed up being raised by someone like her," shot back Mizuki, remembering Momoe's advice: "You do everything to avoid repeating what she says or even might say."

"I have a friend who's a nonstop talker," said Yurie, nodding away. "She's so aggressive that no one can break in. You should see her daughters—they're a bunch of rocks, all three of them. It's beyond reticence. I don't think they could protest a chatterbox like her in any other way. Right, you don't resemble Fū, but ..." After a considerable pause she resumed. "The fact that you understand what I'm saying—in other words, understand Fū's mind—means that you are like her."

"I guess that's why I'm copying Seiichiro," interjected Shōzō, "he knew her like a book, always watching the passing clouds while Fū yammered away. He was like a sage."

Mizuki always referred to her late mother Fū as *ano hito*—

a neutral native third-person pronoun, literally that person. She did not use the recent idiom of *kare*, "he," or *kanojo*, "she," both coined after Japan opened up to the West, but the native personal pronoun, *ano hito*, which sounded more natural to Japanese.

"My mother's supposed to have done things exactly the way she damn well pleased," said Mizuki. "But now that she's dead, I sort of pity her. She accomplished so little of what she set out to do. In other words, her dreams were too grand." The moment Mizuki actually referred to Fū as *ano hito*, something flashed through Yurie's mind and she finally understood why the personal pronouns "he" and "she" exist in the West in everyday usage.

A daughter fed up with an abnormally aggressive mother loses the desire to call her own mother "Mom" or "Mother." Sometimes the daughter wants to push her mother away by using the impersonal *ano hito*. And once she utters the pronoun, the mother begins to exist not as her mother but as an individual.

"The person with small dreams finds happiness. The visionary ends up a complainer," said Yurie, beginning to take active interest in what Mizuki had to say. "Fū stunned people. She made us, the younger generation, realize that there's an alternative lifestyle out there. Oh, that's her photo."

"Yes. In lieu of a Buddhist altar."

Deep in thought, Yurie stared at the photograph. She drew in a long breath, shifting her gaze to the mountain decked in autumnal reds and yellows. "I love the mountains. The air smells different here," she muttered to herself. "I wish I could live in a house with a garden." She then started to complain about living in her tiny condo in Tokyo. "I feel I haven't seen the moon or the stars for a long, long time. The plants I've bought just can't survive in a condo. I think the human race is also dying."

"You needn't worry too much about dying," said Shōzō unhurriedly. "When goldenrod can flourish, Japan's ancient endangered pampas grass will bounce back."

"I'm just talking about a teensy little wish for a house with a garden. Don't distract me," Yurie interrupted him. "You're denying your wife even the smallest pleasure. You just lock me up in a concrete box in a polluted city, hoping that I'll write bestsellers. A man has a duty to build a house and protect his woman, but you're totally disengaged. You say you can't take it to the grave, and, even if you're alive, there's always a chance that it'll burn down."

"Exorbitant real estate prices in Tokyo aren't my fault. All I'm saying is we'd be better off looking for alternatives to this pitiful situation we are born into," he said. "By the way, Mizuki, do you know of any house for rent in the neighborhood?"

One immediately came to mind, but before she could test their commitment, Yurie resumed her abusive tirade. Perhaps it was her way of expressing affection.

"People once lived in palaces and built the pyramids," she said. "I come from the same stock and survived, just the way roses have bloomed on bushes for tens of thousands of years or hundreds of millions of years. As one of those surviving humans, I have a simple desire to live like any wild grass firmly rooted in the earth. Shōzō treats me like a houseplant, feeding me only polluted tap water. What nonsense."

Her seemingly consistent story was peppered with the contradictory, the exaggerated, and the paradoxical. It suddenly broke off and left the listener totally confused.

Shōzō was unruffled. It was as if he was hardly listening to a tune a musician was playing for him. He then responded with what seemed to be the inevitable conclusion of her tirade: "And so, we've decided to travel together before we get too old. Kyoto gives you the impression of—what should I say—hiding the myriad keys to Japan's secrets. There are ghosts wandering about, and you can hear the keys jingling."

The topic has somehow digressed, Mizuki said to herself. So, this is the way Shōzō manipulates Yurie.

Come to think of it, they were constantly on the move. When they had suddenly shown up at Mizuki's apartment in California, the grade-schooler Chie was curled up in a sleeping bag on the rear seat of a packed station wagon.

She had woken up rubbing her eyes.

"Where are we?" she asked.

"Here's Mizuki, your second cousin," said Yurie by way of introduction.

"What's that?"

Chie looked up at Mizuki, eyes devoid of expression.

I was just like that at her age, said Mizuki to herself. She felt sorry for Chie. As a young girl, Mizuki recalled how depressing it was to watch Fū, always on the move, full of life.

Yurie and Shōzō had traveled with Chie to almost every part of the country. This time they were on their way back from Las Vegas.

"Was it fun?" asked Mizuki.

"I watched TV."

Las Vegas wouldn't be any fun for kids.

"Where do you want to go?" Mizuki tried again.

"Nowhere. I'd rather stay home and read books."

"This child doesn't want to go anywhere. When we drove all the way to Yellowstone and pointed out the buffaloes, she wouldn't even look at them," said Yurie. "When we took a ferry all the way to the Statue of Liberty, her face was a complete blank."

"I just want to be home," said the girl gloomily, "but Mommy and Daddy keep saying, Let's go here, Let's go there, they can't sit still without a map in front of them."

After a cursory inspection of Mizuki's shabby apartment, she had pulled some cookbooks off a shelf and said, "I want chili, Mommy never makes me stuff like that."

"She always wants to eat the strangest food. Typical of a kid brought up in the States," Yurie had said with a contemptuous look in her eyes. "When we take her to a French restaurant, she asks for a hamburger."

That little Chie was now married and was studying philosophy.

"Heavens, what's a girl going to do with philosophy? I'd say she'd be so much more appealing if she stuck to fashion and boys." Yurie had mumbled on.

If you were brought up by such a parent, thought Mizuki, you'd be confronted with so many contradictions, no wonder you would want to study philosophy.

"Being the kind of parents we are, we can't really complain about our own child." Yurie sounded reasonable this time. "We've decided to leave her alone. She's been in graduate school for ten years now. God knows what she's doing. Well, I wonder if one day she'll reveal humanity's true potential. For now, she and her husband have to hunt for the best prices, scrounging for bargain-sale toilet tissues. We should, but we really haven't done anything for them. They're supporting themselves with part-time jobs."

The Mama twosome planted themselves on the floor and showed no sign of going anywhere.

"We've decided to go wherever the whim takes us, in search of what have you, until we die," continued Yurie. "I visited Kyoto at eighteen. Back then, I said to myself, I'm going to live here some day. But I don't know why I thought that. People think you're stuck here in the mountains, but isn't Kyoto only thirty minutes away?"

"Why not stay here if you like?" Mizuki suggested casually. "I have an acquaintance who's willing to rent her house for a short period of time. I'm taking care of the key."

No sooner had the suggestion been made than the Mamas came to a decision to take a look at the place.

"That's great, really great," said Karl when he came home, giving their plan a further boost. "You know, by translating your work, Mizuki's hoping to find the key to unlock your heart, so you'd better watch out."

"I'm also looking for that myself. I seem to have forgotten where I hid it. Do you think she'll find it for me if I hang around here long enough?" Yurie cocked her head at Karl.

"She's very good at finding things," he said. "Whenever I've misplaced something, it reappears like magic. Witchcraft has always fascinated me. A woman isn't a woman without magical powers."

Whenever Yurie broke in, Karl picked up the drift of her monologues and connected them with his wife. Invariably he went on to brag about her charm and talent.

An expert in something that apparently linked mathematics, economics or commerce—call it statistics—Karl was doing research at Kyoto University on a project coding Japanese thought patterns into a computer program. Originally from Germany, he had met Mizuki at a university in the States.

"She says she doesn't want to go back to America or Germany," said Karl. "That means I've got to find a job in Japan. I only have a one-year contract. Unless she feeds me, we may have to split up. Let's hope her translation will bring in some money."

Yurie was grinning.

"Get rich, Karl, so that we can publish it ourselves," said Mizuki brightly. "You're supposed to know everything there is to know about the world economy. It should be easy for you to make money."

"Economics is like meteorology," he said. "You don't see many wealthy meteorologists, do you? Well, since life's one big pain anyway, I hope I'll at least be able to live where I want."

Shōzō looked disturbed at Karl's words. After Yurie's tirade, he apparently could not put the idea of renting a house with a garden out of his mind.

After a very quick tour of the vacant house, the Mamas decided to rent it.

## 2 ∽

THE VILLA THAT STOOD HALFWAY UP Mount Hiei had been built as a refuge from the oppressive Kyoto heat. The owner, who had been transferred to Tokyo and intended to return, was willing to rent it on a short-term basis at a reasonable price.

The mistress of the house, who had become friends with Mizuki, left the key with her just in case some foreign academic affiliated with Kyoto University might want such an arrangement, implying that it would be better for the house to be occupied rather than vacant.

Though no foreign academics, Shōzō and Yurie who lived in Tokyo had been looking for a country retreat. The owner considered it a match made in heaven.

The Mamas immediately fell in love with the amenities of the villa. In addition to the kitchen-dining combo, the small house had three Japanese-style rooms. No more than a week later they moved in with two sleeping bags and the bare essentials.

The owner had graciously offered some furnishings for their use: a small writing desk, a mirror, and a set of simple cooking utensils. The house came with a *kotatsu* heater attached beneath a low wooden frame that was covered with a heavy blanket. "This is much more comfortable than living at a hotel," the pair said.

"The air definitely smells different here," said Yurie, looking very content as she gazed at the garden thick with goldenrod and Japanese pampas grass.

Only two sleeping bags, chopsticks, two plates, two tea bowls, and two *zabuton* cushions. Is that all? Mizuki was amazed.

For their brief one-year stay in Japan, Karl and Mizuki had brought a few more possessions than that. When Yurie had learned that her cousin was going to live near Kyoto, she offered some household furniture and belongings that came with the sale of the Myōkō house in Niigata that had belonged to Fū and her husband. Save for some clothes, that was enough to meet Mizuki's family needs.

The fact that the sale of the house and everything that came with it had been forced on Yurie by the aging Fū was well known to Mizuki. She rummaged through what Yurie had lent her, picking out a few things for the newly arrived couple.

"If you like good mountain air," said Mizuki, "Myōkō should be ideal for you."

"It's too remote. Here on Mount Hiei the fragrance of thousand-year-old palaces are wafting through the air."

"I suppose so."

On the following morning after Shōzō and Yurie had moved in, Mizuki hauled to the villa a cardboard box full of useful items. She pressed the doorbell but there was no response. She walked to the garden in the back and found the shutters and *shōji* screen doors for the eight-mat room wide open. In the room were two heads sticking out of sleeping bags like beachgoers buried in the sand.

Dozing shamelessly naked in the zipped bags, Yurie and Shōzō were, thought Mizuki with a chuckle, the very image of mountain monkeys, nibbling on berries and looking down the mountain at a thousand-year-old palace. Yurie and Shōzō had burrowed into the two individual sleeping bags zippered together.

"You appeared from nowhere so suddenly that we had no time to do anything," said Yurie defensively, pulling at a large red knit stole around her shoulders, revealing a patch of white skin.

"Chie made me this stole. I take it everywhere. The yarn's thick and it's perfect for warding off the drafts."

"You wouldn't have that problem if you used the bags separately," suggested Mizuki, but was rewarded with an icy silence.

They had always slept naked. When Mizuki stayed at their house during high school vacations, she thought the absence of sleepwear in their dirty clothes hamper odd, considering how often they did laundry, which was more often than the average household. One day, to her horror, she happened to see two naked bodies parading around the bedroom through its slightly open door.

At that time, they were living in Madison, a college town in the Midwest. With books piled up against her bare breasts, Yurie was trying to draw a desk lamp toward her as she climbed onto the bed.

The significance of the expression Shōzō used to describe one of her activities, "Always reading books, pages rustling—" had finally made sense to Mizuki.

Yurie often complained of the small size of the faux desk shelf attached to the headboard. When tired of reading, she would lie down, dragging under the bedsheet scattered scraps of notepaper and pencils, including dictionaries. All the rustling noises disturbed Shōzō's sleep to no end. Mizuki remembered him complaining that paper, books, and notepads that had slipped off the headboard crowded the pillows, and even his chest.

The bedroom door always remained ajar for their cat, Mani. She loved Chie and could usually be found curled up at the foot of her bed, but once in a while the cat visited Shōzō, her second favorite person, to sleep at his feet.

He knew Yurie didn't much care for these visits, but he gave Mani free access on the sly by leaving the door open just a crack. He probably thought that Mani loved him the most.

Yurie was studying fine art; the bedroom was strewn with art magazines and books on painting, leaving hardly any space to walk. "It is a relentless drain on my energy," she declared, "to drag all those heavy art books onto the bed and then back to the shelf, and besides, it damages the bindings. I'd definitely like to live in a house with Japanese-style *tatami* mat rooms someday. Otherwise, the bindings would go bad, too—" she added.

What nerve! Mizuki said to herself. The way Yurie handled books it wouldn't matter whether it was a *tatami* mat or a bed. She was astounded—chaos must reign in Yurie's head.

Almost every day Yurie checked out the maximum allowance of books. While inserting bookmarks between the pages of those heavy albums, leaving them open side by side, she seemed to be tracing back in time some fragile thread of memory. The bedroom was not big enough for their multiple uses. Mizuki had felt somewhat sorry for the couple, although most of her sympathy tended to gravitate toward Shōzō.

Yurie worked on charcoal sketches every single day; propped against the wall were two or three works in progress. Shōzō often had to pose nude for hours on end, and so they both got into the habit of prancing around the house with no clothes on. To sketch herself in the mirror would give only one view at a time, Yurie complained. She was in desperate need of a female model.

Time and again she had begged her cousin to pose, but Mizuki was somehow not inclined to model. When she thought about it now, she wished she had let Yurie have her way.

Why not sleep on separate beds instead of grumbling about crumpled papers or drafts that chilled their shoulders? But despite the extra beds in other rooms, they slept together on a double bed.

"It comes down to which I prefer," Shōzō had said unabashedly, "rustling noises and cold shoulders, or not having her with me."

They also remarked that such-and-such a couple sleeping on twin beds might split up at any moment. It's been more than twenty years and they're still at it, Mizuki chuckled to herself.

Back then Yurie would explode and take her feelings out on everyone, especially on the teenager Mizuki whenever Shōzō had struck up an extended conversation with her.

"When the blood rushes to my brain," said Yurie, grinning suggestively, "I'm liable to murder someone. You only get a suspended sentence for a crime of passion in the States."

Far from being alarmed, Shōzō had seemed to thoroughly enjoy the rivalry of the two women. And the young Mizuki had experienced a strange moment of elation at being considered an equal.

Shōzō could be very insensitive to young women; he once remarked to Mizuki that she was "as flat as a washboard." Driven by an invisible force of some young plant suddenly shooting up toward the sunlight, the self-conscious Mizuki yelled back, "You skinny horse's ass!" throwing at him everything she could lay her hands on. Yurie had grinned at her contentedly with a look in her eye that could be taken either as satisfaction or admiration, as if to say, You see, you have the same blood in you.

At that very moment, for the first time, she probably recognized Mizuki as her equal, someone she could compete with. She then made Shōzō apologize and say on bended knee, "You're as supple as a rose vine," and ordered him to buy Mizuki some expensive perfume.

Yurie's action had unnerved her, and at the same time she couldn't believe how Shōzō was letting a woman wrap him around her little finger. Mizuki had repeated to herself "You skinny horse's ass" again and again.

The sunbathing in the small villa on Mount Hiei revealed that their condominium life in Tokyo was not much better than that of a college student. Now all this would make sense if they were young freshwater trout, but for a man and a woman, who had already lived half a century, to burrow into sleeping bags-zippered-into-one in a rented mountain villa, would be considered improper. This worried Mizuki.

"I wonder if you can make it through the winter," she said carefully. "Winter on Mount Hiei is pretty harsh, you know."

Yurie countered that these sleeping bags, made of the highest quality material, even kept them warm on a midwinter overnight boat trip to the Alaskan waters. Then they began to reminisce how they would drink the night away with fishing buddies in boats anchored side by side in a quiet inlet.

"On the outgoing tides at sunrise, plenty of crabs and abalone were there for the taking," said Yurie, pulling her white arms out of the stole to convey the size of the crabs, eight to twelve inches in diameter. "At the time of spring low tides a large linen bag would fill up in no time with crabs and abalone this big."

"Interesting creatures, those crabs," Shōzō joined in. "You can see from the boat the real big ones scuttling among the seaweed. If you drop a garden rake into the water from the boat, they grab onto it and climb to the surface in one long procession. Pull it out, you got yourself an easy catch.

"Now, when it comes to abalone, you don't need to go too deep. As long as you're not afraid to get your feet wet, all you have to do is scour the rocks at low tide—which is only ankle deep—gently scraping them off with a metal spatula. Abalone prefer certain kinds of rock, ones covered with moss close to the color of their shell. The way the water catches the light is extremely subtle; with just a slight change in the lighting, abalone disappear, instantly absorbed into the moss-covered rocks.

"If you haven't done this before, even one hour in the water wouldn't get you one abalone. On the other hand, your bag will be full in no time if you know what you're doing. Occasionally you find a solitary abalone washed onto the rocks at low tide, lying underneath a giant seaweed, a disoriented, sun-bleached creature that missed a chance to escape."

The dreamy-eyed Shōzō continued happily: "Why do so many strange things happen in the changing tides? All sorts of creatures once hidden beneath the water are suddenly exposed at low tide."

Yurie too began to describe the Gulf of Alaska: the way gigantic blooming sea anemone on the ocean bottom flutter their tentacles; sea cucumbers that resemble monstrous litchi nuts; sea urchins like frightening dahlia; and how the legless and finless abalone can nimbly hop from one rock to another. Yurie the enchanted raconteur, waving her bare arms, now freed from the red angora stole, her hands and fingers flapping vigorously, was now transformed into one of those strange sea creatures, thought Mizuki.

The dark green of their sleeping bags was the color of the ocean, with their bodies undulating beneath.

Her story continued: The yellow waves pregnant with a large school of herring, beaches carpeted by herring roe, the cries of flapping sea gulls that swarm around the stranded fish trapped between rocks after spawning, bloodied and gasping for a final breath.

As they retold their story, Yurie and Shōzō ceased to be human. Sometimes they were crabs, other times abalone or herring. You could hear the lapping of the waves and see the insides of an abalone's suckers, the scintillating white underbelly of a herring, or the seaweed yielding gently to the waves.

"There were whales, too, spouting water," added Yurie. "Nowadays Shōzō calls me a whale. He insults me by saying I snore like a spouting whale. He's secretly delighted that I'll soon have a stroke. He always tries to dissociate me from anything beautiful. To him, I am a piggy-cat or a whale."

"I know you once called me a washboard, not a rose vine," Mizuki chimed in to remind him.

"It was just a slip of the tongue—"

That's even worse, Stop there, Yurie signaled him with a glare. His body stiffened but he quickly tried to recover. "I wonder if Yuri ever thinks I fantasize about pretty women who look like silvery white fish or cute tiny birds."

"A spouting whale, I see. Shōzō, you're resorting to the stirring images of those gigantic ancient creatures that have survived to this day," said Mizuki. Unwittingly her tone grew caustic as she tried to make up for his lack of imagination about women, while simultaneously feeding Yurie's narcissism.

"His metaphors," said Yurie, "mess up my sense of aesthetics. This sleeping bag, which looks like it's made out of a remnant of some prison uniform, is not really meant for me. The real me is sleeping in a swan's down comforter, wrapped in an autumn green silk gown, resting my head on a pillow stuffed with chrysanthemum petals. You know the fairy tale of the frog princess—that story's real. The difference between dream and reality can be so cruel—," she moaned, but she was actually poking Shōzō in the sleeping bags.

The Gulf of Alaska story sounded like an ancient myth to Mizuki. She did recall receiving a letter containing several photos in which Yurie and Shōzō were all smiles, scooping herring roe off the beach. Their story was certainly a reality then, and you could say similar scenes were taking place elsewhere.

Yurie began to talk about how humans have changed the environment.

"I feel like I was there only yesterday. I hear, though, everything's gone now. The beaches where herring roe washed up have disappeared, harvesting of sprouting seaweed has been banned, and the fishing grounds—now open only once a year—and then only for a few hours—have turned into a battlefield where fishermen shoot each other to grab the choice spots. And all just to serve a few herring roe at a fashionable restaurant in Tokyo.

"From time immemorial humans have understood the concept of a phantom. Those who lived thirty years ago must have grumbled about what they had done to cause the disappearance of something thirty years earlier," she added, laughing.

That's just the way Fū laughed, Mizuki remembered. When she had received a pathetic letter from Fū in which she begged her to come home, she deliberately delayed her departure because of a date she was to have with Karl three days later, a date she did not want to miss. By the time she returned, her mother had died of liver cancer just like Seiichiro. She must have known about it when she wrote her.

A note from Yurie, who was already back in Japan, hinted at the gravity of the situation. Mizuki was still unwilling to spare the time, missing the chance to say farewell.

She often thought about it and hated Karl for it. I am a daughter who's found a man at the expense of her own mother's death, said Mizuki to herself, a perfect match for a philandering mother. Mizuki had heard about her amorous escapades from various sources.

Their heads now completely out of the sleeping bags, Yurie and Shōzō propped themselves up on their elbows, captivated by the abundance of pampas grass, their ripe silver spikes gently swaying in the garden. There was a hint of melancholy about the pair.

"It never occurred to us," Yurie began in her defense, "that you'd sneak into this garden and catch us off-guard—it's bizarre for us to have to expose our old decaying flesh in an aesthetically unacceptable manner; we wish Mount Hiei would erupt at this very moment to bury us in lava." They stared at her reproachfully.

Reproachful or not, they were the soul of composure; they even looked elegant in the fluffy red angora stole they were sharing around their necks. Mizuki ended up closing the *shōji* screen doors for their privacy and went to check on things in the spacious kitchen.

The kitchen was bare save for a refrigerator large enough to hold a human body, and on a shelf, scattered like pieces of a puzzle, sat one frying pan and a lone bamboo tea whisk. Yurie had told Mizuki that she was planning to prepare a formal tea, dressed in a tie-dyed cotton kimono with a *hakata* obi the shape of a seashell tied neatly in the back.

By the time Mizuki had returned to slide back the *shōji*, the sleeping bags had disappeared into thin air, and the room was now as bare as the kitchen.

Shōzō was seated prim and proper in a cashmere sweater near the low table *kotatsu* heater, covered by a quilt in a persimmon-and-black-checkered pattern.

"Go ahead, Honey, shave and brush your teeth."

At this gentle nudge from Yurie, he stepped out of the room.

"Suppose a very glamorous and sensuous female were here," she began, "curled up under an expensive down comforter with the scent of her perfume heavy in the air. You can bet that the insides of her head would be as bleak as a grave. What do you think brings silk gowns, down comforters, and beautiful women into this world? It's the bloodthirsty gaze of men who'd shoot each other to monopolize fishing grounds. This is one calculus problem, Mizuki, that your Karl's got to program into his computer. I wonder what the answer will be."

With scissors in hand Yurie stepped down from the verandah into the garden to cut some aspidistra leaves.

"Sorry, we have no extra plates." On the freshly washed leaves she placed some Kyoto *gyūhi* sweetmeats fragrant with Japanese wasabi horseradish, and poured some boiling water into a conch shell to cool it down for green tea.

Its soft crimson interior, smooth and opaque, instantly sucked in all the hot water.

Well-established shops in Kyoto are very coy about their business: a customer will be kept waiting forever just to make a small purchase. This provokes some people to leave, but there are others who welcome the chance to let their thoughts wander. There you have it, the feel of the ancient capital.

Mizuki, who had dragged Karl all the way from the States, tried to explain this "feel" to him. She was as self-conscious as he was when he had lectured her on the proper selection of wine glasses to match a particular wine. However, the talk of this "feel" of the ancient capital didn't embarrass him at all. He nodded amicably with a knowing look on his face.

The way Yurie cut the aspidistras leaves reminded Mizuki of his aunt who lived in the German countryside, garnishing some homemade sour cream, which she would scoop out from a jar, with dill and chives fresh from the garden.

Now it was time for the tea whisk's appearance, rescued from its exile next to the frying pan on the kitchen shelf. The tea bowl that Yurie was serving, with its flawed white glaze and fish-scale pattern, looked rather attractive.

"You can serve noodles, sweetmeats, pickled vegetables," Yurie explained, "and even arrange flowers in this bowl."

"I bought it on Oki-no-shima Island. I was passing by a teashop where culls from a nearby kiln were on sale for close to nothing. This was only eight hundred yen. Much better than the Hagi ware priced at eight thousand, something I saw on the way back." That was the bowl's history.

"If I keep it in good shape and use it for one hundred years or so," she said, laughing, "it may become a priceless art object. I've named it White Hare, from the folktale 'The White Hare of Inaba.'"

The glaze near the bottom of the bowl had peeled away in clumps, but she still loved its texture and whiteness.

"Well, even if this White Hare became a priceless art object in a hundred years, if I priced it now at eighty thousand yen they'd call me a con artist."

The freshly shaven Shōzō reappeared with a transistor radio in his hand. "Looks like a plane crash in Colombia," he said. "Pilots there are paid very well, you know."

"Why?" asked Mizuki.

"Many planes don't have altimeters, and the repair jobs are done with old parts."

"Why don't they ban flying such planes?"

"Ban? Who'd ban them when the government owns them?"

"I see."

"Russian planes have sliding seats, and when a flight is over-booked, they can seat more passengers. That means the positions of the window seats change accordingly."

"Wow … !"

"I forget which country, but there's some airline that even has a standing-room-only policy. Well, what can I say, you know this is the era of first come, first served."

"Uh-huh."

Yurie immediately took over from where Shōzō left off. "It was a bit like that when we chartered a Cessna in Alaska. The week before our flight, we heard that one of its wings had fallen off, or the plane brushed a mountainside, or something like that."

"There's a good chance of surviving a crash in a Cessna, but a very slim one in a jet," said Shōzō.

"Something really surprised me when I came back to Japan this time," said Mizuki, changing the subject. "Among the usual things listed as banned from coin-op lockers—you know, things like explosives, and so on—were cadavers."

"Yup," said Shōzō. "Thirty years ago when we went to America for the first time, we really enjoyed shopping at supermarkets. Yurie and I burst out laughing when we saw a sign on the wall, No Shoplifting. Well, so thirty years later in Japan, things have come to this, Please No Cadavers in the Lockers."

"When a bus makes a scheduled stop in Kyoto," said Yurie, "a taped voice warns boarding passengers, Please do not carry aboard flammable materials. I haven't heard that one yet in Tokyo."

"Now that I'm no longer in New York City," said Mizuki, "I don't have to wear the handbag strap across my chest, hugging the bag tight the way a school-kid carries a canteen on a field trip. It's so relaxing, too relaxing in Japan—I sort of feel blah. I'm definitely enjoying window shopping, which I haven't done for years."

"Thirty years ago it was perfectly safe for a woman to walk alone in Central Park," said Yurie nostalgically. "Americans were very kind then because we were dirt poor." With an America-is-no-longer-the-same look on her face, she continued her reminisc-ing.

"Lots of things remind us of our trips around the States. From the shape of a drive-in restaurant's roof to the layout of a gasoline station, they all look the same."

"I wonder," said Shōzō meditatively, staring into the horizon that stretched far beyond the spikes of pampas grass. "Is Japan the only country that has narrow streets and high sound-proof walls around houses? But beyond those walls, we now have Disneyland. It was twenty years ago in the States when we spent three days at Disneyland letting Chie enjoy herself."

"On a recent car trip we were very lucky to catch a glimpse of Mount Ibuki near Sekigahara," said Yurie. "The mountain really looks like a white boar. That was where the legendary Prince Yamato-takeru-no-mikoto fell ill after seeing a white boar, as if cursed. Since it still snows a lot in that region, the legend's hail storms give the tale a ring of truth. He went all the way north to Mount Ibuki, but why didn't he pass through Ōtsu on the way to Yamato? It seemed he went back south, and crossed the Suzushika Pass via Mie. Why couldn't he go to Ōtsu in the Ōmi Province?

"I have a feeling there was another reason besides the snow that kept him out of Ōmi. The author of the *Record of Ancient Matters* had Yamato-takeru say as a parting shot, 'I don't have to kill the mountain god, the white boar, right now, but I will on the way back.' What does that mean? This really interests me because the *Record* is not a historical document but a collection of tales about mythical characters. I wonder why the Prince was kept out of Ōmi when one of his consorts was from the place."

Yurie was clutching a copy of the *Record*, her eyes with the glint of a detective writer. It was very likely that their sleeping bags would be rustling all over again.

# 3 ～

"MIZUKI SAYS WE SHOULD HAVE DINNER together while Fukiko's here. I wonder what she's up to," said Yurie.

Fukiko was married to Shigeru Sugano, the younger brother of Mizuki's father.

"Has Shigeru come along?"

Shōzō was busy grinding turnips. All morning he had been gathering the rest of the ingredients with the firm intention of making a very elaborate dish, *kabura-mushi*, steamed fish with ground turnips: gingko berries, *kikurage* mushrooms, *yuri* lily roots, and red snapper. Now he was trying to figure out how he could put it all together.

"Red snapper's darn difficult to fillet; its soft meat is too yielding," Shōzō said in exasperation.

"He's in Sofia, Bulgaria, on a hotel construction project which has been completed, but he won't be back for a while," said Yurie, ignoring him. "That's too bad—just when Mizuki's staying in Japan. I hear he's taking a few days off, holed up in some monastery. What in the world are they thinking?"

"Who?"

"Shigeru, Mizuki, and Fukiko. And Mizuki's begging us to join her for dinner. There's something Fukiko wants to tell us."

"What could that be? Hmm, we might as well plant this *yuri* root rather than eat it."

"Just use pieces of the stalk, bury the rest in the garden. Tell me what we should do."

28

"This is a devilish *yuri* root, for sure."

"You never listen to what I have to say."

"I am. Why do Kansai folks love to eat fish like this? This damn thing's just too soft. I've paid a lot for it; that fish shop's no good. I should have gone to Nishiki."

"What do you think she wants to talk about?"

"I wonder. Don't you have to sprinkle this with salt before filleting it?"

"Tell me what you think, please."

"I should have grabbed some eel instead."

"Snapper's fine with me. Please, what do you think is going on?"

"I can't tell you. By looking at the root, you never know what kind of flowers you get. Maybe it's a demon lily. So, let's eat it. Do we have some pickled plum paste left?"

"I wonder if she's been seeing Mizuki. Why doesn't she join him in Sofia? What's going on with those two? A monastery for the husband, and a grandchild for the wife. You see, Tōichiro and his wife are expecting a baby. Well, I guess a grandchild's more important than a husband."

"It's probably because a husband usually dies first. Well, if that's so, Chie should have a baby fast."

"If you don't want a kid," said Yurie flatly, "no use hanging around a man." For a split second something flashed through her mind: Chie and her husband showed no signs of starting a family.

"We used to badmouth other couples—all they could do was make babies," Shōzō reminded Yurie.

"Fukiko's coming all this way. I wonder what she thinks of Mizuki. Does this mean that things in the past don't bother her anymore?"

"Well …"

"Her husband got another woman pregnant. What kind of woman is she anyway?"

Yurie had met her a couple of times, but for some strange reason, she kept her at arm's length.

Obviously Yurie wanted Shōzō to remember that at the time of Mizuki's birth Fū dropped a not-so-subtle hint that the father was

Shigeru, the younger brother of Seiichiro. She bragged about it as if she had his approval.

Another story that had become a family legend went that when a wealthy but heirless family approached Shigeru Sugano with a marriage proposal-cum-adoption, which for the near-bankrupt Suganos was a heaven-sent proposition, Fū had set off alone to meet with the family to turn down the timely proposal, using the very same pretext of the Suganos' declining fortunes.

This was something that shouldn't happen in the real world, but it does. And as long as something like this happens, there's nothing anybody can do about it or insist that it shouldn't happen. It's like arguing until you're blue in the face that a child born with a finger missing should have all five, knowing full well that four will never become five. And, no one can do anything for the suffering child, either. Since suffering is indeed a given, and part and parcel of reality, you might say that the child, through suffering, is affirming his own being.

Shōzō speculated that Shigeru forced a marriage on Fukiko whom he had met at a munitions plant during the war. He was taking the blame for getting her pregnant. That must have been his way of challenging the authority of Fū, his overbearing sister-in-law.

Now with Seiichiro and Fū gone, there was no way to get at the truth. Considering that Shōzō and Yurie were probably the only witnesses to what had happened back then, was Fukiko coming all the way to Mount Hiei just to air her grievances? What did she mean by requesting that we all assemble in Mizuki's presence?

"Do you think Mizuki told her about us being here?" asked Shōzō.

"Who else? She must have. But are they on such good terms that Mizuki could just call her up?"

"Well …"

"What do you mean "Well"? Be serious."

"I can't tell you. It's obvious she did."

In her pursuit of Shōzō's opinion Yurie often became obsessive about things of this nature. Who cares what other people do? said Shōzō to himself. Of course, you can't know what's on their minds.

I don't even know my own—. A more urgent matter for him was: is this iron kettle large enough to steam two servings of *kabura-mushi* in two separate bowls?

"I wonder if Mizuki's invited us because she doesn't want to be alone with Fukiko?"

"Well …"

"Or, is it Fukiko who wants to see us?"

"Well …"

"Come on, think."

"I can't. You're too obsessive. I'm no novelist. You're the imaginative one."

"According to Mizuki, Fukiko is not joining Shigeru in Sofia because, she said, 'It's no fun to go to a place where I don't know the language. Besides there's nothing for me to do there.'"

"Can't be helped. Everybody has a reason for doing things their way."

"Shigeru's partly to blame. Imagine staying at a monastery between jobs rather than coming home."

"It's his age probably—he just wants to be alone to think about life in general. I know—"

"What?"

"I've decided to take the turnip dish and steam it at Mizuki's place. No utensils here anyway."

"Why did you pick such a difficult dish when you don't even have the right utensils? What a genius. Excel in one art, excel in all others, they say. Please, back to Fukiko and Shigeru."

"I told you. I'm not Fukiko, I'm not Shigeru. How should I know? I'm trying to figure out how to fillet the snapper. Don't distract me."

Yurie immediately snatched away the knife and, with a few quick, deft strokes, the fish was ready.

"Boy, you're good. Well, I shouldn't be surprised after thirty years of toil in the kitchen."

"If you had that much experience, you wouldn't even think about preparing *kabura-mushi* when you're staying at someone else's place."

"Ahh, right, a seasoned cook wouldn't have the foggiest idea about what a novice dreams of."

"I guess that's all human imagination boils down to."

As usual, Yurie's mind began to wander elsewhere.

"You're right. There're no utensils I can use."

Shōzō sighed in despair at the stark bareness of the kitchen. "I thought I could steam it in the kettle."

"Let's take it to Mizuki's house."

"I was going to make use of your tea bowl. A snapper can feed five, and we have fresh horseradish to go with it. Would Karl eat something like this?"

"Probably. Out of curiosity."

THE DISH READY FOR STEAMING, they carried it to Mizuki's house. The hairy spikes of pampas grass, their thick strands now dried white, rustled in the wind.

Dogs at nearby houses began to bark.

"Looks like everyone around here keeps a dog," said Shōzō.

"Nobody's home during the day. I imagine the husbands and wives both have to work to pay the mortgage on their new homes," Yurie speculated.

Villas were mixed with residential subdivisions, making up perhaps a third of the total housing in the area. The residents must have felt a little uneasy leaving their homes unprotected, because every house had a dog chained outside.

The dogs howled, arching their necks as far back as they could as if howling was their only means of exercise. Yurie stopped, staring at a vacant house with shuttered windows, an overgrown lawn where goldenrod swayed in the wind; there was not a living soul around.

MIZUKI WAS SERVING THE TEA and sweet dumplings Fukiko said were from Uji. Karl was nowhere to be seen.

Fukiko in a *kasuri* kimono of subdued brown had positioned herself properly in the Japanese room. Yurie thought she had seen the kimono somewhere and tried to remember just where, superimposing it on the image of the low vermilion-lacquered Japanese table right in front of her.

The furniture and kitchen utensils in Mizuki's household which had been shipped by Yurie for the family's temporary use, had originally belonged to Fū at the Myōkō house in Niigata. Vermilions and subdued browns were Fū's favorite colors. It seemed strange to see Shigeru's wife seated at the lacquer table, assuming possessions Fū loved. Fukiko could have easily passed for Fū.

"How long has it been since your mother passed away?" asked Yurie.

"Thirteen years," replied Mizuki.

"You mean—" Making a mental calculation of how long Mizuki had known Karl, Yurie turned to look at her more carefully. "Things took you that long?"

"I guess so. He was there when you came to see me in California."

"I know. That means it's been almost twenty years. But you didn't marry him until after your mother passed away."

"No."

"You must have given lots of careful thought to it, Mizuki," Fukiko broke in.

"You could say that," said Mizuki, cocking her head. "Or, perhaps, her death did it." Looking back, she really had not wanted to introduce Karl to her mother. "*She* was one of those types who would even make passes at her daughter's boyfriends." The tone of her voice was as sharp as a dagger.

Fukiko's head was gently tilted toward the garden, swaying like a gentle breeze.

Obviously Mizuki's words were meant for her. She ignored them and said, "Shōzō, I've heard you've turned down a job offer at a Japanese bank in the States."

"Yes. I've decided to become a dependent." Detecting her eagerness to remind him of the decision, he gave her what she wanted to hear.

"That's a really prestigious bank. Shigeru-san couldn't get over it," continued Fukiko, taking no notice of his explanation.

Apparently she referred to her own husband with the polite -*san* ending.

"Honey, when was that?" Yurie was completely taken aback.

"Oh my, Yuri, you didn't know?" asked Fukiko.

"No. This is the first time I've heard it."

"I thought you were the one who voted down the idea."

Yurie kept silent.

Is my wife calculating the salary I'd have gotten? Shōzō began to worry as he studied the expression on her face.

"Karl envies you, Shōzō," said Mizuki.

He is actually contemptuous of a man who has no qualms about letting his wife feed him, Shōzō said to himself. But, if you're so envious of me, why not try it yourself? Well, on the other hand, he reflected sympathetically, it takes a near-herculean effort to train a woman for thirty years to do what you want her to do; I guess it isn't so easy to emulate what I've done.

If you want to nurture the woman you live with and at the same time try to live your own life, the same thing could happen to you. If you're despised for the way you live, you might find yourself accepting that. If you're envied, you start wondering about it, then guilt is sure to set in—the feeling that you may be doing something wrong. They wouldn't be talking like that if I were a woman. Take, Yurie, for example. If she were a man, nobody would find fault with her just because she neglected the household chores while she wrote novels, or lived abroad alone for six months.

She didn't surrender to what most people say a woman's life should be because she's a mutant generated by the strains of the very system we live in—a mutation a bit like the earth's topology with its depressions and protrusions. What's in vogue now may become *outré* in the future. A man like me is proof of that—Yurie's lifestyle doesn't faze me at all. The ceaseless movement and connections of things are what life's all about. What would happen to a man if he lived with a woman like Yurie—no, wait a minute—she became what she is because of me. Now here you are, Fukiko, lecturing me like a big sister, Shōzō thought, shooting a furtive glance in her direction.

It's not that we became what we are because something came to our minds unbidden—, he said to himself. Somehow while he was thinking all of this, Shōzō began to understand the kind of presumptuousness women typically display and felt saddened.

Right after he quit his civil service job, he had joined the McKinsey Company, something arranged by Shigeru. Things didn't turn out the way he expected. Shigeru must have felt responsible because he then had broached the subject of an overseas bank position.

"You were an executive," said Fukiko, continuing to lecture him, "which I'm sure exempted you from a set retirement age. So you must have left on your own. Normally you'd be considered too young to sit around the house, you know."

"For a company in the red, it's just good policy to promote employees to executive positions as soon as possible so that they don't have to pay pensions."

"Is that the way companies are run?"

"I really appreciate your concern but it's a decision I made on my own. I mean, it's a big job to be a househusband and a secretary. I'm always impressed by women who demurely accept the dependent label, assuming an air of presumptuousness as an equal trade-off. Their nerves of steel are something I don't have because I've never given birth. Unless you've been in that position, you won't know what it feels like. Whether or not I can come to terms with this remains to be seen. Think about what might happen before it happens, Yurie used to tell me again and again."

"You always say you'd think about it when it happens," said Yurie resentfully. She seemed to have resigned herself to his philosophy, but she was still upset.

"Yuri throws impossible questions at me," he continued, still the picture of composure. "Think about what Fukiko's up to; imagine what Mizuki's thinking; or, put yourself in Shigeru's shoes. How can I when I'm neither Fukiko, Shigeru nor Mizuki? Thinking about what's not real seems to be a novelist's business."

At this point, a thought occurred to him. Yurie, being extremely poor at directions, might feel exactly this way if someone insisted that she should know how to get to a place, he thought. Excited at this discovery, he added aloud,

"Yuri can't even tell which way Kyoto or Tokyo is. 'Not knowing directions is no inconvenience,' she says, 'because I can just ask someone; I've survived so far and asking directions has given me no trouble.' She's absolutely unflappable."

"Whenever I can't find a place I've been to before, Shōzō takes sadistic pleasure in making fun of me. All you have to do is ask. No big deal since I've got the knack of who to ask," said Yurie with confidence.

"What if you didn't run into anybody?" asked Shōzō. "You're the type who'd get lost and die in the mountains."

"You two will have plenty of time to continue this argument later," intervened Fukiko with a laugh. "You try so hard to understand the other person, actually putting yourself in his position," she said gently. "But no matter how hard you try, you still don't get it. Shigeru-san is in a monastery in Bulgaria. He's probably there because he also doesn't understand how other people feel. I reflect on this every time I make my daily climb up Zither Hill to the Kōshōji Temple in Uji, but I still don't get it. Dōgen founded that Zen temple. They call it Zither because the sound of the water running through the rocks on both sides of the hill reminds you of a Japanese zither."

With her plump fair-skinned body, Fukiko seemed buried under layers of flesh. The vacant look in her round eyes with their double-folded lids somehow reminded Shōzō of an otter.

He had been having a problem lately, confusing people with creatures in the wild. Not just other people; he sometimes even had the same confusion about himself. When did that start? He tried to remember.

It probably began the moment he met Yurie. Something of a wild creature, the eleven-year-old Yurie was the very image of a weasel intently observing him in the mist among the dew-drenched grasses.

I wonder why I feel that way about most people, Shōzō said to himself. Is it because I've lived more than half a century, or maybe my brain's deteriorating and I'm becoming senile—? He stared at

Fukiko's round eyes as she tried to play the big sister, nodding in reply here and there.

In his mind the plumpness of her body and pale skin conjured up a mysterious white animal, a creature capable of blurting anything out, and everything at any moment.

"Shigeru-san—"

The way she repeatedly said "Shigeru-san" was not unlike the way one calls out to a favorite dog or cat, "Shiro" or "Tama."

"Shigeru-san, no, I mean, both of us have been trying to understand other people's situations, to really put ourselves in their shoes. Do you remember this kimono?" she asked. Her face suddenly sagged as if a large petal from a peony had dropped to the ground with a thump.

"This is Fū's," she declared matter-of-factly, before any of the people in the room could reply.

Unable to add anything, her three listeners kept their silence.

"For a long time I couldn't bring myself to wear it, but I felt different this morning."

"I sort of remember it," said Yurie, retrieving a thread of memory.

"She wore it when she came to see me in Tokyo, with the infant Mizuki in her arms," said Fukiko. "That was before I married Shigeru-san. In those days women in their early twenties knew exactly how to show off such subdued colors and still looked gorgeous. Fū's appearance was overwhelming."

This baby of mine is Shigeru's child. Do you still intend to marry him—? Behind the plump white otter was Fū smiling, moving closer and closer.

"I was already pregnant with Tōichiro."

# 4 ～

MIZUKI HAD FELT A TREMOR OF UNEASE whenever Fukiko paid a visit or phoned to say hello. After all, her husband Shigeru—Mizuki's uncle—might well be her father.

In such disquieting moments Mizuki would initiate some small talk to break the ice, letting the other side say what was on their mind. Though the inner workings of other people often piqued her curiosity, she was forever vigilant, afraid that conversations might race out of control and entangle everyone in the process.

Fū used to flaunt her past relationship with Uncle Shigeru like a badge of honor, telling Mizuki, "You have a right to demand things from him." The sinister side of the woman who gave birth to Mizuki became unbearably transparent, and the daughter had no choice but to stare with contempt at her own image in the mirror.

In her reminiscences she would become quite emotional about her doting father Seiichiro, but not so about the woman whom she had rejected, someone who thought it was a mother's right to possess her daughter's spirit.

Fū had placed her in the care of a wealthy American—a collector of ancient Japanese artifacts. She was then sent to a private school in the States. It was Fū's way of avoiding her adolescent daughter's critical scrutiny while expecting her indebtedness, Mizuki speculated.

She could not deny the fact that she was more than willing to exploit this opportunity. "Uncle Shigeru might well be your father." In a far away land she had revived Fū's words and replayed them over and over again like an incantation. In spite of this insinuation, she considered Seiichiro her closest relative. After all he had bathed and spoon-fed the little girl every single day. Uncle Shigeru, whom she had met only a couple of times, meant absolutely nothing to her.

This mystery man who might be her father was also the reason she became extremely guarded whenever a new man appeared on the dating scene. She could not help imagining that he was probably doing the same thing as Shigeru did on the sly.

When the new boyfriend turned out to be like Shigeru, a man with an intense longing for women and the ability to blame them for everything that goes wrong, Mizuki almost gave in to torment him just for the fun of it.

Ironically, this fantasy game also helped her understand the nature of Fū's dalliance with men.

Karl appeared in Mizuki's life with a batting average of one marriage, one divorce. He used to talk with much wit and humor about the impossibility of satisfying his first wife, who was enamored by the extravagances that only wealth and status could bring. After his divorce, an aspiring actress entertained the lonely bachelor in a gender experiment, which she claimed was part of a research project. She took it for granted that a man was there to tend to her needs night and day. Considering her firm conviction that she possessed an enormous talent for arousing men and that there was no man alive who could resist her, it was really quite a herculean effort on Karl's part to render personal services, pretending that it was all a spontaneous act.

"A woman," said Karl happily, "who had nothing on her mind but sex is okay, I said to myself. At least that puts me in the mood to test how much stamina I actually have."

He gestured with his hands the way a sculptor kneads clay, greedily swallowing his drool while he described how voluptuous she was, adding that a plaster mold of her back would rival that of a Venus. What did he mean by "her back"?

"There was no expression on her face," he explained, "or nothing in her body language that would challenge you—at least I didn't see any. She was a consummate performer, constantly looking at herself in the mirror."

"Let's face it, marriage ain't for us," the aspiring actress had said to him matter-of-factly. Soon after she began to live with a singer boyfriend. The two came to see Karl and Mizuki and entertained them with a song and dance routine.

"Karl's a real nice guy, you know," said the actress with her Marilyn Monroe laugh. "You're fortunate, Mizuki." That comment humored him greatly. He went on to compliment the singer again and again for taking in the woman. After the two left, he said, "B-o-o-y, I'm beat."

Karl's stories about his girlfriends were not that much different from Fū's. What held more reality for her were the memories of Fū grumbling to the young Mizuki about Seiichiro, or making up stories on a whim about her male friends.

Mizuki experienced a curious sense of calm and security when she was around Karl. What he had told her sounded a bit like the child frog of Aesop's fables who, upon seeing an ox for the first time, rushes to tell her mother, "Mommy, Mommy, Mommy, I've seen someone huge drinking water, much, much bigger than you."

At that moment, she was driven by much the same comical impulse as the mother frog, who said, "Is that right? Was he as big as this?" as she inhaled as much air as possible, puffing up her belly with all her might.

When she imitated the mother frog, she noticed Karl give a perplexed look at her puffed out belly. She was then struck by the insight that it would be better to go out with the child frog and take a look at the mysterious ox herself.

By the time the two started out in search of the ox, they began to see marriage as the natural outcome of their relationship.

Sitting with a vacant stare in front of Mizuki—supposedly the child her own husband fathered by another woman—Fukiko would begin the usual round of small talk. It always puzzled Mizuki as to why she would come all the way from Uji just to exchange chit-chat.

By playing the dumb chatterbox, she might have wished to say, I don't mind Mizuki's presence at all, I'm fully aware of the situation, I married Shigeru with full knowledge of the fact—. At least there seemed to be no sign of malice on her part, and if she had any ulterior motive, it might be to find out that Mizuki had no weird attachment to Shigeru. That again put Mizuki on her guard.

She had assumed that this was another typical visit until Fukiko, upon learning that Shōzō and Yurie were in the neighborhood, formally declared, "There's something I want to tell all of you."

This is the right moment, her words seemed to imply. Mizuki felt she was on the brink of some new discovery. Even if it is something obvious, something everyone knows, there's always a subtle difference depending on who's talking and what's left out.

It was common knowledge among relatives that Shigeru Sugano had impregnated Fukiko, a fellow student he had met during the war at a munitions factory, to escape the relentless demands of his sister-in-law Fū.

As soon as he married Fukiko, Fū cut off the financial assistance his older brother was providing for his college tuition. She argued that the Suganos had already gone bankrupt because of Seiichiro's incompetence. With only a few months left before graduation, the older brother gave Shigeru some valuable hanging scrolls to sell for college expenses. His induction notice came immediately after he graduated, but the war was over.

Fū moved to Tokyo with Seiichiro and Mizuki right after the war and opened an antique art shop in upscale Aoyama.

Shigeru had helped support his brother's family from time to time, and Yurie, then a college student, served as the family courier. He always reminded her to give the money to Seiichiro in person, never to Fū.

Yurie gazed at Fukiko as she revisited these memories.

"I told Fū, I'm also carrying a baby, Shigeru-san's baby," said Fukiko quietly, looking down.

In her mind's eye, Yurie saw the specter of Fū slowly floating by, with the infant Mizuki in her arms.

"I need a husband, too, I said to Fū. You have a good one in Seiichiro, don't you—? That was what Shigeru-san had told me to say. I've given careful thought to this matter, Mizuki. I want all of you to hear me out because I think you've got it all wrong."

"You're thinking that I want to say something mean about Shigeru-san and your mother. I'm what I am for marrying a man like him. Things are the way they are, so I take them as they are, and that's the way I see you, Mizuki."

The three stared intently at her, trying to figure out this woman who would marry a man like Shigeru.

"What you have on your minds right now is not what I'm thinking," she said quietly. "People often reach the wrong conclusions when they judge things only by appearances. I had—there was someone in my life before I met Shigeru-san."

This unexpected confession stunned the three.

"He was drafted earlier than Shigeru-san because he was in the Humanities Department. I had no idea if he was dead or alive when I married Shigeru-san, who decided to marry me in spite of that. Shigeru-san was very fond of him. He was one of his classmates. Shōzō, you must have known him, too. His name was Natsuyama."

Shōzō vaguely remembered this upperclassman, who was a good friend of Shigeru.

"Hmm, I heard he was killed in the war," said Shōzō.

"At that time things weren't so clear. Shigeru-san insisted that, if we wanted, he'd give me up if Natsuyama returned. What do you think? I think he wanted to put himself in Seiichiro's shoes. I can't imagine any other reason."

The idea that her only child Tōichiro may have been Natsuyama's son flashed simultaneously through the minds of the threesome like a bolt of lightning.

However, she simply gazed at their faces, again with a faint mocking smile and continued,

"You three have got it all wrong again. Definitely wrong. When Shigeru-san comes up with an idea, he follows through no matter what. I still like him for that."

She looked as though she was gazing at a mountain in the distance, the gaze of an animal trying in vain to see something impossible to see.

"How strange—" she said meditatively, "I was young—too young to understand. It was intoxicating when Natsuyama had me wrapped around his little finger. It's laughable when you think about it now. At that time there was no such thing as sex education, no books to read on the subject, so I was left totally ignorant.

"I liked him. I think he cared for me too, something you'd expect from young people, but we felt suffocated with the pain of longing and then he had to go to war. I was willing to do whatever he wanted. And it was Shigeru-san who had arranged the assignation for us. But—" Fumbling for words, she blushed.

"He was young, but he was concerned about what might happen to me in the future more than anything else. All he did was press his body against me and he was through. I had no idea what he did or what it meant. I thought he did what he wanted and I remember feeling very sad. And I also felt that I'd done something forbidden for a proper young woman, and if he were to die in the war, I would have no prospects for marriage. You know, you might find this hard to believe—some young women back then were convinced that they could get pregnant just by kissing a man."

Shōzō was listening carefully but the look on his face said he was either smothering a laugh or was at a loss as to where to look. Yurie's gaze was utterly serious, her eyes riveted on Fukiko's.

"Natsuyama's transport ship was sunk immediately after it left Japan," continued Fukiko somberly. "They said he probably went down with it. After I heard the news, I cried every day. Shigeru-san came to comfort me but I kept crying, a hysterical sort of thing, and I told him I no longer wanted to live. He watched me, not knowing what to do. Remembering what had happened at the assignation, I convinced myself that I was pregnant; I began to worry about the imaginary pregnancy and making a living as an unwed mother.

"I lost control, blurted out the stupidest things. Shigeru-san figured out what had happened from my rambling and came up with an even weirder idea. 'If that's the case,' he said, 'Why not get married. I'm still alive. Natsuyama told me to marry you if he died,' he added. Shigeru-san may even have been telling the truth. But his body was never found, I said, sobbing. 'He might show up any time.' I broke into another crying fit. Silent for a while, Shigeru-san was thinking hard and finally said, 'Well, if that happens, then we can get a divorce.'

"At that time he was like a god to me and I decided to go along with whatever he told me to do. Don't ask me why we rushed into it, or why I went along—I think we had lost our wits. I may not be too smart but I finally caught on after Shigeru-san and I did it. I was so confused, I started crying again. That was all I did, cry. There's nothing to do but cry when you don't know what to do."

"Women have it good," muttered Shōzō, "they can cry." Yurie shot him a sharp sidelong glance, jabbing a finger into his knee.

"And, I really became pregnant," said Fukiko. "You know the rest."

"What an innocent, heartrending story," said Yurie thoughtfully.

"No, you really don't know because the rest of the story is even more bizarre and confusing. Shigeru-san said he married me because I was already pregnant, otherwise he wouldn't have. And he tried to get me to say that Tōichiro was Natsuyama's child.

"He thought I was making up a story about what Natsuyama did, and said, 'I'm willing to raise the child because he isn't mine. I wouldn't want to have anything to do with a child of my own.' He also said, 'If Tōichiro were really my son, I'd smother him.'

"That's when he told me everything about Fū and Mizuki. 'I'm trying to atone for my sin,' he said. 'Admit that Tōichiro is Natsuyama's son. If you do, I would really love the baby just the way my older brother showers affection on Mizuki.' Have you ever heard anything so ridiculous? Men out there worry themselves sick about who's fathered whom. I've never heard of a man who is mad at his wife for giving birth to his own child.

"Of course, I'm ashamed of my childish behavior but I was truly grateful for Shigeru-san's kindness and liked him for his eccentricity. So why couldn't he at least try to understand that I had no intention of deceiving him? He kept on demanding outrageous things. He tried to push me onto another man. 'It's unthinkable that a woman can be satisfied with only one man,' he said. 'I have no interest in a woman who clings to only one man.'

"After Tōichiro's birth, he became extremely guarded about sex and said, 'If you want more children, have them with other men. I won't mind feeding them.' He also said, 'You don't show any interest in other men because you're indifferent to them. You don't try hard enough and you're lazy.' But he did say that I looked the most beautiful when I was in love with Natsuyama. What do you think he meant by that?

"Wasn't Fū on Shigeru-san's mind all the time? Can you think of any other reason? After thirty years of such nonsense, anybody would go out of his mind. At one point I seriously thought about taking a lover or two, but I was out of my element. It just didn't work.

"The whole thing was such a bother, so I made a deal with him: 'Let's pretend the gods gave us Tōichiro.' That's how we've somehow gotten by.

"I wonder if Shigeru-san decided to hole up in a Bulgarian monastery because he's unable to free himself of those weird thoughts that plague him. 'You can do anything you want,' he said. 'I'll send you money. I've never tried to tie you down. You're also free. Keep a gigolo, or try a hostess club—do anything you like. Be a woman like that, I'll follow you anywhere. What's boring is a prim and proper housewife sitting at home waiting all day for her husband.' Now that's why he's praying in a monastery. I'm totally confused," she paused, sighing deeply.

"How about his blood type?" Shōzō, always the scientist, suggested.

"That won't convince him of anything because Shigeru-san, Tōichiro, and Mizuki are all type A. It's his soul that is at stake."

Strange, she even knew Mizuki's blood type.

"I'm O," added Fukiko. "Ten years after Natsuyama's death, hoping he was a B, I went out of my way to find out about his blood type just to prove to Shigeru-san that he wasn't the father. It turned out to be AB. What a waste. I resented his not getting me pregnant."

"Well, why not follow Shigeru's advice and go all out?" Yurie blurted, at a loss for words.

"It's too late now. Besides, having affairs doesn't agree with me. I have my own ways."

She jerked her head away from Yurie in protest. "Sorry, Mizuki, you have to hear all this, but I wanted you to know, especially since

I've had the impression that you thought otherwise.

"Also, Yurie, you're Fū's cousin and a novelist. I thought you might be able to give me a better explanation, and Shōzō might shed some new light on the matter as a man. That's why I've decided to share my embarrassing past with you. They say three heads are better than one. What was Seiichiro like, Mizuki? Was he like Shigeru-san? The two were very close."

"I wonder," said Mizuki in a strangely cheerful voice. "I don't know anything about them as brothers. All I can say is my father was very loving to me. As long as my mother was the one who gave birth to me, that was fine with him."

"Go ahead, Fukiko," said Yurie aggressively, "stand up to him, tell him off. 'Whether you're the father or not, it's my child, leave it at that.' He's such a stubborn guy, anyway. But, you know, it may be that he's not happy about your obsession with his past."

Fukiko stared at them with the cute blankness of an otter.

"I was jealous of Fū for a long time," she said, "Mizuki, too. Now that you're married and I've had the chance to meet you and hear you talk so bitterly about your mother, things no longer seem so unnatural. I've changed my views a bit. Now I feel more comfortable talking to you."

After a brief pause, she corrected herself. "I've said a lot of negative things about Shigeru-san, but I think I'm attracted to his complex personality because I'm a simple sort of person, not very smart."

"Things will work out," said Shōzō encouragingly. "He will be back in no time. He just wants to mull things over. Just as you've now decided to try on Fū's kimono, it's probably time for him to reassess what he's taken for granted for so long."

A happy baby's smile brightened Fukiko's face.

"I almost forgot," said Mizuki changing the subject. "Shōzō's brought us *kabura-mushi*."

"My goodness. Such an elaborate dish," said Fukiko, rather impressed. She looked him full in the face.

"He's also made a famous Echigo dish, the traditional *Noppei* stew," bragged Yurie.

"I still haven't gotten the hang of chopping vegetables," said

Shōzō modestly.

"The way he holds a kitchen knife scares me to death," said Yurie somberly. "No matter how many times I tell him not to hold the vegetables with the flat of his hand, he keeps doing it. One of these days he'll chop all of his fingers off," she continued without a pause. "The fact that he quit his job must have really upset me because I had a weird dream the other day."

"A very interesting one," chimed in Shōzō. "You'll like it."

Mizuki and Fukiko exchanged a knowing glance, observing that Yurie and Shōzō really enjoyed a witty repartee.

"A man who turned fifty suddenly decided to get a college education," began Yurie. "He was poor and only had a grade school education. He went back to high school and eventually on to college. He had studied like hell for the college entrance exams and got in; he was past sixty when he graduated. But he couldn't find a job he liked and became rather disillusioned about the world. Everything he'd learned in college seemed useless.

"After giving a lot of thought to his situation, he came up with the idea of becoming a tramp, scavenging food left at graves. At funerals and memorials people leave dumplings and fruit at the graves. He'd sneak in when nobody was around and eat the offerings. It was tough work; sometimes it rained or was very windy, and often he didn't find any food at all.

"In the end the children chased him down like hounds to a fox and stoned him to death. Remember the story on the news of those young boys who hounded a homeless person to death? I guess that had something to do with the dream."

"Oh, but … You don't mean—" said Fukiko, looking stunned. "My goodness, Shōzō, you received an elite education. You'd never be so destitute."

"No. But it's a darn good dream," he said cheerfully. "It's so realistic."

"He's impressed with whatever I say," said Yurie anxiously. "That's the problem. He comes to like anyone I like, dislike anyone I dislike, respect anyone I respect, despise anyone I despise. Don't you think that's weird?"

"Well …" Fukiko was at a loss.

"Yurie's studying how to be unhappy," said Shōzō, "so I'm studying how to be happy."

"If I like a man, he'll like him, too," said Yurie irritably. "That means I can't even fall in love with anyone. He's really crafty."

Mizuki began to laugh.

"Yuri, you've just gone on about how wonderful your husband is," she said. " That's the way I hear it."

Shōzō was grinning from ear to ear.

ON HIS WAY HOME KARL PICKED UP STEAKS from the Hatamoto butcher shop near the Ginkakuji Temple. Mizuki had told him to take his time coming home because listening to Fukiko's complicated story would be too much for him. Mizuki, a self-proclaimed vegetarian, believed that fish was a good source of animal protein. Karl, brought up on a meat-rich diet, picked up beef whenever they had a guest, an excellent excuse for him to indulge his craving.

"You can have your beef when you eat out for lunch." That was what Mizuki had told him, but he insisted that food didn't taste good unless it was shared with friends.

"Shōzō, I really envy you not having to go to work every day," he began hesitantly in Japanese. "I say to myself that working eight-to-five is for eccentrics, yes? I heard about a funny guy the other day. He loves tuna sashimi, yesterday, today, tomorrow, the day after tomorrow, every day, three hundred and sixty-five days a year. No-o-o, it's not just a year, he's been married for twenty years, so multiply that by twenty. He'll go on and on, eating tuna sashimi. Tuna contains PCBs, which are stored as toxins inside the human body. But he still goes on."

"PCBs are also in beef," countered Mizuki.

"Righto. It's in everything. Water's also dangerous. So is eating, drinking, breathing. But this man ca-a-n't help it. By the way, since he eats nothing but tuna, his wife doesn't have to cook for him. That's really handy. Makes her happy."

"How could she live with such a man?" said Yurie.

"She may not be happy, but, at any rate, I see Japanese eat *ine* plants every day—"

"Rice, just rice." Mizuki gave him the correct Japanese word, *o-kome.*

"I thought only eccentrics eat rice, but foreigners—"

"Westerners," Mizuki corrected him.

"Westerners are foreigners, that is, to the Japanese," he muttered to himself. "But, for me, they're not foreigners, but Westerners. Yes, you're right. I, a Westerner, never get tired of eating bread made out of yeast and ground wheat. Eating rice is the same thing, isn't it? So, eating *cow* every day—"

"You mean beef," Mizuki again corrected him.

"I never get tired of beef, but hearing about someone eating tuna every day grosses me out. You could say, nobody and everybody is an eccentric. So, children who refuse to go to school may not be totally delinquent."

Shōzō nodded in agreement. He moved on to a different topic. "All day today I sewed together bunches of cleaning rags. I used to wonder how women could do mind-numbing things like knitting and sewing without getting sick of them, but I now know chores like that aren't so stupid. Take sewing. It's a very simple task and doesn't require any heavy thinking. So, you can daydream while doing it. Your mind's completely elsewhere. As you concentrate on doing the easy stitches, it restores a modicum of reality.

"For instance, since we set up household here, Yuri's bought quite a few books on the Asuka-Tenpyō eras. I picked up some for my own reading. So as I sewed a cleaning rag, I began to imagine that Empress Jitō might have assassinated her husband Emperor Temmu. Apparently Prince Ōtsu was Temmu's favorite son, so if the father had lived long enough, he would probably have given the Crown Prince more power, diminishing the chance of Jitō's own son taking the throne. That may have been her main concern."

"And that was what you were thinking when I was worried sick about you being forced to steal food from graves or stoned to death by some kids," said Yurie, grumbling. "In the animal kingdom, there's a thing called metagenesis, the alternation of generations, where males in some species suddenly turn female. Hmm, I wonder."

## 5 ∾

TOLD BY KARL THAT THERE WOULD BE A SHOWING of Werner Herzog films at the German Culture Center, Shōzō and Yurie came down Mount Hiei by bus to the ancient city of Kyoto.

The road from Hiei-daira to Kyoto snakes down Mount Hiei along the Shirakawa River. The road is also a route to Ōtsu via the Nyoigadake-oka Valley that runs through part of the Higashiyama Mountain Range.

After the bus had turned at Kita-Shirakawa, and again at Betto, and yet again soon after, Yurie didn't have the foggiest idea which direction they were going.

She might have reminded you of a fool sent to buy sweet *manjū* dumplings. He completely forgets what he is supposed to do by the time he comes upon a brook and starts skipping from rock to rock with a jolly ho-ho-ho. Once they got off the bus at Higashi Ichijō, she didn't have a clue which way to go.

If she wanted to go to the famous Kamo River that runs southward through Kyoto, she had no idea where it was. If you pointed out to her, "The river's over there," and if all she saw was the gentle slope of the river bank, she would still walk over and beyond the embankment to confirm that there was indeed a river.

Yet she could at least declare with complete confidence, "We have descended the mountain," a fact that left Shōzō dumbfounded. But it gave him a reason to poke fun at her every time it happened.

"All you understand is the sensation of being up or down or your increasing fat," he said mockingly.

Yurie's response to his jabs was full of wild claims. "You are a pre-Copernican chicken, that's why you make such a big deal out of not knowing east from west, north from south. The earth's round, so if you go far enough east, you end up in the west. It doesn't make any difference which way you go."

She then suggested self-importantly that they stop at the city market either at Nishiki or at the Ginkakuji Temple on the way home, pointing as usual in the wrong direction.

The minute Shōzō walked down a street with her, he would metamorphose into a bully, his face taking on the look of an animal trainer forced to deal with a pitiful brain-damaged creature. He felt the urge to tie a string to Yurie, hold on tight, and hope for the best.

She was staring at the dry bed of the Kamo River.

"In the next life I want to come back as a rock, soak up the presence of the Will of the Universe in perpetual flux," she said calmly. "I don't know why people say there's a difference between organic and inorganic matter. Whether it's organic or inorganic, while the universe is in perpetual flux, every object possesses a free will, individuality, or something like the sixth sense that humans have.

"Take that rock; it's lying still right now, but once the river overflows, it will be pushed along, worn down little by little. No, not worn down, but choosing to entrust itself to a higher power voluntarily.

"Everybody's talking about energy nowadays, but when a camel doesn't want to move, he won't budge an inch. A camel also has his own free will, not much different from a rock that has its own ideas. When it doesn't want to move, it won't.

"The same with birds—if they don't want to sing, they won't, and if they don't want to fly, they won't.

"A camel has a built-in energy supply that enables him to cover a very long distance in the desert hauling heavy loads on his back. But if he doesn't want to get up, you can hit him and kick him all you want, but he won't budge an inch. It appears that mathematicians are hell-bent on trying to figure out what generates this kind of energy, frantically feeding data into their computers. Researchers are studying the behavior of all kinds of creatures in the wild kingdom, photographing worms or other bugs, enlarging the pictures for further analysis. They're mesmerized by their own findings, saying, 'Wow, there's a perfect computer inside every one of these creatures we study.'

"Humans, as the lords of creation with their superior brain and blind faith in man-made computers, are overwhelmed by the information their hardware spews out. They become so confused that in the end they lose all sense of reality, start punching buttons haphazardly until someone trips and his hand inadvertently hits a nuclear button. But damned if they wouldn't come up with a perfect excuse—*That was just a coincidence which we had no way of foreseeing.*"

Yurie tottered as her foot caught the curb of the sidewalk. She abruptly turned around and began to step backward, almost running into a passerby. Shōzō quickly grabbed her shoulders to pull her away.

"In wars," she continued serenely, "men rape women and burn down houses, but sometimes a soldier just shoots into the air. Torture someone all you want to get a confession, but there will always be someone who chooses to die rather than reveal anything. It's so strange. The human spirit is a wellspring of energy for sure, but does that spirit have any substance, any weight? If you weigh someone who's just died, he wouldn't be any lighter.

"You can't say the life force and physical energy are unrelated. A human cadaver turns into soil that will nourish plants, which in turn feed animals, and which humans will consume in turn. We're probably consuming the spirit of these things as well. Humans consume everything they can imagine."

As Yurie walked further down the street, she suddenly reached up as if to grab a piece of the sky. "Spirits have stuck themselves here and there," she blurted out.

That worried Shōzō. Well, now she must have really lost her marbles, he thought. But still somehow what she had said was music to his ears.

And speaking of music, despite the complete absence of musical talent, Yurie never tired of playing the piano. Her performance of a Bach minuet was just a series of sluggish, drawn-out sounds, just the way pebbles no longer roll forward because there is no hydraulic power or wind to push them along.

However, according to Yurie, "Playing the piano gives me the pleasurable sensation of awakening a memory that has been slumbering for eons."

When Shōzō heard her say "spirits," he happened to look up at the roof of a nearby temple. Temples are everywhere in Kyoto, he said to himself, but you don't think about them in Tokyo. What some call spirits may have something to do with what's known nowadays as information.

We're moved by information, and by spirit. A camel in a bad mood says to himself, I won't budge an inch. Living beings are forever making choices like that.

In the distance someone was playing a Bach minuet, the same piece Yurie always played.

"I feel what people must have felt hundreds of years ago," she said, humming the tune. Be that as it may, her performance of the same minuet would be nothing but noise to an outsider.

Shōzō decided to ignore her obsessions because he had heard that exercising the fingers retards aging.

THE THREE WERNER HERZOG FEATURES were *Even Dwarfs Started Small*,* *The Great Ecstasy of Woodcarver Steiner*, and *La Soufrière*. The first was a drama, and the other two documentaries.

*Even Dwarfs Started Small* was a fantastical story of a concentration camp uprising by dwarves. Somewhere in the countryside, inside a white-walled building dwarves who resent their daily mistreatment rebel during the warden's absence. They go berserk, committing every imaginable act of destruction; the insanity is repeated scene after scene.

Everything the dwarves seize, they smash and burn; what happens in the film is not so much a performance as a drunken brawl

---

* This is the official title given in the Internet Movie Database (IMDb).

gone awry. During the film Yurie would doze off every fifteen minutes or so, wake up, mumble, "Not bad," and then fall right back to sleep.

For the two documentaries, however, her eyes had stayed wide open.

"He's gifted," she said, quite impressed.

She apologized for having fallen asleep and explained that it was due to a post-ovulatory rise in body temperature and an abnormally high dissipation of energy—both of which were beyond her control, and that she had not intended to show any disrespect to the director.

"Whenever I dozed off you had to knee me, which I didn't appreciate," she said.

"This director," she added, mumbling like a sleepwalker, "may be attracted to fascism—he's also cynical."

Shōzō found the two documentaries extremely interesting. One was about the ecstasy and loneliness of a Swiss ski jumper named Steiner who could almost fly through the air like a bird, the other a profile of three men who had chosen to stay behind in a doomed, abandoned town near the volcano, La Grande Soufrièrel, which, they were warned, could erupt any moment.

The same volcano erupted in the early part of the twentieth century and a town had been engulfed within minutes by a highly toxic gas. The vintage black and white footage evoked the muteness of a town trapped in the deadly fume.

The sight conjured up the ghastly aftermath of an A-bombing, an image long familiar to every Japanese. Plates of bread and spaghetti shared space with humans, immobilized into stillness like blocks of dried clay. No lava had oozed over them; toxic high-temperature gas had frozen them as they sat over a meal.

Because of their memory of what had happened to the neighboring town, the townspeople began to desert the city when told that the volcano might erupt any day. Some television sets were still on, front doors left ajar, with Herzog's camera peeking into every nook and cranny. What a perilous venture. Why would some people take such risks even when they know in advance of an impending disaster?

Three men had refused to evacuate the town no matter how many times the authorities warned them.

The neighboring town that had been instantly destroyed had one survivor. How did he survive? He was a hardened criminal who had been locked away and forgotten in the deepest dungeon. Rumor had it that he was sold to a circus in the United States and lived into the 1950s.

The old photograph of this criminal was superimposed on the images of the two towns.

One of the three men, who had rejected the authorities' warnings and stayed behind, was napping with his cat, using a tree root for a pillow.

"Aren't you afraid?"

"Nope. A human dies only once anyway. Not just me—everybody dies someday. If I die, it's God's will. Where do you suggest I go? I've got no money, no place to go. Are you rich?" he asked cheerfully and began to hum a song.

A dog was wagging its tail. Two donkeys were walking down the quiet, deserted street.

Another man was tending a pig; his fifteen children had already been evacuated.

"Aren't you afraid?"

"Nope. But if you insist, I won't mind going with you." This man, unlike the first, looked as though he was waiting for an invitation—Let's get out of here together.

"I don't mind going with you," the man repeated, but his expression betrayed no sense of urgency. It was hard to tell what he really meant.

After this suspenseful scene, the voice-over intoned: "These shots, however, turned out to be totally useless. After many days of waiting, the eruption never came, and, scientists found that even the previous danger signs had disappeared. The residents began to drift back to town a few weeks later. And what remains is a documentary of a catastrophe that never took place."

The audience burst out laughing as the deep baritone finished his narration.

"Yup, it was quite good," said Shōzō.

"A volcano also has a free will," declared Yurie, smoking. Once ensconced in a chair in the lobby, she didn't budge an inch, just like a camel. Most of the moviegoers were young elite college students. A group of young men and an attractive female student were engaged in a polite conversation.

He was trying to remember when Yurie had been as slim as this student. During their courtship he had invited her to the May Festival at the University of Tokyo and they talked for two hours at the Sanshiro Pond. What had they talked about?

She had mentioned something about being very lazy. She was indifferent to the student movement, but she wouldn't mind letting friends who were engaged in illegal activities hide flyers and newsletters under her bedding. The idea was that she was so tone-deaf to politics that even if the authorities had conducted a search, they would leave her bed alone. That was the opinion of an activist friend who had asked for a favor, Yurie told him.

She also cut classes to lounge on the bed reading D.H. Lawrence's *Lady Chatterley's Lover*, Joseph Kessel's *The Noon Face*, and Van de Velde's *A Compleat Marriage*.

Shōzō also remembered when she came to see him in Sapporo. She had run away from home with the money she borrowed from a kimono shop owner she knew. Back then she was skin and bone like a TB patient. But now she looked like a pig or a porpoise. He shook his head. It was strange, he thought, her cells were working against her will, accumulating fat in her body at a steady rate.

Here were college students, young and slender, in the midst of a polite discussion. Their voices seemed to project the confidence that the onslaught of fat would never overtake their bodies.

"That can't be helped," said the female student in a clear soprano voice. "I know that's just the way it'll turn out." In a down jacket with a white wool cap she bore a striking resemblance to Audrey Hepburn. That put Shōzō at ease.

Yurie's smoking didn't particularly bother him when she was young, but now he was irritated that he hadn't insisted back then that she quit. He couldn't stand secondhand smoke—let alone smoking.

She sat rooted in the chair, her sensations sharpened by an ever-growing awareness of an expanding bulk.

"Aren't we going to Nishiki?" asked Shōzō. At his urging, Yurie slowly raised her body.

"We'll go to the Yoshida Shrine to celebrate the coming-of-the spring *Setsubun* Festival, and stop on the way by the market at the Ginkakuji Temple." Surprisingly, she was unusually clear on how to get there.

Heavy snow had covered the entire Japanese archipelago, and the drifts were deep on Mount Hiei. But in downtown Kyoto most of the snow had melted. There were only a few vendors left at the Yoshida Shrine by the time Shōzō and Yurie arrived. Making a dead stop in front of a vendor of sweetmeats, Yurie, just like a camel, would not budge an inch until she had one.

"I'm dying to eat bean candies," she muttered to herself. "Unlike the other kids, I wasn't given an allowance to buy what I wanted. Today I'll eat what my free will tells me to eat."

This was her way of justifying a carb craving.

She was a very sickly child who had contracted dysentery three times. As a result any food sold by vendors was off-limits to her. When no antibiotics were available in postwar Japan, this precaution was necessary because any outbreak of dysentery was considered an epidemic.

The disease boosted her immune system to the point that she would welcome food that even Shōzō would not touch—whether it be Southeast Asian, African, or Indian.

So she bought the candies, and they took off to Daigengū, a sacred precinct on the premises of the Yoshida Shrine dedicated to the veneration of the eight million gods of ancient Japan. There was a time when each region of the country was assigned an appropriate number of gods. The allocation of gods probably had something to do with the population of ancient Japan and the powerful influence of the Yamato Dynasty.

ON THEIR WAY DOWN FROM ŌMOTOMIYA, Shōzō and Yurie ran into Karl and Mizuki with their two children, Mary and

Leonard. English was their first language but they were also conversant in German and Japanese. The parents had made arrangements for them to stay with a Thomas Mann specialist on weekdays. The German scholar and his wife had lived in Germany for several years, making things easier for the children to keep up with German when Japanese failed them.

Fond of children but childless, the couple was thinking of an adoption. This was to be a rehearsal for them.

Mary and Leonard were not Karl and Mizuki's biological children. They had been adopted through an agency in the United States. Karl held the belief that to be a true human one has to bring up a child. Mizuki agreed with him and went through with the adoptions because, considering her own traumatic childhood, she wasn't so sure about having her own baby. And she was also concerned about the problem of overpopulation: she felt it would be more meaningful to take in orphaned children.

Karl and Mizuki knew they were perfectly capable of having their own children, but they had reached the conclusion that not exercising that option would be the most humane thing to do.

In the late 1970s the hordes of wandering hippies from the Counterculture Movement began to re-embrace the mainstream. Some communes survived—mostly around college towns where down-and-out hippies eked out an existence. That was where Mary was born. Her mother, a self-proclaimed poet from Scotland, decided to have her first baby in her mid-thirties. Evidently expending her last ounce of energy in the delivery of the baby, she died right after the childbirth.

Before she died, she supposedly voiced what the Virgin Mary would have said, "This is God's child." At the height of the Counterculture, it would have been a commune's responsibility to take care of a motherless child, but the movement was already on the decline when Mary was born. The local authorities, acting on a request from the commune's landlord, evicted the hippies and took in the orphan until they could find a foster home.

When Fukiko had said, "Well, then, let's say Tōichiro is a god's child," Mizuki was reminded of the briefing the authorities had given her about Mary.

Soon after Mary came into her life, Mizuki, who disliked being an only child intensely, decided to adopt another baby. Mizuki and Karl both worked at a university, and had to rely on a babysitter for their children. Such decisions, however, are what child-rearing is all about. Or rather, they began to realize that only by letting others live could they also live.

Leonard was found in a desolate American town in the gold and vermilion entrance hall of a Taoist Temple, its inner sanctum dark and musty with the smell of burnt incense. The baby boy was wrapped in a poncho. On a piece of paper someone scribbled: "Father maybe Japanese or Chinese." According to a Welfare Department official, considering the note's poor English and the poncho, the infant's mother was probably a migrant Chicano farm worker.

"In other words the mother felt the baby should be rescued by a Japanese or a Chinese god," the official had said with a shrug and a quick glance at Mizuki. "I don't think she knew the ethnicity of the man who fathered him. Probably it didn't make any difference to her." The official was probably clueless about the difference between Chinese and Japanese, Mizuki thought. To Americans all yellow-skinned people belong to one general group, which is more or less Chinese. It is the same reaction Japanese have toward whites, to whom they automatically start speaking in English, or asking a Dutchman or a Swiss to give them English lessons.

Karl had once said, "When Central Americans meet a German, they tell you: 'My grandfather was German.' When they meet a Japanese: 'My mother was Japanese.' " Mizuki felt Leonard's mother wouldn't have said that and decided on the spot to adopt him.

When the children were about to start first grade, Karl and Mizuki told them that they had been adopted. They offered a simple explanation, thinking that dissembling was not in the children's best interests.

"You see, your father and mother were in a very difficult position and could not bring you up. So we took their place. We are your Papa and Mama. Your parents asked us, Please take care of our children." At that moment Mizuki felt almost like a god.

The adoption signaled the beginning of Karl's interest in Taoism, which, he theorized, was an essential factor not to be ignored in any analysis of Japanese industry.

"So, it looks like you've got to research the Loch Ness Monster, too," said Mizuki, laughing.

The children were slow to use Japanese when they were around Karl, who was also reluctant to speak the language. That was why the parents boarded the children with a Japanese couple and placed them in a Japanese school. At least that was Mizuki's rationalization. Mary and Leonard had just begun elementary school in the States, and were now having fun at the Japanese school.

Mary, a pale-skinned Northern European, was no blond but her enchanting blue eyes certainly matched her light brown hair; and Leonard had a dark complexion and jet black hair.

The two children greeted Yurie and Shōzō in accentless Japanese—"How are you?"—bowing politely in the Japanese style. Karl and Mizuki spent every weekend with the children at their house on Mount Hiei, and on Sunday night took them back to Kita-Shirakawa where the German scholar lived.

"Snow again?" said Karl, flakes fluttering into his open mouth.

# 6 ⁓

ON HER WAY HOME from the nearby supermarket, Mizuki saw Shōzō prowling around in front of the beauty parlor. The curtains were drawn so it was very likely that the shop was closed for the day.

"Oh, something's wrong?"

"Yuri said she was going to have a haircut. She said she'd be through in an hour, and it's been three hours but no sign of her."

"Maybe she had something else to do."

"I think I should talk to the hairdresser." He peered hesitantly through an opening in the window drapery.

"This is just where she works. She's probably gone home by now."

"Well, I see some movement inside."

For some reason he looked pale. Mizuki was still wondering what to make of it when he began to bang on the front door. A woman in her thirties, maybe the owner, poked her head out.

"We're closed for the day—" she said, in a decidedly unfriendly tone.

"Excuse me—my name is Mama. Didn't my wife come here?"

"Well, I don't know all the customers by name."

"In her fifties, short, fat—in a suede overcoat."

"Short hair?"

"Yes, you could say that."

"There was someone here by that description, I think, but she left two hours ago. I've just closed the shop."

"Which way did she go?"

"Well, I couldn't say."

Shōzō, now even more suspicious, peered into the shop. Mizuki quickly pulled him away from the door and apologized to the owner. "Sorry to bother you. We'll look elsewhere."

Now looking frightened, he was obviously convinced that Yurie was already a missing person.

"She must have gone on another errand. She might even be home by now."

"I've already been to the supermarket to look for her," he said desperately.

"Well, I certainly didn't see her there. No need to worry so much. She might be having coffee somewhere."

"Yuri wouldn't even think of stepping inside a coffee shop alone," he snapped. Now he definitely sounded on edge. "She might have been murdered inside the beauty salon."

Mizuki was decidedly taken aback by the serious tone of voice. It was no laughing matter for him.

"You've got some weird ideas, Shōzō. Why in the world would anyone murder her at a beauty salon? Besides, it's only six o'clock. She might have gone down into Kyoto on the spur of the moment. She might be trying to phone you even as we speak."

"You think so?"

"Something's wrong with you. The hairdresser must have felt terrible the way you kept peering into her shop. Just because your wife's been missing a few hours. She's not a child. It's possible she's at my house."

"Is Karl home?"

"No."

"Without him, she can't get in. I also stopped by your house, too, but nobody was home. That worries me even more."

"Would you worry if Karl was by himself?" asked Mizuki, laughing.

"I wouldn't if he were there alone, talking with Yuri."

"Well, then, what are you worried about?"

"What do you mean? I'm worried because I don't know where she is," he said angrily and looked away from her. His usual composure was in tatters.

"So you don't know where she is. No use suspecting the hairdresser, though," observed Mizuki, watching him as he repeatedly glanced back at the shop.

Lo and behold—it was none other than Yurie who slowly emerged out of the gathering darkness.

"Where in the world have you been?"

"I was taking a stroll."

Shōzō was speechless.

"I had a long talk with a real estate agent," she said indifferently. "I like it here, I really want to live here."

IT WAS AN EARLY FEBRUARY MORNING when the water in the toilet had frozen solid at the rented house. That drove them back to Tokyo. But they returned after the equinox ushered in the first signs of spring.

According to climate studies, the relationship between the carbon dioxide generated by industry and the oxygen produced by plant life is far out of balance, and the level of carbon dioxide is on the rise, which causes global warming. However, that warmth was nowhere evident on the Japanese archipelago. In fact the winter was so severe that many parts of the country were buried deep in snow, and the abnormally low temperatures were driving people to despair.

Mizuki recalled how Shōzō and Yurie had scrambled back to their tiny concrete box in Tokyo when they could no longer endure cooking in a bare kitchen or diving into sleeping bags, teeth chattering. However, the arrival of spring brought them along with it to try again.

The first phone call from Yurie after their return went something like this: "The water from Lake Biwa tastes like chlorine in this warm weather. We're drinking a concoction of rotting organisms and chlorine. I meant to treat you to some very good *gyokuro* tea I've bought, but this water won't do," she complained.

Then, with her customary leap of logic, she abruptly switched to the possibility of a meltdown of all the earth's glaciers as temperatures rose. She went on to say that most of the land would be covered over by the rising ocean.

The extinction of the dinosaurs was partly due to environmental changes. Even so, the real reason they were able to thrive for millions of years was probably because of their exceptionally tiny brains. By contrast, what's called human history is barely two or three million years old, and brain size and the length of time a species will survive do not seem to correlate.

For example, in human history, the mere appearance of a powerful dynasty or a political figure never guaranteed a long life for that dynasty or person. It simply left a memory of castles in a twilight dream. In Chinese history, the reigns of Qin Shi-huang Di and Kub-lai Khan were much shorter than those of other emperors. Germany's Hitler and Japan's Nobunaga bequeathed only ruin to posterity, certainly nothing that would earn them the title of savior. Those historical figures were quite adept at knowing how to push those emotional buttons of human instinct that can be so easily manipulated. When a man acquires even the semblance of being a hero, his actions become a cautionary tale for all of us who want to avoid destruction.

What is considered an almost interminable stretch of early human existence was devoid of heroes, a time when human beings mouthed nothing but incomprehensible incantations. Wasn't it the small, less imperious, skittish creatures—the mammals—that destroyed the dinosaurs?

"There's nothing to say that humans won't be overrun by cockroaches," Yurie was still on the phone, speaking in a pitifully sad monologue. She began to cast contempt upon the dinosaurs biting the dust right and left. All the while the humans, the exemplar of mammals, continued to reproduce with fear and craftiness in their eyes. They would destroy bit by bit the bountiful good earth that had nurtured them, using the scientific method that they had conjured up with their overdeveloped brains. In the end all they could leave for posterity to prove they ever existed would be their fossilized bones.

Yurie, herself one of those humans, was wandering in the mountains in search of a hideout like a frightened dinosaur nearing extinction. The fact that she didn't like Biwa water apparently did not translate into a total rejection of the Mount Hiei area, and on the spur of the moment she had consulted a real estate agent. On hearing about this impulsive move, Mizuki thought to herself, Oh, not again.

"You worried me to death," complained Shōzō, definitely embarrassed.

"He thought you might have been murdered in the beauty shop," said Mizuki, chuckling. "He was ghostly pale and almost broke the door down."

"Weird guy," said Yurie, looking away.

"If you'd told me you were going to a real estate agency in the first place, I wouldn't have worried."

"I couldn't help it. I hadn't planned on it when I left," she said petulantly and continued walking.

"Where are you going?" Shōzō stumbled after her quickly as if chasing a runaway kite. She was going the wrong way. Their house was in the opposite direction.

"Please, Mizuki, come with me," she pleaded. "The agent told me about a house for sale. I just want to see what it looks like from the outside if I can. He said it's located on the Ōtsu side overlooking Lake Biwa."

Mizuki and Shōzō gave in. They followed her as she turned the corner with a map in her hand.

In the lavender mist of early dusk you could almost hear the imperceptible murmur of nature about to take its first breaths of spring.

"The house is in a totally isolated hamlet, perched halfway up the mountainside," said Yurie excitedly. "The place is so hidden amidst rows and rows of hillocks that it's invisible from below, yet once you're up there, a lovely panorama will take your breath way. That's what I like about this area. So conveniently inconvenient."

Shōzō grabbed the flyer Yurie had pulled out of her pocket and took charge immediately. "I knew it," he said decisively. "You're going the wrong way." She let him play the tour guide, accepting this as the most natural thing in the world.

Dogs began to howl as they walked past a row of houses, where many of the residents were gone for the day. They finally came upon what they were looking for, a house vacant with an overgrown garden and a large wire mesh pigeon coop. Gray feathers clung to the mesh, and lay scattered here and there in the tall thick grass. A lone abandoned sandal lay on the veranda; ivy nearly obliterated the closed shutters from view.

"Ah-ha," said Mizuki, remembering something at the sight of the pigeon coop.

"Was this actually a pigeon coop?" asked Yurie.

"Yes, the former residents kept pigeons."

"Oh my, you've heard about them, Mizuki?"

"Yes, very eccentric people. He became a pigeon—I mean the husband."

"What do you mean?"

"He became so obsessed with pigeon racing that he quit his job. I understand he was just an ordinary white-collar worker. So, his wife had to go back to work while he spent his days with the birds. Quite a few of them, they say. I heard she used to complain about the cost of the feed. She even helped raise them. All he saw day after day were his wife and the pigeons, and they somehow became one and the same in his mind."

"Became one?"

"He lost interest in humans. He never spoke to anyone except his wife. He began to behave exactly like a pigeon."

"What do you mean like a pigeon?"

"The pigeon is a very fastidious bird, so they say, and bonds only with a mate of its own choosing. No matter how hard humans try to control their breeding behavior, they won't accept anyone they don't like."

"Trying to breed them?" said Yurie, surprised. "Humans themselves don't do things the way others want. But I also heard from someone who kept free-range pigeons on her veranda that they aren't particularly chaste."

"I don't know much about pigeons, but this man must have imitated some deranged pigeon because he rejected all humans except his wife," Mizuki continued with the story. "She worked hard every day to keep a roof over their heads, and once she came home, her husband overwhelmed her with his smothering affection. By the end of the day she was totally exhausted.

"Even though he may have learned pigeon speech, he no longer understood human language, and she was the only human he could communicate with, or so it was said. He even imitated a pigeon's habit of not letting his mate out of his sight."

Yurie's worried look told Mizuki that this was no laughing matter.

"Remember she had to work with humans in the outside world," Mizuki went on relentlessly. "Living with him exhausted her, both mentally and physically. Then the pigeon man insisted on mating with her every day until she gradually wasted away, her face ghostly pale in a house that reeked of pigeons. Finally, one morning, she went down the mountain and never came back."

"What happened to him?"

"I wonder. I heard they divorced or, well, maybe they didn't, but once the wife left, his health failed rapidly. Rumor has it that he's in a mental hospital."

"What happened to the pigeons?" Shōzō broke in, recoiling as he peered into the cage. "I wonder if they all died."

"I heard all sorts of stories, that the wife secretly left the door open, and that the husband found out and closed the coop. Some might have escaped. But I'm sure most of them died, the way the owner was behaving."

The pigeon down caught in the wire mesh were fluttering in the wind.

"Let's get out of here." Averting her face, Mizuki started to walk away.

"A pigeon or a crow, it makes no difference," said Shōzō flatly. "I've never liked birds. That's one thing I've no desire to keep in the house. When I think about angels and try to imagine where the wings are attached, my skin starts to crawl."

Speaking of wings, Mizuki recalled that Shōzō was very proud of the model airplanes he had assembled. Their house in the United

States was full of them.

"Yuri calls me a duck," he said.

"Why a duck?" asked Mizuki. She could not quite see the connection between a duck and a pigeon. She cocked her head, puzzled.

"She says, when I'm asleep, I keep my head tucked into the sleeping bag like a duck bobbing for fish."

"Since he sleeps on his side, his shoulders leave an opening in the sleeping bags and the draft chills me," mumbled Yurie.

You could fix that by sleeping in a separate bag, Mizuki said to herself.

Long ago, around the time of her father's funeral, Mizuki remembered seeing a family of ducks swimming in a paddy field in Kambara. It was early spring, just the time of year in snow country when all the rice fields were flooded, forming a vast expanse of water like a lake. The water level rose because the farmers back then did not have subsurface drainage. Many of them kept ducks.

She also remembered what Uncle Shigeru once said. "Ducks are good substitutes for dogs around here. They all start quacking at the first sight of a stranger, which makes them good watchdogs for farmers."

She was reminded of something else. As they returned from her father's funeral, Fukiko had pressed her infant son Tōichiro into Shigeru's arms, intent on repelling Fū, who was inching her way toward him.

"I used to eat Kambara duck eggs," said Yurie, breaking Mizuki's reverie. "Eggs were extremely precious in postwar Japan. The farmers gave them to us wrapped in straw, which often ended up as special gifts to friends and relatives. Of course, they were huge, much bigger than chicken eggs, and when you fried them, they looked really spooky."

Yurie held her shoulders just like Fū. Mizuki instinctively recoiled, averting her eyes.

The house up for sale, with the pigeon coop, looked like a mirage in the early spring twilight.

"This is too spooky," said Mizuki, nudging Yurie's shoulder. She hoped the comment would dampen her whimsical spirit. "Isn't that why it's still on the block?"

"They're asking thirty million yen," said Yurie. "That's cheap, isn't it?"

"Cheap?" shot back Shōzō, staring at her incredulously as if to say, Who's got that kind of money? "We can't use this house as is. We would need another ten million to renovate."

"We can sell our condo in Tokyo."

"We won't have any place to stay."

"Do we have to live there forever?"

—You work in Tokyo, don't you? Shōzō almost blurted out. But held his tongue because he didn't have a job.

"This would be perfect for someone with a regular job in Kyoto or Ōtsu—otherwise, it's just a vacation house," Mizuki broke in, trying to help out Shōzō. If he became a duck and Yurie skipped town, then the job of taking him to a psychiatric clinic would be mine—. She said urgently, "I think there are lots of dead pigeons inside." That was meant to impress upon him the improbability of the situation while his reason still remained intact.

Now apparently determined not to become a pigeon, Shōzō looked away. "I hate birds," he said, "because I have a funny feeling that they may have been my ancestors. They say you hate your own kind. I don't like to eat chicken, either—I guess I find it a bit cannibalistic."

"Shōzō loves fish," said Yurie. "He reads up on them all the time. I don't have good reflexes but I can still swim, so he says my ancestors must have been fish, specifically coelacanths. When I swim I really feel like I have gills. My shoulders and thighs do their thing just like fins, moving and cutting through the water. Fish have been on this planet much longer than birds."

As their conversation focused on fish and birds, all three of them stood peering into the coop, craning their necks like hungry Komodo dragons.

"I don't want to become a bird," repeated Shōzō firmly. "I have no desire to devolve into one of my ancestors." He wiggled his head definitely like a bird.

What popped into Mizuki's mind at that instant was the image of a human embryo. Its shape slowly grows and changes into a scary four-limbed fish-like creature—like an illustration in a science book—that eventually takes the form of an amphibian, crawling out of the water to become a monkey-faced infant. Don't people scream and shout, baring their teeth like monkeys, or furrow their foreheads in deep, suggestive wrinkles?

Because of his instinctive hatred of birds, after he heard the story of the unfortunate man who regressed psychologically into a pigeon, Shōzō grimaced, thinking about his dead bird brothers and braced himself as if to keep his distance from their imagined carcasses.

Was the depressing story really the source of his fear? Mizuki wondered. He said he didn't want to devolve. But was it possible that he actually longed for this retrogression while that very yearning frightened him? Hadn't he been seen peering suspiciously into the beauty parlor like a duck chasing after his mate?

"So, what do you think, Mizuki?" asked Yurie in absolute seriousness, switching the topic back to the sale of the house. She carefully compared its exterior with the blueprint in the flyer.

"Won't the condo in Tokyo be a problem?" asked Mizuki.

She didn't know much about real estate in Japan. By American standards, listing a house that looked more like a log cabin buried amidst the packed row of houses on the mountainside for an exorbitant amount of money would be unthinkable.

Japanese only seem to feel alive when putting down hundreds of thousands of dollars on a matchbox house with flush toilets that would freeze in the winter, or when paying several thousands of dollars for a kimono to doll up their daughters on New Year's Day. They will drink coffee that costs more than a dollar a cup—with a tiny sliver of cake thrown in for an additional dollar. Neither would they bat an eye to pay one hundred dollars per person for a meal at a fashionable Japanese restaurant.

According to Karl, these strange phenomena were all economic in nature, and in them lay the key to unlocking the mystery of Japanese prosperity. "And it requires," he had added, "far more complex math than that used in designing a spacecraft."

Yurie was intently looking at a few trees that stood behind the house where the woman had left the pigeon man and disappeared for parts unknown. "Take a look," she said. "I don't think I've seen that species before." She walked along the fence all the way to the back of the house, with Shōzō trailing behind.

"It may be a metasequoia," he said. He had a lively interest in trees. He drew near, looking up at the dry needles and the thick branches that shot straight up. "Sure looks like it. Did the former owner plant it? A metasequoia all right. Why is it growing here? Botanical gardens have them, but in general it would be very difficult to get them unless you have special connections. I think it was 1944 when they were rediscovered in Szechuan. They're now protected nationwide by the Chinese government. I never expected to see one on Mount Hiei."

Was the man-turned-pigeon interested in ancient trees that were fast disappearing from the earth?

"A house with a metasequoia," said Yurie, encouraged. "That's nice. The layout of the landscape up to the front gate isn't bad, either."

The same crude stones were used for the gate and the path leading to the front door. It was clearly the work of an amateur.

"A metasequoia grows very fast, you know," said Shōzō. "I think this one's twenty or thirty years old." The house appeared to be as old as the tree.

It was soon after Mizuki had moved to Mount Hiei that the occupants of the pigeon house had left. All she knew about them was what the neighbors had told her.

Yurie was smiling to herself. Apparently the conversation reminded her of something. "Did you hear about the young man and the metasequoia from your mother?"

"What?"

"He came from Hokkaido and was Fū's favorite. There was a question about a metasequoia on a company entrance exam he had to take. He had never heard of it, so he wrote down that it was a cross between a *medaka* killifish and a *koi* carp. I don't know if that had anything to do with it, but he failed the exam and didn't get a job. Fū hired him on the spot for the boutique she had opened in Tokyo."

I wonder if he was one of those men Fū was intimate with, Mizuki thought.

"Fū was rather fond of scatterbrains," said Yurie, gazing up at the top of the tree. "I wonder what happened to the young man? He might have planted this tree. He could have become a pigeon, too. You remember him, don't you, Honey?"

"Nope," said Shōzō immediately, shaking his head: "That reminds me, though, there was someone who helped Fū out when she was dying in the hospital."

It was painful for Mizuki to hear anything that had to do with her mother's death. It might have been the same man who showed her the shop's accounts after it had been sold. Fū must have known instinctively that death was near; everything was in good order.

Only a few shares of stock had been left to Mizuki; the house was already mortgaged. The young man took care of all the details and turned over what remained after the debts were paid. He quoted a very small sum when she asked how much she owed him for all his services.

Some people tried to urge Mizuki to take legal action, saying that the young man had in fact swindled her and gotten rid of the shop for his own gain. But she had no desire to check into the matter. She just wanted to forget everything about her mother. Uncle Shigeru only gave general advice about the business and never even referred to the young man.

Mizuki found it very moving that a single tree could elicit a totally different memory from each person.

"The metasequoia is in the fern family," explained Shōzō, obviously now impressed by the house now, if only for the tree. "It's amazing to see it grow on a mountain."

"I guess this house is out of our reach even with the sale of the Myōkō house," said Yurie. She had not quite given up finagling a way to purchase the strange house.

"Sleep on it," advised Mizuki. "Shōzō's easily spooked—imagining you might be murdered at a beauty parlor—if he lived in a house like this with such a gloomy history behind it, he might very well turn into a duck."

She found it hard to go along with Yurie's wild idea. The two of them sleeping in this vacant house in their old gray-green sleeping bags—it conjured up the image of a graveyard. It was all very vivid to her. Shōzō's head tucked inside a sleeping bag was, in her mind, the very image of a duck thrusting its head into the water.

"By the way, Mizuki, two American friends wrote me that they want to visit Japan next month on their way back from China, and stay in Kyoto," said Yurie abruptly. "If it's not on a weekend, I'm wondering if we could borrow Leonard and Mary's bedding. The couple's fairly well off, so they could stay at a hotel. But we'd still have to take care of them. They might as well stay here provided it's only a night or two, considering the trouble of driving them up and down the mountain. That would be much more convenient for us."

Mizuki thought that lending the bedding was no problem, but given the lack of amenities at their rented house, she wondered how they could possibly entertain guests.

"They have traveled all over the world, and been to Tokyo three times, but for this trip they're just visiting Kyoto. The wife asked me to make a reservation at a Japanese-style inn. English may pose a problem there. All things considered, that might be the easiest solution. If things don't work out, I don't mind having them here."

Mizuki couldn't keep up with her. One minute she talked about purchasing a house with a pigeon coop, and in the next breath she wanted to entertain foreign guests at their house when they didn't even have any extra bedding.

"Their 1939 canoe trip down the Columbia River was featured in *National Geographic*. The wife had a Chinese grandmother and married a China specialist. The couple has been shuttling back and forth between China and the United States since their retirement," said Yurie, adding that they were both around seventy.

My parents' generation, thought Mizuki.

As if on cue, Yurie said, "When we first met Lynn Ann twenty-five years ago, she was younger than I am now. It was right after she lost her first husband."

Evidently, Lynn Ann was the wife's name.

# 7 ∽

Yᴜʀɪᴇ ᴡᴀs ᴏʙᴠɪᴏᴜsʟʏ ɪʀʀɪᴛᴀᴛᴇᴅ ʙʏ Sʜōᴢō's lack of interest in the pigeon coop house. She wanted to drop by Mizuki's house but insisted this time on going alone.

"You go ahead," she said. "There're some books I want to borrow from her and I've got to get the bedding for our guests." She added quickly. "I'm dying for eel."

Eᴠᴇʀʏ Tᴜᴇsᴅᴀʏ ᴍᴏʀɴɪɴɢ ᴀ ғɪsʜ ᴠᴇɴᴅᴏʀ drove his truck up Mount Hiei. That very morning Mizuki had run into Shōzō buying conger eel. Apparently the job of buying the seafood fell to him. He was eyeing every fish with affection and longing. He could assess the freshness of the seafood with a quick once-over. "That one looks good, this one, no," he said, showing Mizuki how to pick the best. "It's horse mackerel season. I wonder where the mackerel's from?" Checking the van's license plate he mumbled to himself, "Oh, from Mie Prefecture. I thought maybe Wakase." When he found out that the fish actually came from Karasu-chō, he said, "That's good, close enough to the sea."

"Is he a college professor?" asked the vendor after he had left with his purchase of eel. It must have been a very rare sight to see a man buying fish during the day.

"Uh-huh," mumbled Mizuki with a quick nod, finding it a bother to answer.

"Does he teach at the university or work in an office?" he asked again, not skipping a beat.

"Probably both."

She thought the vague answer would suffice, but it didn't seem to satisfy him.

"I think he's here to do research on Mount Hiei, working on a book, I gather," she added.

Because of poor transportation, residents of this area often held jobs at the nearby university or were self-employed. Many of them were potters and painters. Mizuki's answer must have finally done the trick because he asked no further questions. However, a few housewives nearby pricked their ears up.

Mizuki realized that a man in his prime hanging around at home really sticks out and invites suspicion. Loafing was just not socially acceptable in Japan for a man.

"I wonder why her memory improves so suddenly when it comes to what's in the fridge." Shōzō muttered to himself, leaving for home alone grudgingly after Yurie had declared she had to have eel.

"He even follows me to the hairdresser," groaned Yurie pitifully as she watched him go.

"Remember what he told me about a murder being committed at the beauty parlor," said Mizuki in earnest.

"Me murdered? How ridiculous. He once placed a call to our daughter Chie ten times and when he got no answer, he set off for her house at two in the morning to roust her out of bed. He kept banging on the door, oblivious to the ruckus he was making in the neighborhood. Chie and her husband were furious. They had returned home around one o'clock and had just fallen asleep. But leave it to Shōzō. His usual paranoia snowballs everything into a murder. He called them every hour on the hour. When he'd said, 'I'll go and take a look,' I asked him, 'What's so unusual about a young married couple staying out all night?' He dismissed me with—'You have no maternal instinct.'"

"If you two lived in a house with a pigeon coop," pointed out Mizuki bluntly, "he'd turn into a pigeon for sure."

"He even peeps into my study. He pretends to be tending the garden, but he's actually spying on me. He complains later that he saw cigarette smoke in my study. He might as well try to hypnotize me to quit smoking, but he can't."

"Well, aren't you writing novels because you're under his spell?"

"What did you say?" said Yurie quickly. For once she was at a loss for a response.

"He must have quit his job to be my overseer," she added unapologetically.

"You let him do it, didn't you?"

"I wouldn't have to write novels if he did things the way I wanted."

"What did you want him to be? A financial wiz, a political wheeler-dealer?" asked Mizuki, casting her a withering look.

Pondering this for a bit, Yurie responded, "Well, how about a king, so obsessed with a woman that he ruins his kingdom? Or, a man pursued by a rebel army, eulogized in a poem—'A pear blossom on a branch, a drop of spring rain.' I also like the idea of Shōzō turning into a red poppy fairy. At least women can say with certainty they don't chase after phantoms of Beatrice or Gretchen like men do. The women in the lives of Napoleon, Socrates, and Tolstoy, even Caesar, never worshiped men. If those women were moved by anything, it was their man's divine idiocy. What else can you do but hug a frightened man?" There seemed to be tears forming in Yurie's upturned eyes.

"For instance, women may dream about Buddha or Christ, but both men actually existed," she went on. "Men on the other hand have refashioned a woman who gave birth to an illegitimate child into a virgin mother, a child-devouring goddess into Kannon, the goddess of mercy.

"Men are different creatures. Because they're unable to give birth, they need a different reason for their self-identity. They're afraid they won't be men anymore unless they use their brains to reason things out. It's tough for them. Intellectualizing doesn't agree with me. Because if I overuse my brain, I lose my instinct. When I run into a man who says I'm the intellectual type, I don't know what to say. Men are certainly gifted at rationalizing something utterly irrational."

"They're hopelessly romantic, I should say," rejoined Mizuki carefully. "I understand that the phrase, a 'romance for older men,' is very popular in Japan now. I've heard about sperm banks in the United States. Lesbians and self-proclaimed single women are seriously thinking about having babies without men."

Not a good judge of the opposite sex, she more or less agreed with Yurie. "Well, if you're worshiped as *the* Virgin Mary day and night, you may as well end up becoming *the* Virgin Mary yourself," she said.

Yurie cast a disdainful look heavenward. "Shōzō believes anything I say," she said. "That's why I get anxious and have to distract myself. You aren't very smart if you think happiness has everything to do with being accepted without question. None of those guys who swallow everything a woman says and love her for it are worth having." Yurie's way of speaking had suddenly turned rougher than usual.

What she's saying is close to the argument that the truth is that there is no truth, Mizuki said to herself and took a deep breath.

"I never, ever, went over to his office to spy on him outside his window," said Yurie bitterly, staring into the middle distance with deadly seriousness. "I always gave him freedom to do what he damn well pleased. But look at me now. I'm constantly on edge worrying that any minute his head might pop up at my window. Even if it doesn't, I'm still worried. The whole thing really bothers me. The only way I'm going to find peace of mind is to get used to it. Mizuki, every person must come up with a way to find peace.

"I don't know why all this happened, but it just did when we began to live together. He shouldn't have married me. But he says, 'Nothing's more fun than hanging around with you.' Is that possible? Who knows, he may just be lying or fudging the truth. I think about getting a divorce every three minutes."

"But, you won't divorce him. You rather like the way things are."

"I'm doing it for him, not for me," she said, shaking her head. "I've tried everything to encourage him to get rid of me, but it doesn't work. No matter what I do he just takes it in silence. I didn't want to ruin him, so, it was all for his sake that I tried very hard to cut him loose—I'm just not the housewife type."

Wasn't she admitting aloud that she used to have many affairs, in hopes of falling in love? Mizuki wasn't sure.

"In the end," said Yurie, "I somehow must have gotten on his good side—pampering him, letting him take a good thing too far. I don't know how it happened, but I've ended up overnurturing his self-confidence. He now believes firmly that I can't do a thing without him, and that it's his duty to keep an eye on me. I feel suffocated."

To Mizuki's way of thinking, however, the fact that Yurie never bothered to spy on Shōzō at work might have been the very reason he quit his job.

Of course, there was no actual need for her to camp outside his window, but the fact that she showed no interest in what he was doing made him quit. And he had become so worried about his wife, who sat at her desk day after day filling her head with wild fantasies, that he decided he might as well join her in the world of make-believe, instead of being forced to worry about her.

Men often say in public that they dislike women interfering in their work. In reality, however, if women showed no interest in what men did, they wouldn't do anything. They are all a bit like the little boy, completely engrossed in play, who cannot believe that what he's doing has any value unless he looks up once in a while to get his mother's attention and shout—"Lo-o-k, lo-o-k, Mommy!"

"Don't you think the reason Shōzō quit his job was that you lost interest in his work?" said Mizuki. "You can continue with your writing because he takes a peek through the window once in a while to see how you're doing. Otherwise, you'd have given it up long ago. He always supported what you were doing without saying a word, and that's why you can continue to complain about him.

"You made him do what he really didn't want to do so that you could do what you want to do. He brought home the bacon by cutting down trees, figuring out the cost of lumber and finding buyers, while life for you was free and easy. No wonder you can afford to gripe about what's wrong with the world." As she spoke, she recalled what Shōzō had once told her in Yurie's absence.

"How can a woman be so carefree when she sends her man to the salt mines everyday?" he had said. "Women are so presumptuous. Most men can never be as calm and collected as women. I'm a novice at how to keep a woman trembling in fear. I'm supposed to bully her, but I'm the one who's bullied. I try to tell myself—She's my slave, just my slave—but I end up giving the slave a personality.

"Well, that's what gender relationships are all about. One side's driven to meet the other's demands but they hardly get any appreciation for it. It either makes you paranoid, or you just want to sleep it off and forget about it. But when you wake up the following morning, you start thinking about how presumptuous and lazy she behaved the night before—and it makes your blood boil."

Mizuki had wanted to chuckle at the delicacy of these bedroom revelations but pretended she didn't know what he was talking about. She covered it up with a neutral "Uh-uh."

She wanted to tell him that some men grit their teeth to stay awake after sex but Shōzō wasn't someone she was scheming to sleep with. Even if she did, she thought to herself, the idea of him remembering that she had said such-and-such and acted accordingly was rather unexciting. Instead she opted for silence.

With some melancholy, she began to reminisce about the affairs she'd had in the States with a few fledgling Japanese scholars, especially the way their hands had grabbed for her, discovering as it were a hidden treasure; or the way they pretended to be world-famous sexual athletes, how they had displayed techniques they'd picked up in the men's weeklies with utter confidence, unwittingly exposing themselves as inexpert liars, but with affectionate personalities.

When it came to gender relations in Japan, what she heard and what she actually saw were two different things. She was equally confused about Japanese women's selfish demands and the behavior of Japanese men who allowed these women to have anything they desired. Take the case of a junior high school classmate she had met in Tokyo the other day. When this classmate had visited her husband in Kyūshū, the southernmost of the four main islands in the Japanese archipelago, where he had been holding a job for fifteen years, there had been cobwebs dangling everywhere in his house, entangling her hair in disgusting, sticky strands. When she stepped into a hallway her footprints were clearly visible in the accumulated dust. She had never visited him after that. True, he was never tardy in sending her money. But she would not want the company to give her husband special consideration because of the hardship of spending so much time away from life, and have them send him on an occasional business trip to Tokyo because, she said, "My skin breaks out in hives when I see him—cedar fever doesn't even compare." At that Mizuki immediately asked—"Why not get a divorce?" The friend replied with perfect composure, "We've got children, and I hate to work a desk job. I also hate to be poor." Her face betrayed not the slightest hint of guilt, acting as if she had been the one forced to endure misfortune.

What was more astounding was her conclusion: "In the event that my husband finds a common-law wife in Kyūshū, he's agreed to register our house and lot in Tokyo in my name and my children's. This arrangement is nothing unusual in present-day Japan," she added matter-of-factly.

Thoroughly shocked by these comments, Mizuki had thought to herself that no American man would be crazy enough to put up with such a marriage. It couldn't be male instinct to allow that, either. She had scrutinized her friend long and hard. Then, as if to justify herself further, the friend added: she had found that every dish in her husband's kitchen was chipped. Considering the fact that she had bought a brand new set of everything just for him, she knew then and there that her thoughtfulness was totally wasted on him. A rather unenthusiastic "hmm" was Mizuki's only response.

Much later, still disturbed by the fact that Japanese men would quite willingly accept such outrageous self-serving behavior from women, she had mustered enough courage and bluntly asked an acclaimed Japanese novelist she had met—"How do men explain such gender relationships?"

"Frigidity is contagious even for men," said the old novelist, grinning sardonically.

Yurie, a rather comically egocentric creature, seemed oblivious to Mizuki's silence.

"You know, it's easy for women to convince most men that they're no good, but not so with women," said Yurie. "So why are men so eager to make women think ill of them? They're a strange bunch." She paused for a long moment and continued, "Shōzō's never, ever in his life wanted to work. He did it for a while, he said, because it seemed a woman wanted him to do it. All he wanted to do was catch fish or make some unusual lures. The only thing he tried very hard to do was satisfy a woman. That's what he said."

Was that woman Yurie?

A look on her face proudly proclaimed to the world, I'm not frigid. It was not the leer of a nymphomaniac continually urging a man to greater efforts, her hunger eternally unsated, which amounts to frigidity.

"Nymphomania is also contagious," Mizuki said half to herself as an image flitted across her inner eye: Shōzō befriending a man who had obviously been intimate with Yurie. With an exchange of sympathetic glances the two men were asking for each other's forgiveness. And what was Yurie doing at this time? Ever the woolgatherer, she simply gazed at the sky, and when her lover's wife had joined the threesome, behaved not as a rival but rather as a companion with whom to share the misery.

Whether it be frigidity or nymphomania, nobody knows what causes such phenomena. It seems that both thrive with the rise of civilization.

"To be born on a South Pacific island feeding on bananas from a few trees growing in the garden would be just fine for Shōzō. That's him," said Yurie. "He doesn't need much clothing, either. He thinks I'm a banana tree that produces year round. He says that if he were born in a place like that, he says he'd never be the king because it's such a bother."

"Bananas, I see. Well, sometimes men would have to fight in a war, wouldn't they?"

"I wonder what he'd do. He'd be finished off quickly by an arrow, or he'd immediately surrender. He'd be captured and made a slave in no time. He's so narcissistic that he'd think that his enemy's daughter might take a fancy to him. I just can't figure out a man like that. When I say—'Don't have an affair,' he obeys. He says he doesn't want to see me unhappy."

"I feel so anxious, I feel I'm going mad," she continued in total despair. "He says to me, 'Why do you have the jitters all the time?' I get anxious because I'm around a man who's paranoid about his wife being murdered. He says that I have a formidable talent for making people angry—by ignoring them, for example—I know I don't listen to people carefully enough. I only talk about myself and that also irritates people. So one of these days I may provoke someone, and end up beaten to death.

"According to him, I'm such a half-wit, a disaster waiting to happen, that he has to keep an eye on me. A car might run over me because I walk looking over my shoulder. Besides, I often trip and fall. But, if I really do show any of those signs, it's because I'm worried about a man who's obsessively worried about a woman."

Mizuki's thoughts turned to Karl, and she somehow felt guilty because he had been forced to leave his homeland and follow her to America. It was a bit frightening to imagine what the future might bring for them.

It won't hurt him to stay in Japan for a year, she thought, but that's probably the limit. Then we have no other choice but to return to New York. Keeping my distance from Japan wouldn't be a bad idea for me as a translator. If that's what we've got to do, that's how we should look at it. It's the best way out.

"Well, if that's what you want," she said, actually commenting for herself, "you should think of it as the best possible option."

Even though she was much younger than Yurie, she always found herself playing the peacemaker.

Remembering the imminent arrival of Yurie's American guests, Mizuki showed her the bedding Leonard and Mary used on weekends. The sight of the light bedding, perfect for a night in a log cabin, seemed to spawn a memory in Yurie's mind. She stared at the pattern of the fabric.

"I once slept in one of these *futons* at the Myōkō house," she said.

The muslin outer layer had the pattern of a traditional spinning wheel. Spinning wheels are now museum pieces. The pattern was also quite out of fashion. When textiles were in short supply during the war, Fū had reused one of her kimonos or previously discarded long underskirts to make the *futon*. Several patches were visible.

It was Yurie who had sent the *futons* to Mizuki. Now the children were making use of them. The furnished house the university had found for Mizuki and Karl came with a bed.

# 8 ~

IT WAS DURING ONE OF SHŌZŌ's overseas assignments that Yurie had met Lynn Ann in a tiny Alaskan town on an island, one of many that dotted the southeast coastline.

"My Forest Days"—That was how Yurie referred fondly to the Alaskan sojourn.

"I heard Japan's anguished cries echoing in the forest as it tried to rise from the ashes of war," she recollected thoughtfully. "Beyond the Pacific Ocean, my parents were toiling away in threadbare clothes with disheveled hair. I saw their reflections at the fjords edge, the smell of the lush grasses wafting through the dark forest. That was when I met Lynn Ann.

"The town had an Old Russian Orthodox church that often held tea parties. In a samovar like the ones you see in Chekhov's plays, we boiled water and poured it into cups that were filled with jam at the bottom."

"Really?" Mizuki was all ears.

"It was a mixture of Russian rose berries, sweet briar, and pears. I also saw jars full of salmonberry and blueberry jams. Wild rose berries and strawberries grew everywhere. In our backyard we were able to pick a year's supply."

"Wow, it sounds like a dream."

"It certainly was. And what I'm telling you now will sound even more so in another twenty-five years.

"Lynn Ann often talked about the Great Depression that swept through the United States when she was a young girl. Her story of what happened during the Depression—I was born around that time—was like listening to some tale of prehistoric times. The Stock Market Crash and the long lines of the unemployed. I listened to her while thinking about old Chaplin films and the stories I had heard from my parents about the hard times of early Shōwa.

"There was something called the New Deal, but, according to Lynn Ann, the real recovery only came after the Second World War had begun. Ultimately what Germany and Japan did gave America the best excuse to go to war. With a sigh and a wry smile she always spoke plainly.

"The United States in its post-victory euphoria was eagerly assuming the role of world leader, sending everybody into a frenzied scramble for U.S. dollars. In an effort to rebuild industry, a low-key, obsequious, defeated Japan, whose main selling point at the time was poverty, sidled up to Americans with transistor radios, hand-made trinkets, cultural artifacts—whatever might make Americans happy—all of it made with dirt-cheap labor, blood, sweat, and tears. I watched my country like a child who would steal a sidelong glance at her helpless, wretched parents. I was often tempted to overcompensate for this by talking down to Americans. They were very kind to the poverty-stricken Japanese and didn't know how to be as high-handed as they are now. Well, I guess, at least back then they felt they shouldn't.

"Such was the world when I had a chance encounter with Lynn Ann. She was teaching painting at a vocational school for American Indians. Back then the whites said Indians and Eskimos don't have marketable skills and all they do is hang around on street corners with beer bottles and cokes in hand, sponging off welfare. They're good for nothing.

"A quarter of a century later, things have reversed and now the voices of Indians are being heard. The American continent belonged to us in the first place, they're saying, we are what we are because white men stole it. I understand they've been able to wheedle out quite an indemnity. Oh well, they'll be conned out of that in no time. And it will all be very legal—mind you—they may be tricked into making questionable investment deals. There are ways."

Mizuki was impressed by Yurie's line of argument, which was very similar to Shōzō's.

"Tell me more about Lynn Ann."

"She always used a middle name with her first, Lynn Ann, because I think it sounded a bit Chinese. Her grandmother was Chinese, quite an intellectual and a graduate of Wellesley College. Wealthy Chinese in pre-Revolution China sent their daughters to women's colleges on the East Coast. While studying in the United States, the grandmother met a Brit and married him, shuttling back and forth between England, China, and America. Lynn Ann was born in Cambridge. Not the Cambridge in England but where Harvard is."

Many cities in America are named after famous European cities. Alaska's Petersburg, of course, comes from the capital of Imperial Russia.

Mizuki recalled the questions Americans had often put to her. "What is the Japanese version of Margaret?" or "How about Katherine?" Her answer was, "We don't have any because the two languages are linguistically unrelated."

Those same Americans cast her contemptuous looks that implied she was ignorant and uneducated. They insisted that since in different countries Margaret became Margarite, Katherine Katerina, Japanese should also have equivalents.

Recalling with amusement a linguistics class she had taken in college, she wondered if several hundred years from now the American name Lynn Ann might be seen as being derived from the Chinese Lin-an.

"So, that Lynn Ann—continue your story."

"She looked genteel."

"A genteel lady, hmm."

"She was married to a biologist who specialized in earthworms and taught at a Midwestern university. She had just lost him, I mean, when I met her."

Hearing that she was Yurie's age at that time, Mizuki began to look for any obvious sign of Lynn Ann's so-called elegance in Yurie. Because she chose to write manuscripts with a traditional brush, one side of her nose was often smeared with ink.

"I see a stain on the side of your nose."

Yurie began to rub the spot vigorously with a tissue.

"I still can't get rid of it."

Mizuki also noticed that Yurie's sweater was inside out.

"Your sweater. It's wrong side out."

"Oh, you're right."

She didn't seem to care.

"Once in a television interview I wore a sweater wrong side out but didn't realize it until the interview was over," she said. "You couldn't really tell. I don't think anybody noticed."

It seemed that she was proud of the fact that things of that nature didn't bother her, thought Mizuki. Her logic probably ran something like this: If that's the way it is, you might as well make the most of it, as something positive. Under particular circumstances a sweater wrong side out was no big deal. That was probably what she really wanted to say.

Her looks are far from those of an elegant lady, more like a dotty housewife, concluded Mizuki.

"When you ask Eskimo children to draw a picture," continued Yurie, "they invariably leave the entire sheet blank except for one corner where they depict a person the size of a dot in a sleigh or catching seals." Her eyes once again took on an abstract, dreamy look. "If you tell them to add something else, they simply look at you with a blank stare and reply, 'The rest is snow, so why not leave the space as is.' I had heard that from Lynn Ann at the Russian tea party I mentioned. I was the only housewife who had shown any interest in her story and she immediately took a liking to me. A short while after the party I received a phone call from her, inviting me to her home."

"She lived on one side of a duplex surrounded by sweet briar. The first floor, twenty-*tatami* wide, had a living room and a kitchen, the second a few bedrooms. It was the sort of perfect and comfortable house every boarding school would provide their teachers at the time. I saw Lupines and Bleeding Hearts in the front yard. The Bleeding Hearts—those were my favorites. I've never seen them in Japan, though. What would be the Japanese name?"

She seemed to be groping for something elusive, no longer within reach.

"Columbines, too. The Japanese call them buttercups. Exactly the same as we have in Japan. So many different flowers in the garden. But, once inside—" she hesitated.

Her expression suddenly changed, as though she had seen something very peculiar.

"It was a strange house. I'd never seen anything like it, ever."

Mizuki's curiosity was piqued.

"What was so strange about it?"

"No-o-o-thing extra in there. Just what came with the house. It was stark, like a vacant house. When I went inside the bathroom, a pair of hose was drying in the bathtub—that was it. With all that fuss on the phone about me coming over, she only served me instant coffee."

"Just like you and Shōzō," said Mizuki, grinning.

"What do you mean?" snapped Yurie with a puzzled look.

"Your place looks just like that. All I saw were tea cups and a frying pan."

"Well, Ye-e-s. Lynn Ann must have had some pots and pans in the cupboard. Americans usually keep their kitchen utensils out of sight."

Totally unfazed, Yurie picked up where she had left off, continuing her critique of a house she had seen twenty-five years ago, but with a renewed look of astonishment.

"Over two cups of instant coffee Lynn Ann talked for almost two hours about her husband who had died in a tornado. She was inside the house when it hit. It ripped off the roof which landed a hundred feet away but left her completely unharmed. She spent two hours telling me about the tornado and how wonderful her husband had been. He researched earthworms. Did you know that of all the creatures on earth, they collectively occupy the largest space?"

"Hmm."

"This earthworm scientist had almost made it to the house when the tornado whisked him into the air and then hurled him to the ground. He died instantly. His clothes were ripped to shreds and his body was riddled with twigs, dirt, and glass fragments."

Now here was Yurie staring vacantly into the distance, sipping her cup of instant coffee. It was the drink Mizuki just happened to serve when Yurie had stopped by on the way back from the spooky pigeon-coop house.

After she lost her husband, Lynn Ann had taught painting in Alaska for a while, and then remarried, this time to a China specialist.

"Even if our relationship is as tenuous as the ritual exchange of Christmas cards once a year, she's someone you'd never forget," added Yurie, thinking hard. "So, I'll be meeting her second husband for the first time. It's all a bit like finding something I had misplaced a long time ago.

"Her story about the tornado immediately reminded me of the A-bomb devastation. She was embroidering lace only several hundred yards away from where her dead husband lay, with fragments of glass and twigs lodged in his body. But she was perfectly safe. The roof was thrown a hundred feet from the house yet all the porcelain in the cupboard survived intact. She was in fact serving me instant coffee in one of the English cups that had survived.

"I wonder why she's decided to come to see me. Why now? Her Christmas card said she's married a Henry Coleridge. He's interested in China but used to do cultural anthropology—research on the family systems of American Indians. I may have met him somewhere."

As if trying to solve a mystery in a detective novel, she paused and then continued on to say that Lynn Ann's letter was very cryptic. She read out a few passages to Mizuki:

> … I want to come with Henry and see you because I feel we have something in common to talk about.
>
> He used to live on an island called Yolka. Do you remember Yolka? We have to tell you more about it when we meet.
>
> There's something else: we've met a Japanese named Fumiko, a college classmate of yours. She's apparently doing some bibliographical work on Japanese and

Chinese art in a library in Seattle affiliated with an art museum.

Yurie said that she must be her college roommate, Fumiko Yamashiro. "Yolka was a real strange island. Yolka means Christmas tree or fir tree in Russian, but there're no firs anywhere in the area. Apparently it was named by a Russian who had lived on the island and planted a fir."

Nastasya, a beautiful blond with the same name as one of Dostoevsky's characters, lived on that island.

Alaska was once Russian territory. In 1867 the United States bought a landmass four times the size of Japan for two cents an acre. After the completion of the sale all the administrators sent by the imperial government returned to Russia, but some of the settlers stayed on and became Americans. For that reason, many older Alaskan residents had Russian names.

After several generations the descendants knew only a smattering of their mother tongue. However, some remnants of Russian culture were evident in names such as Sonya and Pecha, including Nastasya. As a blood relative of a chieftain of the Tlingit Nation, Nastasya was extremely proud of her native heritage. But with her blond hair and piercing blue eyes she was technically a Caucasian.

She chose to live on Yolka after the Second World War probably because one of her Russian ancestors had married a native woman and lived on the island. A house built by her then live-in boyfriend had stood all alone on this deserted island.

She planned to develop a resort, a group of fantasy hotels among the hot springs bubbling in the marsh. But nobody except her close friends would think of vacationing on such an isolated island. No jets flew over the Pacific in those days.

Alaska won statehood finally in 1959. The United States government, eager to develop the new state, put the deserted island up for sale to anyone who was willing to homestead—all for a few hundred dollars.

Thrice-divorced Nastasya lived with her two breathtakingly handsome teenage sons: one was blond, the other olive-skinned with dark hair. Only one year apart, the boys were inseparable. Their closeness was the source of the town gossip that they were homosexuals. Another rumor circulated that these brothers were allegedly involved in kidnapping a female classmate.

It was just before the kidnapping when Nastasya had sung the leading role in a musical. Yurie and several people in charge of the staging were invited to her house on Yolka and treated to an outdoor white-night party. They could roast king crab, king salmon, and abalone over rock-banked fires, soak themselves in a river hot spring or enjoy a sauna at her house.

A small sand dune lay between some rocks. There they were, the two brothers, making a long rectangular box out of a hemlock tree. Someone asked, "What's it for?" They replied, "A coffin."

The guests lounging nearby thought it was a sick joke but otherwise ignored the boys. However, a few weeks later a girl was kidnapped, buried in the well-provisioned coffin and kept alive with a breathing tube.

After the father had listened to the voice coming from the buried coffin, he scraped up every penny he had for the ransom. Around ten thousand dollars, it was said. And in the 1950s that sum could easily have purchased a decent house.

The girl was returned unharmed, but the kidnapper was never identified. Officially that is. The whole town whispered that it was a scheme cooked up by Nastasya's sons, and that the kidnapped girl was an accomplice.

What also captivated the townspeople was the revelation that the girl's father was Nastasya's lover. The story bandied about was that the desperate father had turned to her for help to put together the ransom. The rumor persisted for years that he asked his lover to marry a wealthy oilman for the money. Nastasya had always wanted to be an oil-magnate.

Even after things settled down, the kidnapper remained officially unidentified. The story kept circulating that Nastasya knew her sons were the perpetrators and decided to pay the ransom. Nobody ever found out what actually happened, but the speculation making the rounds may well have been true. Soon after the incident the two sons had left for college in California and the unharmed girl had also left the island. More outrageous rumors followed: the brothers attended the same college or they didn't; they became transients or they had been sent to reform school.

Back then the town had only a few policemen, who were probably under the influence of the wealthy families. Few of the crimes that did occur were ever solved. There were several homicides when Yurie lived in the town, but no murderers were ever caught nor victims identified.

If a body was abandoned in the woods or thrown into the ocean, there was little chance it would ever be found. In divorce cases, even if the court awarded child support to the woman, it rarely materialized. Unless a big celebrity or someone extraordinarily honest was involved, the man could simply move away, never to be seen again.

Those unfortunate divorcees mumbled to themselves, shrugging their shoulders, "The United States is such a big country, how can anyone ever find a deadbeat Dad?" It was hard to tell whether they were boasting or complaining about the size of their country.

"Coleridge, Coleridge—Samuel Taylor Coleridge is a famous Romantic poet. Well, Henry Coleridge—" Yurie was trying to remember something.

# 9 ～

ALL THE HOTELS IN KYOTO ARE BOOKED SOLID during cherry blossom season. Yurie tried several major ones, even Japanese-style inns, but in vain. She gave up and said to Shōzō, "They can stay with us."

"Lynn Ann's the sort of person who invites a friend over for a cup of instant coffee, so our log cabin shouldn't be any surprise to her."

When Lynn Ann telephoned from Tokyo, Yurie explained the situation in excruciating detail:

"Japan is now in cherry blossom season and people make reservations months in advance to visit Kyoto for that. If you still want to come, be prepared for Japanese noodles in a cottage. You know Thoreau's cottage on Walden Pond. Hotels in Kyoto—all the Western hotels and even the Japanese inns—are booked. We aren't that well off, so we can't put you up in style.

"I really want to see you, though. When you get to Kyoto, would you call us from the train station? Are you with me so far? What I'm trying to say is that we want to live the simple life just the way Thoreau did, so simple that you can count everything you need on two hands. Well, if need be, just throw in another ten toes.

"They say Japan is number one in computers, but what's the use of being told what to do by a machine that will be obsolete in a year or two? Speaking of brains, a friend's son is doing research on frog brains. Ultimately what he's concerned with is the human brain. According to him the capacity of the male frog's cerebrum is larger than a female's.

"Well, Lynn Ann, I don't mean to make excuses for ourselves just because we're female, but, if it's true about frogs and humans, don't you think we're truly blessed for having a bit smaller brain capacity? I dream about losing my brain all the time. When it comes to counting figures above ten or twenty I'd rather round them off to the nearest ten. Otherwise, I somehow don't feel right. Well, it comes down to that, we're constantly forced to do things that are extremely complex but ridiculously unimportant.

"In any case, would you give us a call from the station? If I tried to explain where we should meet inside the station, it would only confuse you more. The layout is utterly chaotic. So would you take a taxi as far as the last stop on the Hieidaira bus line? We'll meet you there. Just tell the driver that Hieidaira is on the way to Mount Eizan." Yurie made her copy down the name, spelling out Hieidaira in the manner of a telephone operator, h as in house, i as in ink, e as in end and so on.

The fact that Lynn Ann was American made Yurie feel very comfortable telling her what to do. Japanese either expect you to do everything for them or take charge and plan everything in advance to avoid any undue inconvenience for their hosts.

Karl and Mizuki, who happened to be visiting, exchanged glances at the way she was hammering away at her points to Lynn Ann, her mind simultaneously leaping in many different directions.

"They're rich. They fly first-class all over the world, and own a villa in Mexico where they live half of the year," said Yurie after she hung up the phone. "Lynn Ann told me, We would feel lonely stuck in a hotel. We'd rather barge in on someone like you—someone we'd feel comfortable with talking to our hearts' content.

"I wonder if they want to burn the midnight oil with us and reminisce about things that happened a quarter century ago. Oh Yuri, Lynn Ann said, sleeping bags, grass mattresses, so what? I'm coming to hear your voice. Absolutely no sightseeing, I could care less about Kyoto."

After hearing so much about Lynn Ann, Karl and Mizuki's curiosity was at its peak.

"I'm really fascinated by the Yolka story," said Karl. He was referring to the kidnapping incident involving the two boys who buried the girl alive in a coffin fitted with a breathing tube.

"How many hours did they keep her in there?"

"Well, not more than a day, I should say," replied Shōzō. "I heard there was a stockpile of food and water in the coffin. They say some townspeople actually saw the boys speaking to the girl through the tube. They were atop a piece of driftwood in the tall grass at the edge of the forest where Indian paintbrush, Indian celery, and black lilies were in full bloom."

"I wonder what they were talking about?"

"Probably it went something like this—" said Yurie with a gleam in her eyes. "The boys were talking about snatching Nastasya from the girl's father and selling her to some rich oilman. Am I right?" She turned to look at Shōzō. "Nastasya was somewhat of a seductress, don't you think?"

"You could say that," he said.

"His memory's always good when it comes to women. Isn't that right?" said Yurie gleefully, nudging his shoulder. "Can't you fill Karl in with more details, Honey?"

Shōzō was slowly rotating his neck as if relieving a crick. That was what he did when he was embarrassed.

"I think it was five or six years after the incident. I was on a business trip, first to Seattle, and then eventually to Alaska, where, I happened to see her hostessing at a nightclub in a leotard with black fishnet stockings," he said.

"I had no idea you went to a nightclub. When was that?" asked Yurie.

"I don't quite remember. She must have been close to forty then. When the coffin incident took place I think she was in her early thirties. She once told me that the kids were born when she was around seventeen or eighteen."

"I told you. You do remember a lot about her."

"Coffee shops, where the hostesses would light your cigarette with matches tucked into their panties, was all the rage with young salarymen in Tokyo when we were leaving Japan. Shigeru took me to one, but I just watched him indulging himself since I don't smoke. Such naivete."

Whenever conversation drifted to Uncle Shigeru, Mizuki could not help feeling a little uneasy. After all, it was just a rumor that he might be my father, and even if it were true, so what, she said to herself,

"Shigeru must have taken you to lots of striptease bars," Yurie rubbed it in. "Back then the Japanese Anti-Prostitution Law had not yet been passed."

"He always showed me around Tokyo whenever I came down from Sapporo," said Shōzō quietly, rotating his neck again.

"What in the world was Nastasya doing in a nightclub?" asked Yurie. "I wonder if she broke up with the oilman."

"Well, I guess showing off her, uhh, attributes, was a hobby."

The Nastasya story again—it all went in one ear and out the other for Mizuki who had never met her. Her mind was elsewhere, going over a phone call in which Fukiko had told her that Uncle Shigeru would soon be returning from Bulgaria.

He had taken design jobs mostly in the Kansai region after a stint at the Osaka World's Fair in 1970. Fukiko might have engineered the move because at that time Fū was still living in Tokyo, the Kantō area. Fukiko's mother was a dyed-in-the-wool Kyoto-ite, and many of her relatives were still in the Kansai.

"Shigeru-san says he'll work in the Tokyo office after his return," Fukiko had told Mizuki on the phone. "It seems I will soon be leaving Uji. I'll wear out my welcome with my son if I live too close to him." What she had said could imply: Since Fū's daughter Mizuki is now in Kyoto, we'll have to go to Tokyo.

Mizuki had noticed Fukiko's tendency to mix the present with what had happened long ago. Her slow and deliberate way of speaking had the feel of someone delivering a well-written speech to make sure that you understood what she was telling you. It reminded Mizuki of peering into a vast, mysterious cavern that could be seen as the embodiment of a Kyoto woman. Bats and other small creatures held their breath in this stalactite cavern, their vigilant eyes gleaming in the dark crevices of the icy walls.

Mizuki tried to superimpose the image on what Yurie fondly called "My Forest Days." When were my forest days? She had left Japan in the 1950s when people barely had enough to eat, and barracks hastily erected on vast scorched fields were a common sight in Tokyo. The inhabitants of that great metropolis could not afford to stay in the forest; they were desperately trying to rebuild their world with bricks retrieved from the rubble.

In the dormitory of an American prep school Mizuki had shut herself away like the seed of an exotic plant that happened to have fallen in the wrong garden. Mine was a cactus forest, she said to herself. Were those days in America "my forest days"? She was not so sure. How about those days when I was fifteen and lived at an old house near the Yoyogi forest that was ravaged by the bombings, when my mother kept nagging Seiichiro about planting saplings in the garden? Suddenly she remembered what Yurie once told her about the seed of a *hamanashi* sweet briar transported by ocean currents all the way from Japan to the beach of an island in Alaska where it had sprouted and borne fruit.

Also, there was the story of Rapunzel—the German word for rampion, well known for its excellent bouquet. Karl had raised it for salads in his garden in the States. He had remembered to bring the seeds with him to Japan and after settling into the Hiei house, the first thing he did was to dig a plot for a garden and plant them.

Mizuki heard Yurie saying, "Will you join us for dinner the night Lynn Ann and her husband arrive?"

Karl jumped at the invitation. "Yes, we'll look forward to it," he said. "I'll bring a rapunzel salad. The season's just started."

Yurie mumbled to herself—"Rapunzel?"—as if trying to remember something. "The word sounds so familiar," she said.

"It's one of Grimms' fairytales," explained Karl. "The leaves are so delicious that you'd risk stealing them from your neighbor's garden."

THERE WAS SOMETHING ELSE YURIE remembered. It was Peter who had told her the tale. Rapunzel, Rapunzel—. The fragrant plant growing in the neighbor's garden. You'd risk stealing some—

oh, yes. Peter and Monika were our neighbors when we lived in Stockholm. Over the years she had wondered why her Stockholm friends never mentioned Peter the aspiring writer. Even though she had the same literary aspirations, he had never thought of her as a writer because she had not told him about it.

Back then, those aspirations had taken the form of her painting. Perhaps in her mind the two mediums were the same thing. She did not recall discussing art with him. He had once said something prophetic, "You're an artist. No way could you put up with a conventional husband like Shōzō, running an ordinary household. Even if you tried, sooner or later you'd fall apart."

Out of the countless things he had whispered in her ear, those prophetic words were what she remembered most clearly. He had assumed that Yurie was not a writer. The thoughtless assertions he had made on that premise embedded themselves deep in her memory like massive cores of black granite.

She had yet to become a full-fledged writer back then. She had neither told him her aspirations nor showed him any of her writing. There was no reason for him to think of her as a writer. Yet he disappointed her deeply. Although he desperately wants to be a writer, he may not make it—she had said to herself. Why? Because he couldn't see beyond the flesh-and-blood woman he was trying to seduce.

For a very long time she knew that she had not been able to speak her mind. Day in and day out things would slip off her tongue, things that, she told herself, could not be said openly. But she knew she had been lying to herself the whole time. Worse still, her duplicity caused not a ripple of agitation among people because they had no inkling of what was really on her mind. She thought she would go mad.

She had escaped madness only because she had put pen to paper in secret, writing about matters that had nothing to do with everyday chit-chat. That was when she decided to submit a story to a literary magazine in Japan. Had she not continued this daily ritual, she would have gone insane long ago, walking out the front door on a whim in the middle of the night to set fire to a house or commit murder.

She had got it into her head that if she actually said and did the things that were really on her mind, people would see her as nothing but a bundle of aggression, anger, and sadness, offending everyone, and a threat to those around her. That left her with no choice but to keep on lying.

For her, lying meant: to say "Yes, fine" about something you find distasteful; laugh when you don't want to laugh; put every ounce of energy into things that you find are absolutely boring; keep up this charade until it finally paralyzes your brain.

However, that was nothing to take anyone to task for. When she looked around, everyone was more or less doing what she was doing. In the end she had to readjust her thinking—mutual deceptions might have their own intrinsic value.

In her dreamy reminiscences, the story of Rapunzel once again meandered through her mind. When Yurie and Shōzō lived in Sweden, Peter had taught her Swedish using Grimms' fairytales. She remembered a poem in one of the fables that repeated the name, Rapunzel, as if it were part of an old favorite melody.

Once upon a time, there was a man and his wife who were childless for many a year, but were finally blessed with a baby. Heavy with child, the wife watched a fragrant rampion called Rapunzel that grew next door in a witch's garden, craving it day and night and pining away until she almost died. Knowing that it was wrong, her husband climbed over the wall into the garden, hastily pulled up a handful of juicy, delicious leafy rampion and prepared a salad for his wife.

Once she had it, she could never forget its taste. She begged for more, so he climbed over the wall again and again until he was finally caught by the witch.

Despite his repeated apologies, the witch demanded that the unborn baby be given to her as compensation. When a beautiful baby girl was born, the witch immediately appeared and snatched her away, naming her Rapunzel. When she was twelve years old, the witch shut up the lovely Rapunzel in a tower, which had neither a staircase nor doors, the only aperture being a little window high up in the wall.

Rapunzel had long golden hair as fine as spun silk. The witch stood every day at the foot of the tower, calling out to Rapunzel to let down her hair and then using it to climb up the tower.

One day while riding through the forest, a young Prince passed by the tower and heard Rapunzel singing with a voice so sweet and lovely that he fell in love. He sought for a door, but there was none to be found. Feeling at a loss, he kept a long vigil below the tower. One day a witch appeared, calling out to Rapunzel to lower her plaits of hair and then climbing up to her. After the witch was gone, the Prince repeated the words and was able to meet the lovely girl.

She had never set eyes on a man before, but she was so enchanted by the Prince that she let him come and see her every evening.

However, their happiness was short-lived. When she learned of their trysts, the witch seized Rapunzel's beautiful hair in her rage and cut it off. She then drove poor Rapunzel into the wilderness. The witch fastened the plaits she had cut off to a hook by the window and then let them down. Unaware of what had happened, the Prince climbed up and found the witch who swore that he would never see Rapunzel again. The Prince, beside himself with grief and anger, leapt out of the window only to have his eyes scratched out when he fell into the briars below.

The storyteller must have felt pity for the two lovers because he let them reunite in the wilderness. Rapunzel and the twins born to her went to find the blind Prince in the forest. When two of her teardrops fell on his eyes, he could see as well as ever.

Peter had recounted this tale to Yurie years before she met Lynn Ann in Alaska.

Although it had seemed like just another fairytale when she first heard it from Peter, now the tale took on the strange freshness of a reality, merging countless images in her mind.

A man who steals fragrant leaves from a neighbor's garden for his wife; an imprisoned girl in a tower who lets her lover climb up plaits of her own hair; a prince's sight restored by his lover's tears. Yurie felt she had somehow stumbled upon the reason why such stories had been passed down from generation to generation.

"Rapunzel! I can finally meet her," said Yurie, oblivious to the conversations going on around her. "The Rapunzel I've met only in my dreams."

WHEN SHE WOKE UP THAT MORNING Yurie experienced a dull, heavy band of pain around her head, as if someone was physically squeezing it. She was reminded of her mother who had had similar complaints, and tried to connect this pain with the story of Rapunzel and Lynn Ann's impending visit. When Yurie's mother was her age, she often complained: "My hands and feet feel numb, my neck is stiff like an *omochi* rice cake's been glued to it and I can barely raise my arms half way. When I hold something, I lose control and drop it. I don't know how many teacups I've broken." This was exactly what Yurie was experiencing now.

"If my mother were alive, she would be Lynn Ann's age," said Mizuki, gazing at Yurie the way her mother Fū used to. The look in her eyes reminded Yurie of what Fū had told her a few weeks before she died—something that also involved Yurie's mother.

"Not long before she died, your mother was reciting a poem by Ariwara no Narihira, the very last one in *Tales of Ise*," said Yurie, talking half to herself:

> I have always heard
> this is the road we all must travel at last
> But I never dreamed
> it would come so soon.

"After she recited it, she said to me: 'Yuri, your mother also talked about this poem. My memory of her redeems me.' That was what she said to me. She gazed at me, thinking about my mother."

Yurie fell silent for a while. Why am I telling this story at all? I must be feeling the way my mother or Fū felt, or even Narihira.

"She also recited another poem from *Tales of Ise* for me," Yurie continued:

> "My innermost thoughts,
> saying nothing, I will just give up

and let them be,
since there is no one
who feels the same as me.

'You're a novelist and know all about this, she had said to me. It's not my place to say it, but in the end people fail to express their true feelings no matter how much they think they've tried. I really understand that now.' That was what she said."

Fully aware that she was dying, Mizuki had delayed her return as long as possible and missed the chance to be with her when she died. She had probably been talking about her daughter, and expressing her painful awareness of what her child was doing to her.

Yurie had heard her mother recite the very same poem when she started feeling dull pain. The memory of the mumbling recitation of the poem weighed heavily on Yurie. Despite a stroke that had left her in a coma, from time to time she was heard to wail like a baby—a baby with a paralyzed tongue. She bawled like an infant clutching at its mother's sleeve, her glazed eyes boring into Yurie's.

Fū had died of cancer, but her faculties remained intact until the very end. It seemed she kept repeating, through sheer willpower, the same poem Yurie's mother had recited. Yurie knew then that Fū was thinking about her own daughter, a daughter in a far away land who refused to return home, even knowing her death was near.

"You see, Yuri," she had said, "I really don't want her to come home while I'm alive. That's why I don't call her to come back. If she did, if she were at my bedside staring at me with those reproachful eyes, no, worse, if she tried to avoid looking at me, excusing herself to get out of the room, I would find that even more painful."

The way she had said pa-i-n-ful, slowly drawing out the syllables, was how people in the Niigata region, where both Fū and Yurie's mother had grown up, expressed grief—trying to convey the heart-rending nature of it all.

"I, I remember every nasty thing I did to people long ago. And I'm frightened now that someone may do the same to me." She cackled her loud, haughty, malicious yet somehow forlorn laugh.

That was what was racing through Yurie's mind when Karl, oblivious to everything but his own curiosity, said, "I'm really interested in Yolka Island and that strange incident involving Nastasya. Who in the world is Henry Coleridge? You may have met him once, right, Yuri?"

"Apparently I have."

"Henry, Henry, hmm, didn't Nastasya call someone Henry?" said Shōzō, suddenly joining in.

It is customary for Americans to use first names, and even if they forget your family name, they often remember what they call your Christian name. It is the complete opposite in Japan. Unless you are on intimate terms, Japanese will only remember your family name.

"You have such a clear memory of Nastasya," said Yurie teasingly, but a remark like that nowadays was nine times out of ten pure flattery. She sensed he wanted her to be jealous.

That had not always been the case. She recalled with a touch of nostalgia the days when she saw any woman as a potential rival. When a young and sexually attractive woman walked by Shōzō, and his eyes automatically drifted after her, Yurie said to herself—Oh, how it used to set me off.

In a split second her blood would begin to boil, and she would summon all the abuse she could muster to hurl at him. She had a clear memory of how it had frightened him and yet how it had also given him an obvious thrill; these days she simply kept it up out of habit to reassure him.

The act was in no way automatic for her; it was all very touching when you considered how much effort it took on her part. She gave a wry smile. It appeared that she was trying to have some fun with Shōzō by stirring him up with images of a sensuous woman.

"That was him. That was Henry," said Shōzō suddenly. "The guy passing around the liquor like a good husband should."

"I'll bet Lynn Ann's husband is that same Henry," said Karl, emphasizing his point with unexpected enthusiasm. "I don't know either of them, but I feel I'm right."

"Looks like Yolka will be a hot topic when Lynn Ann comes," said Mizuki in a level voice.

"In other words the boys wanted to get rid of their mother's lover," chimed in Karl. "That lover was Henry Coleridge, the father of the kidnapped girl. He sank so much into Nastasya's schemes that he was bankrupted. When he begged her for the ten thousand dollar ransom, she sold herself to a rich oilman who had long been lusting after her. It's possible she was aware of what was going on. In the end the boys killed two birds with one stone: they forced their mother to sell herself to another man, and at the same time made her break off with her lover. And what's more, Henry's daughter probably wanted it that way. She couldn't stand watching her father being wrapped around Nastasya's little finger."

Karl's hard-boiled detective work temporarily freed Yurie from the coils of the Rapunzel story and she now found herself going along with him.

"The tale of a little girl who makes her father sell his lover," said Yurie, nodding, "Uh-huh. I see." Somehow, she thought, everything in the world is linked together curiously.

## 10 ～

IT WAS SOON AFTER HER FIRST CALL when Lynn Ann called back to tell Yurie about a change of plan. "We had no intention to stay over in Tokyo—if possible I'd love to come over right away. But Henry's worn out from all the traveling and I want him to rest before heading for Kyoto."

Yurie gave a sigh of relief. Thank goodness, there's no reservation to cancel. That would have complicated things. Once cherry blossom viewing's over, fewer people will be around, and with the weather getting warmer by the day, I won't have to worry about rounding up more blankets for them.

Spring had been late in coming this year, and tourists who had made reservations months in advance had to go home without seeing a single blossom. Of course, the buds had not forgotten to open, and by the time Lynn Ann and Henry had arrived, the tiny petals were already fluttering to the ground in the quiet rain.

Darkness had descended when Lynn Ann stepped out of the taxi. She immediately caught sight of Yurie, who was absent-mindedly waiting at the bus stop. She rushed to give her a bear hug.

Releasing Yurie, Lynn Ann said, "Oh, my, you're like someone from a dream. The cab driver was really nice. He understood English and we asked him to stop the car to take a look at the cherry blossoms. They have a frightening, even spooky sort of beauty at night, like flower nymphs. Now I know why Japanese love cherry blossoms.

"I was overwhelmed by the sight of the pale pink petals, dancing all around us in the mist—Oh, we've come to a far away land—no,

105

we're still on our way to that place, almost as if some spirit is sweeping us along."

As they moved away from the bus stop, she snuggled up to Yurie, her steps quick and buoyant as if walking on a cloud.

"You're very lucky, making it just in time for the late-blooming flowers," said Yurie cheerfully.

She was already feeling very comfortable with the straightforward English personal pronoun "you," with which, unlike Japanese, she could address a much older person.

Once a pale brunette, Lynn Ann was now a platinum blonde and her shiny hair was speckled with wet cherry petals. She was proud of her shapely legs—even in her forties she had looked chic in the mini-skirts that were all the rage. Her pride still communicated itself in the graceful way she carried herself in a skirt that fell just below the knees. Her every step seemed to show off the gorgeousness of her legs. She could easily pass for sixty, even fifty. At least that was the way she must have felt about herself.

The supple movement of her hands, precise and elegant, showed she was well practiced in presenting herself. In contrast, Henry Coleridge, who looked pale like most Northern Europeans, appeared to be ill. His translucent blue eyes, the color of antique glass, held a strange indefinable poignancy. Shōzō greeted him at the *genkan* foyer, trying mentally to connect the man before him with the husband passing around liquor at a party twenty-five years ago. The two images did not quite fit together in his mind.

Yurie lumbered in unceremoniously with tea on a tray, which she accidently spilled. Shōzō lowered his eyes.

"Barbarian!" he wanted to shout, but she had been complaining lately of a heaviness in her body. If he had actually said it, she would have retorted, "My sensitivity is in revolt, manifesting itself with a destructive force."

Her speech and manner tired him in the company of others much more than when they were alone.

He noticed that she was hardly paying attention to Lynn. As usual her mind was elsewhere.

Lynn Ann started talking about Fumiko Yamashiro, Yurie's

classmate in college, and went on to discuss China. But Yurie's blank look told her that she would not get the attention she had surely expected.

"Why didn't she marry?—I mean Fumiko," said Yurie suddenly. "As far as I know she's studying Yin-Zhou bronzes," she continued, completely ignoring Lynn's attempt to start a discussion on Chinese Buddhism.

"That's what Henry's interested in. That was why the three of us had such a lively conversation together," ventured Lynn quietly.

Henry said that they had visited Mount Tiantai and the Guoqing Temple in China, where they learned that a high-ranking Japanese monk by the name of Saichō had once studied. Now that Yurie was living on Mount Hiei, they wanted to see the Enryakuji Temple that Saichō had founded on the mountain. Henry wrote down the *kanji* for all the names he mentioned, pronouncing each with a heavy accent.

Shōzō was experiencing *déjà vu*; Yurie seemed to possess the mysterious power of bringing different people together, the kind of people he normally would never have had the chance to become friends with.

Here they were, folks she had met only a couple of times twenty-five years ago, barging in on her with hardly a greeting, talking their heads off, assuming that their listeners knew what they were talking about. Why should I pay attention to them? Yurie seemed to be saying to herself. My lifelong strategy has been to concentrate on my own world.

"No, no, Fumiko's no lesbian, just a romantic," mumbled Yurie, her eyes fixed somewhere in the middle distance. "I can't believe she has no boyfriend."

"Well, I guess he's somewhere," said Lynn Ann indifferently.

"She's a very nice woman. I'm sure she's got someone as nice as she is. A conventional marriage isn't her thing, that's all," interjected Henry. "In the old days men felt compelled to marry to please women. But some of today's women reject that sort of thing. If I'd been born thirty years later, I would have lived differently. Nowadays people do the most daring things—things people my age just dreamed of—acting as if it's absolutely normal. But then their radical lifestyle creates different sorts of problems. I find it all rather pathetic." Henry looked you straight in the eye when he spoke.

"Yuri, we got married because of you," said Lynn Ann.

"Heavens, what do you mean?"

Finally the conversation seemed to be getting somewhere.

"We met at a marina in town. We learned that Dr. Morgan was your family physician. He and his wife invited me out on their boat. Henry happened to be one of their guests. We had such a good time with them. Remember what I told you at a Russian tea party about Eskimo children drawing pictures? While I was telling the hosts about the story, a conversation drifted to an operetta, *The Mikado*, in which you and Nastasya had played, and then to her Japanese *sumi-e* ink painting, which was on display next to your drawing at an exhibition, and so on and so on.

"Henry remembered meeting you at Nastasya's house on Yolka. Henry, dear—you couldn't remember Shōzō, but you certainly did Yuri," said Lynn Ann. Henry was after all Nastasya's lover.

"There were so few Japanese in that town. Yuri was the first I had ever met," said Henry.

Yurie didn't have the heart to tell them that Shōzō also remembered Nastasya. Lynn Ann seemed to take it for granted that Yurie and Shōzō knew all about Nastasya and Henry, the town's celebrities. That made things easy for the listeners.

Among Japanese there is an unwritten rule that when conversation turns to sex one should only make indirect references to it. As a result verbal exchanges lose their edge. After many years of living in the States Yurie and Shōzō felt rather relaxed and nostalgic about the casual way Americans talked about sex.

It probably had nothing to do with being American. It just so happened that Yurie's close friends always exhibited this casualness. It was Lynn Ann's way of saying that she had no intention of hiding their past. Did she mention her current husband's old flame because she wanted to know what Yurie and Shōzō thought about the woman who was obviously still on Lynn Ann's mind?

"You remember that incident, don't you? About Annabelle?"

Annabelle? Yes, yes. It was all coming back to Shōzō. That was the name of Henry's kidnapped daughter.

"Well, I don't know how much of the story you know—she's forty now," said Lynn Ann. Shōzō couldn't quite imagine an older Annabelle.

Yurie was now listening eagerly to Lynn Ann.

"Guess who she's with now."

She lowered her head and gave a long sigh.

"She is with Ivan and Antonio of all people—Nastasya's sons, the kidnappers themselves. They were in cahoots. She's living with two men."

"Ivan and Antonio—" Shōzō repeated the names to himself. Hmm, that was it. Those were the names of the two attractive boys on everyone's lips. The scene came back to him like an object once sunken surfacing slowly from the bottom of a river.

Nastasya had married several times: her first husband was a Russian who fathered Ivan. The younger boy, Antonio, was the son of a Spaniard, or possibly a Mexican. Every teenage girl in town would swoon over the two extraordinarily handsome boys.

"Annabelle's living with them. My guess is that they're making a living off her."

"Making a living off her?" queried Yurie.

"Prostitution."

Henry looked downcast, his eyes full of pain.

"Poor Henry. I just can't bear to see Annabelle do this to herself. She's your only daughter, Henry. She's a good girl. But I think that lovely, luxurious blond hair of hers trailing down to her hips, and those violet blue eyes, drove her to this. I told her, 'You're making Papa miserable.' Do you know what she said? 'I don't worry about him because you're with him, not Nastasya.' Even now, she really hates Nastasya with a passion. She's quite attached to me, though, because I'm so different from Nastasya.

"Lynn Ann, make Papa happy, Annabelle told me, I've got to decide my own future." It appeared that Annabelle called her step-mother by her first name. It was clear that she could not possibly imagine addressing a woman who was not her biological mother in any other way.

"In life you do what you've got to do," said Henry, nodding, his eyes fixed on something far away.

"Ivan and Antonio must be gay. Whether the relationship is physical or not, when a number of men share one woman, they more or less have that psychological tendency," he said almost to himself. A shrill cry split the night, and his eyes followed the shadow of a bird darting across the garden. Puzzled at the unfamilliar call, Shōzō cocked his head and wondered aloud, "That's no bush warbler."

"What's the point of trapping a wild bird born to fly, born to cry, training it like a parrot to mimic human speech," said Henry dryly, staring into the darkness. He must be thinking about Nastasya, Shōzō thought to himself.

"So, how's Nastasya doing?" he asked hesitantly—Nastasya who wore a black leotard and fishnet stockings, and sang in a nightclub.

"I wonder how many men that woman has gone through after you? All we know is that she was with a black pianist or piano tuner the last time we saw her," said Lynn Ann, pressing Henry. She referred to Nastasya as "that woman."

"Well, quite a few, I'd say. She just has no luck with men," said Henry.

"No luck? Was that what happened to you, too, Henry dear?"

"Some women can't be saved," sighed Henry.

"Nastasya bled him dry. With that scheme of building a fantasy hotel or something on a god-forsaken island, she even had barges haul in lumber and a diesel engine. And you remember that house, don't you? I hear nobody came to the island except her own personal guests, her party friends. At the time Henry was doing research on a native Alaskan family, and became captivated by the story of the woman's background. Her grandmother or great grandmother—I'm not sure which—was the daughter of a chief of the Tlingit nation. Henry spent all his money on that woman, everything the poor scholar had."

Nothing to do with family lineage, Shōzō said to himself, careful to hold his tongue; it was Nastasya he fell for.

"To make things worse, there was that kidnapping incident. She always ran things on a shoestring, living off one man after another. Ten thousand dollars came and went in no time and all she wanted was to get rid of Henry, who was stone broke by then."

"I had to do it for Annabelle. Nastasya broke up with the oil tycoon in two months." Henry was clearly defending her.

"What happened to the boys was all her fault."

"It may also be the sons' fault that she turned out the way she did. It's a chicken-and-egg thing. There's a reason for everything that happened to Nastasya and her sons. The same is true with you and me. We might be the reason for someone else's problems." Once again Henry seemed to be protecting Nastasya.

Lynn Ann shook her head in resignation. Yet, she continued the story in her dispassionate voice even with the hint of a faint smile on her lips. With her careful attention to rhetoric, potentially vulgar stories turned into quiet running water or even a suite of lovely melodies. Yurie realized how talented this friend was.

"Poor Henry," said Lynn Ann to her husband who sat right next to her, as she cradled his bald head in her arms. "It's too much for me to see him go through this."

Looking at his watch, Henry rummaged through his pockets for some pills and popped them into his mouth.

When he had left for the bathroom, Lynn Ann whispered to Yurie, "His liver's in bad shape. Since he can't process protein, the ammonia buildup has damaged his brain; he sometimes loses consciousness. Don't say anything if he doesn't touch any food, okay?"

Although still not quite sure what really ailed him, but remembering his awful skin color, Yurie nodded. "Is it all right for him to travel like this?"

"What remains of our life together is a little something extra. Just lying in bed won't cure a disease. We're having a good time one day at a time. It's like caressing your favorite worn-out doll," said Lynn Ann laughing, rubbing her shoulders. She added that she had received an inheritance five years ago when her mother died, and as former teachers she and Henry also had good pensions. They were comfortable.

Karl and Mizuki arrived with the rapunzel salad, which he had promised. Lynn Ann had stopped talking for the moment, but standing on ceremony like some newly arrived guest was not her style. She began again:

"My, seeing someone Annabelle's age makes me feel meditative," she said. "She's Henry's only daughter, and because she was traumatized when she was a child, she feels insecure unless she hurts herself or is hurt by someone else."

Henry fished out a photo from his wallet and showed it to Mizuki. The Annabelle in the photo, with her hand nervously raking luxuriant blond hair that reached her hips and her innocent wide-set eyes, was the very image of an ingénue.

"Do you have grandchildren?" asked Mizuki.

Lynn Ann shook her head.

"No. Young people nowadays talk about the uncertainty of children's survival," she said. "They don't even try to make babies. They can't help it. I once thought that way myself. Of course, I was ahead of the times. That was the era when people thought the bigger the family the better off they were, and streets were packed with cackling hens leading long processions of little chicks behind them. I tried to avert my eyes, sneaking a peek at them now and then. But I was a real minority. Well, how about you? Any children?"

"Yes, two. I'm not their biological mother, though. They were abandoned and we adopted them."

"Well, dear, being brought up with biological parents doesn't necessarily mean kids turn out right. The important thing is how you raise them."

Imitating Henry, Karl extracted from his pocket a photo of Mary and Leonard. "This one," he said, pointing at Leonard, "seems to have Asian blood in him, so I'm very interested in things Asian."

Then the conversation shifted haphazardly to Yin-Zhou bronzes, Taoist Immortals, and yin-yang theory.

Karl mentioned that some sophisticated math problems, including what could be considered modern calculus, were part of the *keju* civil service exams in early China. He didn't think calculus originated in Arabia but wasn't sure which country had actually discovered it first.

"I've been studying Zen since I came to this country, playing the *shakuhachi* flute, and seeing *kabuki* and *bunraku* plays," he said. "It all has everything to do with the distribution of my energy flow. That one is Mary. Her mother was a Scot, so my wife says I need to do some research on dragons."

Instead of "Mizuki," Karl referred to her as "my wife."

"My wife teaches Japanese at a college in the States. Speaking of languages, she says deciphering linguistic codes can be a lot of fun."

Mizuki took up the thread and began to tell the story of a very bright student whom she had helped read a Japanese novel in the original. In one paragraph a soldier says "Shimatta!," as he is irritated at missing a curfew and facing a closed gate. The student had mistaken the expression "I blew it!" for "[The gate] is shut!"

"That also has something to do with the way a circuit in the brain processes information," said Karl, shrugging his shoulders.

## 11 ～

LYNN ANN'S STORYTELLING NEVER LET UP even after the arrival of Karl and Mizuki.

She would abruptly trail off and then start anew without warning, backtracking to Nastasya or Annabelle, or switching suddenly to an account of chanting Buddhist monks in a procession that meandered through the outer court of a Chinese temple.

"The service at the Guoqing Temple was not what you'd call structured, but you would come away transported as if countless tiny streams had merged to form one mighty river.

"I understand many Buddhist paintings and statues were destroyed during the Cultural Revolution. Inside the temple, I had the feeling that the quiet murmurings of those persecuted Buddhists have now slipped out of the past, their chants pouring at last into the open air of the present. I have no particular interest in religion—haven't been to church for a very long time—but being in that temple made me a bit nostalgic. All at once I remembered the church I had attended as a little girl, wondering aloud if the adult Christian plaster saints had the same fervor and faith as the Chinese Buddhists of those chaotic days. When I was growing up, many people challenged the hypocrisy and fanaticism of those same sanctimonious churchgoers, and when young people refused to go to church, many adults sided with them."

At that moment what had taken hold of Mizuki's mind was Shigeru's return from his monastery hideaway in Bulgaria. While I'm here in Japan, there might be a chance to see the man who might be my father, she thought. Sentimentalism played no part in her curiosity about what he now looked like, or what he believed in. Rather, she wanted to carefully study this exemplar of the warped soul, a likeness of which must also reside within her.

On the eve of Shigeru's return Fukiko had sounded calm and collected on the phone, with her mind apparently intent on the move to Tokyo.

"You never know when Shigeru-san might start talking nonsense again," she had said, clearly finding Mizuki to be someone she could confide in. "When that happens I'll be counting on you. My son Tōichiro just—" Fukiko trailed off.

"By the way, when will you and your family return to America?" she had asked. One could infer from the innocent question that she was opening up to her because she would soon be leaving for a faraway country.

In the meantime the story of Henry's old flame was capturing Karl and Shōzō's undivided attention in direct proportion to the intensity of Mizuki and Yurie's negative response to the story. Somehow in their minds Nastasya's tale linked with memories of Fū.

"I'd like to excuse myself," said Henry after dinner. He scrutinized the Japanese bedding Mizuki had spread out for him with intense curiosity, and promptly lay down.

When fabric was scarce during the war, Fū had made *futon* covers out of her kimono undergarments. Unlike their modern synthetic equivalents, prewar *futons* were made of heavy, absorbent cotton batting. Yurie had seen the pregnant Fū making them at the Myōkō house just days before Mizuki's birth. Yurie had shipped Mizuki two of them when she arrived in Japan with her family. Both covers had traditional patterns: one of them spinning wheels, the other a thousand cranes.

Mizuki's children used them every weekend. Henry flashed an OK sign, smiling contentedly, half buried in the fluffy sun-drenched *futon* that Yurie had given a good airing in anticipation of the guests' arrival.

With his exit Lynn Ann perked up, looking much younger and showing no visible signs of fatigue from travel, and her storytelling took on a livelier pace, flowing on deep into the night.

"You know, I said all those nasty things about Nastasya in front of Henry, but I really think she's quite a woman. He knows it, too, so I don't think he lost much going through that mess with her. That's how I comfort him when nobody's around.

"Every woman dreams of living her own life. We're just intimidated by the possibility that we might end up like Nastasya's sons, feeling anxious about one thing or another, avoiding risks, living a life of no gains, no losses. You know, dear, I'll tell you something about children," she said, suddenly turning to Mizuki. "A child needs his mother only when he's a fledgling. My son died at the age of eleven before he had a chance to test his wings; in my mind he's forever an eleven-year-old boy. Whenever I see a child around his age I want to be near him. But when I see how Ivan and Antonio turned out, I say to myself—There's no guarantee the same thing wouldn't have happened to my boy."

After the death of her son in an accident and her first husband in a tornado, it must have occurred to her that everything in life is forever in flux.

"Henry took a great interest in Alaskan folktales on Yolka, the world in which humans are interchangeable with forest creatures and sea life—a bear might become a human in an instant, then a mysterious bird would tear through the sky like a bolt of lightning. I think his encounter with Nastasya was a little like that.

"I happened to show him an art book on Yin-Zhou bronzes soon after he broke up with her. That was the beginning of his interest in China. I'm no expert on ancient Chinese bronzes or Indian sculpture, but regardless of the topic or the time period, I feel both cultures represent the spontaneous expression of a belief in the magic of the primordial world.

"Henry's relationship with the university went sour after that mess with Nastasya and since then he's been working at things in his own eccentric way without ever expecting much recognition. But I don't care about that sort of thing. We've lived the way we like, enjoying every minute of it and we couldn't ask for more. Now on this trip, you've let us stay at your place—yes, so many people all over the world have been good to us—in Africa we were saved from being killed by a Masai warrior. But when we think about it we feel it's much better to have had that chilling experience than none at all."

Cocking her head, she turned to Karl and said, "When I was much younger, I used to have a great respect for the social animal in a man, but nowadays I'm having second thoughts. You men should be pitied. A man's social nature is something akin to a half-crazed mother totally consumed with caring for her child; there's nothing very unusual about that, but it makes you look away in disgust. A mother who destroys herself for the sake of her child isn't particularly laudable. It's instinct, you know. Some women may want to romanticize the tragedy of a vanquished lord, but a man trapped inside a pathetic corporate structure, seething with an inner rage, is quite similar to a woman losing her sanity over a child."

Karl was listening with a grin.

"Your Mom was just like that with your sister Taeko, wasn't she?" said Yurie, challenging Shōzō. Mizuki thought the tone in her voice had turned a bit hostile but he looked unaffected.

"It's best to stay away from a mother bear with cubs. A mother would rip somebody else's kid apart to feed her own," said Yurie venomously.

"Well, all of us had a mother," responded Shōzō. "You might say we've all survived and thrived by feeding on that meat."

Lynn Ann smiled, nodding in agreement.

"I absolutely go crazy when it comes to my mother-in-law. I felt my skull was being crushed by her jaws when she was around," said Yurie cruelly, in a tone at once sadistic and masochistic. I guess I can talk this way, she thought, because Lynn and Henry are foreigners and I'm speaking in broken English. For them, conversation isn't a zero-sum game, so they may be experiencing the same sort of liberation. Otherwise, why in the world have they come all this way?

Yurie forged on. "Women are really disgusted with how men switch the concept of motherhood, *bosei*, for that of the virgin mother, *seibo*. To make things worse, when Shōzō introduced me to his mother for the first time, he proclaimed proudly that I was an intellectual type. I drew a blank."

"Some people think you are," said Mizuki, grinning.

"What I have in mind when someone says intellectual," said Shōzō, "is a homophone character with the 'disease' radical enclosing it, which means 'idiotic.'" He was obviously very pleased with himself. Often the real discoveries come to you in the heat of the moment.

"Nowadays, to call someone an intellectual isn't a compliment— it's sarcasm," said Karl. "I think it's because humans are being destroyed by things intellectual."

"When I say, I'm not intellectual, some people think I'm being modest," protested Yurie again. Her mouth gaping idiotically, she seemed to have forgotten the attack on her mother-in-law but soon picked up where she had left off. "Shōzō never added the 'disease' radical when he called his mother an intellectual," she said, noticeably once again on the offensive.

"You don't really respect that disease *radical* anyway, Yuri, do you?" Karl teased her with a devilish sarcasm that surpassed even her own.

"You let Yuri get away with anything, Shōzō," joined in Mizuki, "because you've been raised by a woman just like her." She nodded with a look that said, Aha—I see, quite pleased with her own comment.

Yurie suddenly became agitated as if her brain waves had temporarily stalled; she quickly downed a cup of *saké* to stimulate her circulation. As the drink took effect she began to laugh, seemingly more content with herself.

IT WAS SOON AFTER THE DEATH of her second husband that Shōzō's mother Michiko began suddenly to lock horns with Yurie. Totally preoccupied with her youngest daughter Taeko, she began to wheedle Shōzō to make various extravagant purchases. His inability to refuse her requests always frustrated Yurie. From Taeko's formal kimono (worn only once), college tuition, trips with friends, marriage (lavish wedding costs), to hosting her husband's family, her long list of demands never ceased. Apparently Yurie still harbored resentment at how much they had overextended themselves just to meet the demands.

Mizuki, who had heard all about it from her, felt that she could have flatly told Michiko, We don't have that kind of money, and besides, it's just wasteful. Instead, she continued to criticize Michiko behind her back, wearing the contorted expression of someone who only had herself to blame for giving in to such unreasonable demands.

Lacking the imagination to create a world of her own, Michiko let a relentlessly acquisitive society dictate her life and fan the flames of her fancy, all the while dreaming that her son would fulfill her every desire.

Yurie had met her for the first time just before she married Shōzō. She must have been Yurie's present age. At first she had said things that sounded quite admirable. Her remarriage was to spare her son the financial burden of the young Taeko and herself. She often joined the young married couple for concerts at Nichigeki Music Hall. Yurie's early impressions were that she was a quite practical, unsentimental sort.

However, with the loss of her second husband she underwent a sudden metamorphosis, screeching loudly like a threatened mother hen to protect the chick under her wing. This reckless protectiveness disgusted Yurie.

"She should marry again. It seems a woman turns weird without a man around," Yurie used to say.

This comment had failed to elicit any response from Shōzō. Didn't we have to live abroad for such a long time, she said to herself, because we had to keep on sending money to Michiko? She felt sick to her stomach.

The daughter who had driven Michiko to such extreme measures was now a mother herself and talked about nothing but her child's college entrance exams, treating her aging mother as something of a nuisance, despite all the sacrifices she had made, sacrifices that had been the target of Yurie's utter contempt.

"Staying with Mom even half a day wears me out. How can she go on and on all day just talking about herself?" Taeko once said, possibly intending to humor Yurie. But as far as she was concerned, Taeko's criticism of Michiko also applied to the daughter herself.

It seemed obvious that what she really wanted to say was that it is a son's duty to take care of his mother. But, for one thing, Michiko was letting her daughter's family live in the house left by her second husband, and also not to be forgotten was the fact that her late step-father had raised her for more than ten years. She had reluctantly taken in her mother for those reasons.

Taeko packed off Michiko to Shōzō from time to time, begging him to give her a breather. When her own children were toddlers and she needed all the help she could get from her mother, she was full of bravado, boasting, "I'll take care of Mom for the rest of her life." It now seemed that she had forgotten she ever said anything of the sort.

Yurie was easily overcome with pity on seeing Michiko's wrinkled sunken eyes. "I wonder if someday I'll look just like that. I can't help but look away and stare into the sky," Yurie had once mumbled to Mizuki.

On the surface at least it seemed that Yurie treated Michiko rather kindly when they were together, which confused Mizuki and made her wonder what lay deep inside this mysterious cavern of kindness. As with an abandoned bonfire that flares up during a gust of wind, a strange glow would flash from Yurie's eyes at the slightest mention of Michiko, the way smoke rising from a mound of charred leaves bursts instantly into a forest fire. That look and the incomprehensibility of Yurie's behavior always disturbed Mizuki.

In the aftermath of Michiko's extended stays, Yurie would call Mizuki and fall into a predictable tirade. "A man can never refuse his mother when she's young and in control—even the most unreasonable demands—but once she grows pitifully senile, he's cruel to her in the name of reason, audaciously declaring that reason is the governing principle of life. To their mothers or wives and to every woman in the world, men are in fact nothing but bundles of sexual fantasies driven by their hormones and metabolism."

She would eventually target Shōzō, scattering sparks of vitriol like a runaway forest fire. "He didn't even feel a tenth of the pity for my father that he showed for his own mother. And even if I had had a younger brother, he wouldn't have done even one hundredth of what I've done for Taeko. It's a fact—everything obnoxious about his personality has been passed down from Michiko."

Yurie's abusive tone, rivaling the screech of a woodpecker, made Mizuki want to cover her ears.

However, once Yurie calmed down, she would turn conciliatory. "I can analyze his mother the way I do because, deep down, both of us are alike. Besides, the way he's obsessed about me isn't quite normal. If a man is blind to what his own mother's doing, the same goes for his wife. Shōzō's now trying to make me cast the same sorts of spells his mother used."

Her tirades ended almost always in the vein of the Mother Goose nursery rhyme "This Is the House that Jack Built." Jack builds a house and makes the Malt, the Rat eats the Malt, the Cat kills the Rat, the Dog worries the Cat, the Cow with the crumpled horn tosses the Dog, the Maiden milks the Cow, the Man who's dazzled by the Maiden marries her and builds the House, and, so the cycle begins all over again.

Indeed, that is how the spark of a story is ignited. Well, let me see, how did Nastasya's tale begin? Wait. We don't have to start the story with Nastasya at all. We can, but we may also begin with the cat, or the dog, the cow, the maiden, or the rat. In other words, you can start anywhere you please.

THE TALE THAT LYNN ANN HAD RELATED on a drowsy early spring evening lasted until dawn, penetrating the walls and *tatami* mat floor like the gentle, intermittent murmur of a drizzling shower, fading, then starting all over again.

Mizuki remembered what an old neighbor had said that very morning. "The long rainy season's just around the corner. The *hototogisu* will soon come to call. They'll appear with the rain once all the cherry leaves are out."

Yurie had been playing the Cuckoo Waltz on an old out-of-tune piano in her rented house. "I don't know why but my fingers remember the tune even when I can no longer read music," she said.

Her words triggered Shōzō's memory of the singing *kakkō* birds when he had gone with Shigeru to visit her at the college dorm in Musashino.

*Kakkō* also came to sing in the trees surrounding the house where Mizuki lived as a girl.

"I understand that Nastasya's last live-in had no formal training but was able to play Mozart and Chopin just by listening to the melodies," said Lynn Ann, picking up the thread of her story. "He often played his own arrangements of those pieces at a nightclub."

With Henry out of the picture, she talked about Nastasya in a more favorable light. One was given the impression that Henry had taken possession of his wife. No, it was more like she was becoming Nastasya, enraptured by the pianist's Mozart arrangement. "He played Chopin and Mozart à la Negro spirituals. I wonder what they're doing now. I've heard they're in San Diego," Lynn Ann added.

In her mind's eye Mizuki was facing the phantom Nastasya, a woman she had never seen before, whose image she would recognize instantly as Fū's. If she were alive she would have started fierce arguments with her daughter; her eyes full of hatred and fear would lock onto Mizuki's, sparking yet another altercation.

A few generations ago old people in the West had learned much earlier than their counterparts in Japan not to count on younger people. Those same aging Westerners have the courage to remove children they don't like from their wills and write in a favorite cat as a sole benefactor. Even in their seventies, they are still vigorous enough to look for new mates. In any case, who in the world would take time to talk to these aging people? Decidedly not their children.

"On our second date," said Lynn Ann happily, "Henry brought along an old magazine that featured a canoe trip on the Columbia River I made with my first husband."

That was the year, she continued, when the United States in a wartime boom finally recovered from a long depression. Turning to Yurie and Shōzō, she said, "You were born around the time of the Great Depression. I was a young girl then. I remember the long lines of the unemployed all over town.

"I was too wet behind the ears to understand what was going on. It was only after the fact when I realized that economic recovery meant sending my husband off to war. He was drafted and fought against your country. Up until then I barely knew where Japan was. And he lost a leg in the war. Sometimes I can't help thinking that if he hadn't lost it he may not have died in the tornado the way he did. Well, lots of people with all four limbs died in that tornado, too. It was his fate—I guess I've got to accept that.

"Young people were really anxious when the war was just about to break out. We may have thought up the canoe trip just to forget the whole mess. As old as I am, I still can't bear to keep seeing history repeat itself. I don't think humans are much wiser," she said in a soft faltering voice. "Now that American prosperity's slowly declining, I think it's a great opportunity for us to stop and take a good look at ourselves."

"Don't tell me all you and Henry talked about during your first date was your first husband's research on earthworms," said Yurie, changing the subject.

"Of course not. My goodness, you remember that? I guess what is said between women is different from what a woman will tell a man."

Lynn Ann gave a quick shrug of her shoulders with an amorous glint in her eyes. "The truth of the matter is, women really want men to listen to what women tell other women, but men have such limited imaginations," she mumbled after a long pause in a slightly quieter voice. "Henry's been telling me all about Nastasya. All I can do is listen to him as if I were her. It seems it never occurs to a man to talk to a woman about any other man besides himself."

Mizuki suppressed a laugh as she recalled how she had listened absentmindedly to Karl talking about his former girlfriend. Shōzō for his part began to smile sheepishly, saying to himself—What about me? He then rebutted Lynn Ann's statement. "Yuri is not a man, but I have a feeling she's about to accuse me of never remembering the men she's slept with." I've got no time, he thought, to remember all the details of that sort of thing anyway.

There's not even one time when you tried creating an atmosphere where I could really put my heart into telling you a story, thought Yurie, suddenly sympathizing with Lynn Ann after Shōzō's disappointing rebuttal.

Karl took out a *shakuhachi* flute he had brought with him and began to play.

# 12 ∾

HAVING SLEPT ALMOST TILL NOON THE FOLLOWING DAY Lynn Ann and Henry left for a walk in the woods in the late afternoon. Yurie let out a long sigh of relief.

They must have walked about half a mile or so into the mountains near the *Jizō* roadside shrine at Ike-no-tani because Lynn Ann came back with a peony-red *shōjōbakama* blossom in her hair, a flower plentiful in the area. On the way they had met an English-speaking foreigner, who told them that Ike-no-tani was famous for Chinese herbal arthritis remedies, Lynn Ann said. Several foreigners besides Karl lived in Hieidaira; the passerby they had spoken to was a Finn.

"We didn't find any herbs for the liver, though," she said disappointedly. Henry's condition seemed always to be on her mind.

"We heard the water at the shrine's really good and walked all the way to the cavern," she continued. "Lately I've been thinking about what our ancestors must have known about the mysterious and elusive forces of the universe. My mind also keeps tossing up the image of a calcified black liver in which so many things have been bottled up for so long. You Japanese keep things to yourselves while Westerners get anxious unless we can talk about something that's bothering us. Your way of doing things might strike one as rather uninspiring but it's actually quite audacious."

The tone of voice and the look on her face seemed to declare that it was her way of reaffirming the Asian blood that coursed through her veins. In fact, she displayed the fearlessness common among the Chinese whom Yurie had met in the States, an attitude reinforced by China's long history. Yet Lynn Ann referred to herself as a "Westerner."

"We Westerners are overconfident about our innate abilities. On the other hand you see nothing extraordinary about things made by humans. Isn't that so?

"Instead of oils you use watered-down *sumi-e* ink for painting and watch it run haphazardly here and there. You know the ink fades, but you also know it can't be erased no matter how much you try to wash it off. You seem to take it all in stride, yet you do so with a haughty conviction of superiority that says, Everything rots away in the end. The temple we've just visited, for instance—is it really a temple? It's so nondescript that it could be mistaken for an ordinary house. By the way, the walk through the woods was wonderful. The trail seemed to go on and on forever. You say to yourself—if I keep on going a little further maybe I'll see something—yet there's nothing but trail. It was a strange and lonely path with a promise of something in store for you. We have plenty of natural beauty in America, but walking on a deserted road in the woods would be a dangerous proposition, tantamount to not having any natural beauty."

"We don't want to do any sightseeing, no crowds. We've come all this way to talk with you," the two guests had said. So, around noon the following day, Shōzō and Yurie drove them to the top of Mount Hiei, only ten minutes away by car. For lunch Shōzō fed them *kitsune-udon* noodles with fried tofu in his extra special *kansai*-style seaweed soup.

Smacking their lips with obvious pleasure, Lynn Ann and Henry said they had never eaten such delicious soup and would be very happy if that was all their hosts served for the rest of their stay.

That wouldn't quite do for Westerners, but going along with their request for light meals Yurie served them eggs and oatmeal for breakfast. She was determined to show the guests, as she had told Lynn Ann on the phone, the kind of unpretentious lifestyle she led with Shōzō, a cottage picnic forgoing the formalities of plates and utensils.

Wherever he went, Shōzō had to look for the highest spot that would offer him a panoramic view. He must have assumed other people were as curious as he was because he never failed to invite guests to the top of a mountain or a tower to take in the view. Pointing out Lake Biwa to Lynn Ann and Henry, with his gaze fixed in the general direction of Ōmi and Mino, he began to talk about the fourteenth-century warlord Oda Nobunaga, who had set fire to Mount Hiei.

"He was said to be a genius. If you stand here, you can see Kyoto meeting the eastern part of Japan—there, the Sea of Japan beyond the north side of Lake Biwa—you can almost feel the movement of the forests and hear the murmurings of the sea.

"Nobunaga really wanted to conquer this region. He was hot-tempered but one of his retainers Toyotomi Hideyoshi, cool-headed and shrewd, pretended at the crucial moment not to have seen disobedient vassal lords deserting him. No wonder Hideyoshi was able to unify the country after his death," he explained, sketching out his version of Japan's medieval history and the geography surrounding Kyoto, the center of a thousand-year-old kingdom.

"Our water comes from Lake Biwa," Yurie broke in. "But pollution is a big problem now. The way humankind is going, we may experience something much worse than what Nobunaga tried to do."

Shōzō invited the guests to take a look at the Eastern and Western Pagodas, but Lynn Ann shook her head. "I've had enough temples and shrines," she said, as she strolled toward a pine grove with Yurie.

"She's more interested in the people who're explaining the history than the old historical buildings themselves," Henry said to Shōzō, chuckling.

"Only thirty years after the Revolution, China's current regime seems to be scheming up some big modernization projects, but according to conventional Western logic it won't be so easy for a nation that takes its lead from Marxism-Leninism to change directions.

"I'd say that food shortages in the USSR could be solved in a flash if they privatized farming and reduced the number of bureaucrats. But, that would cause a riot. Such a scheme may come to nothing but they can always start another revolution in a hundred years. I wish I could live long enough to witness all the changes that will happen in the world. Well, talk is cheap when you're not putting your life on the line," said Henry.

He gave an enigmatic smile lodged deep inside his translucent blue eyes, which were made conspicuous by the jaundiced skin around them.

"By the way, torching skyscrapers for the insurance money has become routine in the States," he continued on a new tack. "I hear arsonists will do it just for a few thousand dollars. I have no doubt that the head offices of the insurance companies—packed with enough art objects to put a king to shame—have figured out how to cover their losses to the last penny. While visiting an acquaintance at an insurance company, I ate in the company restaurant and watched a female professional with legs as beautiful as Dietrich's. At a table all to herself she was going through some papers, as the crêpes suzettes she had ordered flambéed on a serving table right beside her. She didn't even give one glance at the flame. Its fiery reflection in her glasses was probably enough to satisfy her. But as soon as I lit a cigar, she fixed me with a glare that would easily surpass Medusa."

Shōzō recalled the wonderful aroma of brandy, orange rind, and butter from the crêpes suzettes he had once eaten. Yup, that'll be next on my list, he thought as he swallowed a bit of saliva. He also tried very hard to superimpose Dietrich's legs on the pair that belonged to the young Lynn Ann, but they didn't jibe.

"You see, you've got to be very careful what you say to women and blacks in the States," Henry continued. "They'll slap you with a long list of their demands faster than you can say 'discrimination.' Well, I can say the same thing about Chinese women. When I was buying some silk in China, the female vendor picked up a pair of scissors and cut the fabric with the swift efficiency of an executioner, glaring at me with an expression that seemed to imply I was nothing more than a criminal. All the while she spouted something with the shrillness of a screeching woodpecker, her eyes gleaming like those of Jiang Qing, Mao's wife.

"And what a gorgeous figure that silk vendor had! Three generations after foot binding was banned, here she was a perfect specimen with long, beautiful legs, a straight back and breasts as hard as rubber balls. She looked me straight in the eye. Ha, ha, ha," he said, guffawing.

"A woman like that wouldn't just appear from nowhere after only three generations. She had the look of a survivor, someone swept away with her house and all in a Yangzi River flood; someone who had to struggle for thousands of years in the filthy flood waters. And if manna fell from heaven, she would swallow it without a second thought, claiming it as her birthright.

"A Westerner wouldn't have the slightest idea what's going on in a Chinese woman's mind just by looking at her face. Other whites may think they do, but it's quite beyond me. Lynn Ann has Chinese blood. I don't know if blood has anything to do with it, but now that she's married to me, she sees and hears things that are totally outrageous, yet nothing surprises her. She'll just pick up a blade of grass that's shooting out of the good earth and say, How pretty, and then decorate her hair with it. Henry, dear, she says, people can act like a tornado, too, you know. That's all she'll say."

"It's not so much the difference between East and West as between men and women, wouldn't you say?" said Shōzō.

Henry turned to him with an I-find-that-hard-to-believe look and fired back. "But, aren't you a man?"

"Eh?"

"You're a man, but your life is not dictated by foolish masculine reasoning. The proof is that you quit your job while still in your prime and now you sit back, absentmindedly watching whatever your wife's doing. You certainly are in command of the situation. I could never do that."

"I don't think I'm in command of anything. Inside I may just be completely flustered. Noise bothers Yuri, so I use earphones to watch television. If I don't, she moves out of the room. When I sense that she wants to be near me—"

"Eh? You mean you want her to be near you. Well, it really doesn't matter. Second-guessing what the other person may want you to do is the stuff of male-female relationships.

"You expend every drop of energy to please, wrongly believing your partner wants you to do so, strutting around, convinced you have the final say, and unexpectedly confirming your own survival—a happy ending for everyone. Rationalism would write it all off as simply wasted effort. You could say it leads to abandoning one's ego. But one's ego means someone else's ego. Well, so, you watch television right next to your wife even if you have to resort to clumsy earphones. What egos, both of you!"

"These days she says the glare from the screen hurts her eyes, so she reads sitting some distance away from the set."

"I see. My hat's off to you. So, you keep the television on and watch what you want no matter what."

"Well, I don't know whether I deserve your praise. To me an individual is just like a boulder; you can't possibly move him."

"I'd figure out a way to obliterate the earth if need be. Of course I know that's absurd, but I guess that would make me feel like I'd become the sun, the center of the universe."

"Hmm. The sun—the word is feminine in German. I remember Yuri behaving a bit like you. She was what you'd call Westernized. I guess I had found that exotic."

"The sun is masculine in French, as well as in English. How about in Chinese?" continued Shōzō, parrying Henry's assertion. "Because of their yin-yang philosophy, they might have hypothesized about something much brighter than the sun, another sun invisible from the earth. Even if they saw the sun as something awe-inspiring, I wonder if they would consider it as absolute as the West touts it to be. To say something is absolute means you end up dwelling on the things that are not absolute, so it's the same thing."

He began to ponder what he had just said. Well then, how about Japan? Amaterasu-ōmikami is a sun goddess, but a very different deity from Apollo. She's rather nondescript but some people have claimed that in the beginning women were embodiments of the sun. Speaking of power, he mumbled on, American women can't hold a candle to Japanese women. Look at the way they control and utterly spoil their children; if I bring this to Henry's attention, he might find it to be of some consolation.'

"You sit there prim and proper, looking like a cat who's just swallowed a goldfish," said Henry with a vigorous shake of his head as if warding off a fly. "I wish I could slit open your stomach to see what's in there." He paused and then muttered, "It's all this *reason* rubbish—tying us in knots." But he changed the subject as the womenfolk had caught up with them.

"We've been to a temple where Dōgen stayed," he said. "They called it the Tiantong Temple." He pulled out a notepad and scribbled down four Chinese characters, two for Dōgen, the other two for the temple.

"Remember the temple that offered lodging to pilgrims?" He turned to Lynn Ann, trying to jog her memory, and then described the typical Chinese Buddhist fare the temple had served.

"The Chinese food was a little too much for Henry. And it was tough for him not to have a salad," she explained to Yurie.

Shōzō began to point out the attractions of the area, the Eastern and Western Pagodas, the Yokawa Main Hall of the Enryakuji Temple, and the Kurodani Temple, all nestled within the folds of the surrounding mountains.

"The Tiantaishan Temple had much better music for morning prayers. Do they have the same rituals here?" asked Henry.

Neither Shōzō nor Yurie had the slightest idea whether Japanese temples held early morning services. But if such things happened anywhere, it would probably be at a Zen temple. From what the couple had said earlier, it was clear that Lynn Ann and Henry would not stay in Japan long enough to look for one.

Back from Mount Hiei, Henry said that if there was a Zen temple nearby that served meals, he wanted to invite Shōzō and Yurie for supper. Shōzō immediately suggested that a panorama of Kyoto from the mountain gate of the Nanzenji Zen Temple would be a must. They drove to the gate while it was still daylight. In case the temple did not serve meals, Shōzō had called Karl and asked him to find some suitable restaurant near the Nanzenji and make a reservation.

More hungry than Mizuki for knowledge of anything related to Japan, or Kyoto for that matter, Karl was much more knowledgeable about eateries and old shops than the average Japanese. That had also been true with Yurie and Shōzō when they lived abroad. They traveled the length and breadth of their new homeland so frequently that they had discovered places unheard of even by most Americans. Nowadays they relied on Mizuki and Karl as guides to the ancient capital.

From the vantage point of the Nanzenji Temple gate, Shōzō rattled off the famous sights of Kyoto enthusiastically: "That's the Shimizu Tower, there's the Museum, the Kyoto Tower, Kyoto University, the Imperial Palace, and the Tadasu-no-mori Forest." He went on to point out the famous temple known as the Ginkakuji Silver Pavilion, and the Shinnyōdo. Given that for Henry and Lynn Ann, listing so many famous tourist sights would go in one ear and out the other, it appeared that his real intent was to educate Yurie.

It was utterly futile. No matter how many times, and how patiently, he tried to instruct her as to what was where, the minute she turned and climbed down a temple stairway, she wouldn't have the faintest idea in which direction the Eastern or the Western Hill lay. Even in Tokyo, where she had resided for decades, once inside their condo she could not tell you the direction of Tokyo Bay, which lay not so very short a distance beyond their house.

On the other hand, she was astounded by Shōzō, who for thirty years had persisted in pointing out tourist sights to someone who had no sense of direction. She pretended to be impressed by his display of knowledge but as a matter of fact never listened to him.

Henry was different. He was persistent about finding out the exact position of every place he had heard about: Osaka, or some famous river meandering through the mountain valleys. Sometimes he muttered to himself, This must be latitude thirty five degrees.

Oblivious like Yurie to Shōzō's description of downtown Kyoto, Lynn Ann abruptly changed the subject to liver, saying that nowadays a broiler chicken was as fatty as foie gras. Even though in the old days Sunday brunch was not Sunday brunch without chicken liver, she now ate it only after removing all of the yellow fat. She stared at Yurie's chest with a look of acute concern about the imagined accumulation of fat around her heart.

Walking away from the two chattering men on the grounds of the Nanzenji, Lynn Ann came up shoulder to shoulder with Yurie and casually whispered into her ear, "We met somebody else besides Fumiko six months ago at San Francisco Airport—an old friend of yours, Peter Frisch."

Startled, Yurie froze.

"But why? Why him—how did he know you knew us?" She stared at Lynn Ann.

"I didn't, but Henry did. I decided not to mention it in my letter, but there's something that happened twenty years ago after that incident with Annabelle and Nastasya's two sons. I heard this much later myself, long after all the parties concerned had left, including you. Peter came looking for you. That's what Henry told me, and I don't know how true it is. I understand that you and Nastasya both submitted paintings for the same exhibition on the East Coast."

If you say so, I guess we did, Yurie said to herself.

"I think Peter Frisch happened to see the exhibit and then found out where you lived. He had probably visited the town on business or something. You were gone, of course, so he figured since Nastasya was in the same show she would know where you were. That's probably why he showed up at her place. Henry had not completely broken up with her and things were still pretty messy. Well, I don't have to go into all this. It's such an old story."

She hesitated to go on, but Yurie wanted to know the rest. She urged her on, but she found out soon enough that the reason for the hesitation was unrelated to anything that was on Yurie's mind at the moment.

"Nastasya—"

Yurie realized the minute Lynn Ann began that she had misread her earlier hesitation.

"What about her?"

"Nastasya—"

She tried to continue, but paused again as she studied Yurie carefully.

"Uh-huh. Peter, no, Nastasya had seduced him, hadn't she?" asked Yurie, meaning to prod her on, with the firm intention of putting an end to the awkward silence. The certainty that the answer would be in the affirmative gradually consumed her.

"Nastasya had invited Henry to her Yolka house, but never came home that night after she took Peter to town for some entertainment," said Lynn Ann. "She brought him back the following morning while Henry was waiting patiently. Well, at least that gave him the perfect excuse to break up with her. I don't know any more than that. So, I see now that she had never given Peter your new address or contacted you about him." She nodded as if things finally made perfect sense.

"She and I were not that close, you know. We never wrote to each other after I left." Yurie tried to sound indifferent but was surprised at the nasty edge in her voice.

For some reason Lynn Ann's tone also grew more caustic. She glared at Yurie with smoldering eyes. That was the cold, superior air of the Chinese that Yurie had detected from time to time. There she goes again, she said to herself.

"Henry had never forgotten that meeting with Peter. That was why he stopped him at San Francisco Airport. Peter didn't recognize him, though. He tried to pass him with a you-must-be-mistaken look on his face when Henry called after him. 'Do you still want to know Yurie Mama's address?' Sorry, Yuri, I hope you aren't offended."

"Oh, no, not at all. It's ancient history."

She still couldn't figure out what Lynn Ann was really driving at.

"He then turned to face Henry, walked over and copied down your Tokyo address and telephone number. That was the first time I was introduced to Peter Frisch. Now what do you think Henry said to him at that point?"

She looked over her shoulder to make sure that the menfolk were out of earshot.

"He said, 'I don't have a fucking idea where Nastasya is. Ask her sons if you want to find out.' He then fished out a photo of Annabelle, the one you've seen, and showed it to him, saying, 'My daughter's with them.'"

Yurie was stunned.

The elfin face of Annabelle suddenly crowded into her mind, together with the image of Henry showing off the photo with the clear intention of exciting Peter. Henry might have reasoned, If this is the man who came to see his old flame Yurie and decided on the spot to seduce another woman, if he was the cause of Nastasya breaking up with me, this same man may succeed in snatching Annabelle away from Ivan and Antonio.

Goodness gracious, Henry couldn't possibly have thought of giving Annabelle's pimps more business. Besides, they wouldn't make much money off Peter, Yurie said to herself.

She stopped short, looking up at the sky. A raindrop fell on her eyelid, another on her lips. Henry was dreaming up more trouble through Peter's possible encounter with his daughter, she thought.

"A father can come up with the strangest notions," said Lynn Ann with a heavy sigh.

"Was there a woman with Peter at the airport?" Yurie purposely steered the conversation back to herself.

"Let me see, he could have been with someone, definitely not a white woman. I thought she was standing a bit away from him, but he never introduced her to us. It was hard to tell whether she was even with him. At least she was pretending she wasn't."

Not introducing someone accompanying you wasn't so unusual in Japan, but that definitely meant something to a Westerner, thought Yurie. She could almost imagine the kind of life Peter was leading in the United States.

"Did he look rather roguish?"

"You mean Peter?"

"Yes."

"Well, there was something of the ex-hippie about him, but with his European accent he sounded very proper. I think he's the serious type. It was Henry who was talking like a *yakuza*. I felt I didn't know him at all. I was really shocked."

So that was what Lynn Ann really wanted to tell Yurie.

"I was worried that this whole thing might put you in a spot—Henry giving your telephone number to Peter and all that."

She then continued, making excuses for Henry—that the only reason he gave out the number was because Peter had told him Shōzō and Yurie were good friends of his. "So, you knew him when you were in Stockholm?" she asked.

Yurie nodded in silence, and then after a long pause explained, "His ex-wife worked at the same research center as Shōzō."

The two women's conversation stopped when Henry and Shōzō caught up with them.

Still unable to figure out exactly what Lynn Ann was trying to tell her, Yurie was now even more confused. It was also unclear what she and Henry thought of Peter. Did they consider him just some fickle man, in search of Shōzō and Yurie, who once happened to show Nastasya a good time, or vice versa? Was Lynn Ann letting her imagination run wild about Peter and Yurie? Wasn't it possible she was only pretending she didn't know anything? What did Nastasya tell Henry after she had heard about Shōzō and Yurie from Peter?

There are many different ways to spin a tale. It can go in any direction, its final version usually unlike anything you anticipate.

After dinner the party drove back to Mount Hiei. Lynn Ann and Henry looked the overly conscientious Americans with their seat belts securely fastened.

At the wheel Shōzō began to talk about Shigaraki, a nearby village he had told Yurie that he wanted to show Lynn Ann and Henry.

"Well, we've had such a good time, quite enough for one day," said Lynn Ann, looking anxiously at Henry.

"It's only a few hours drive, we'd be back by early evening. Of course, it wouldn't be such a bad idea to take it easy at home, either. In that case I could mow the lawn," said Shōzō.

Yurie remembered that they always wound up fighting on a trip because he would drag her to every tourist spot highlighted in the guidebook.

"When Shōzō insisted that I go up the Leaning Tower of Pisa with him, I refused to budge an inch, and stayed put at the entrance, listening for half an hour to a woman who just happened by. She was walking her dog. Of course her Italian was all gibberish to me. To this day I'm still clueless as to why she was able to go on talking to someone who obviously didn't know a word of Italian."

Lynn Ann offered an answer.

"You must have stared at her long and hard, trying to unlock the source of her mysterious vocal energy, until your stare could have drilled a hole in her head. She kept on talking, convinced that you were impressed by her story."

"When he finally came down the tower, Shōzō asked me what the conversation was all about. I told him that I couldn't pick out even one Italian word. All I did was watch her like a tone-deaf person listening to an aria, admiring her cute ribboned little dog that looked like a stuffed toy, her paw raised like a point-setter."

Lynn Ann did not relent. "But I thought you were trying to find out why she was so determined to keep on talking, weren't you?"

"Oh, I see."

Impressed by the simplicity of her question, Yurie felt that the mystery had finally been solved. Uh-huh, she said to herself. Another new discovery was being made: the question of why Henry and Lynn had come all the way to Kyoto seemed at least partially answered.

Henry who had shown very little interest in Yurie's Pisa story said, "I'm not that tired. If it's only a day trip, I'd like to see Shigaraki."

In response Shōzō emphasized the fact that the town was on the site of an ancient imperial villa, and with only the ruins of the foundation unearthed, it could hardly be considered a tourist attraction. The two guests nodded and said, "Well, we'll stay here one more day and leave for the States right after we visit the ruins."

"The Emperor Shōmu had tried to build a villa and the Hall of the Great Buddha at Shigaraki," explained Shōzō, "but his plans were scuttled because of frequent forest fires, which were manifestations of protest, a fiery symbol of the people's anger." Henry was all ears, nodding away.

"The Mikado was married to a brilliant woman from a powerful clan, who was probably the real power behind the throne. I imagine that the Empress Kōmyō was fascinated by what a group of sophisticated monks returning from China had told her about Buddhism. No doubt their intention was to disseminate the new knowledge they had acquired in that civilized country. It is very likely that the birth of the resplendent Tempyō era had everything to do with this powerful empress."

Declaring many times during his twenty-year reign that he wanted to move the capital, the Emperor built one new palace after another, wandering from place to place. It would appear that his own ministers eventually refused to support further projects, and in the end he had to return to the old capitol, Heijōkyō.

Henry's interest was piqued immediately when the topic shifted to eighth-century Japanese Buddhism. And when Shōzō mentioned that Shigaraki was also well known for its ceramics, Lynn Ann became equally animated.

"As I mentioned before, an imperial villa once stood in the area, but there's nothing left to tell of its past grandeur," he said. All the more reason to see it, the two visitors responded, now even more excited about the trip.

"I hope it's not too much of a tourist spot," said Henry.

"I don't think so. Getting there isn't easy, either," replied Shōzō.

I'm sure trains are available, but if we drive, we can also hike around the countryside, he said to himself.

In the old days he always jumped at the chance to be at the wheel but now he found it a bother and would not even think of driving in a crowded city unless it was absolutely necessary. Yurie remembered those days when they had driven thousands of miles crisscrossing the American continent, and how Shōzō could hardly wait to rent a car after they had flown to a place.

This was his first outing by car since he had quit his job. Viewed from the window of a moving car, the landscape of Japan is entirely different from that of, say, a train.

"Long forgotten places are the best to visit," chimed in Yurie. "When there's too much to take in, you won't be able to see what's beneath the surface."

"Let's start right after the morning rush hour and come back before the streets jam up in the evening," suggested Shōzō.

Once the cherry blossoms are gone, the weather fluctuates from sweltering heat to freezing cold. Yurie told the two visitors to take along cardigans.

The early spring leaves along the road were reflected in the clear calm water of the Uji River. It was picture perfect.

"Oh, natural beauty you don't see in America," commented Henry and Lynn Ann as they admired the view.

Barely a clearing in the mountains, Shigaraki was a quiet, sleepy hamlet, with the Uji River meandering through it.

"This is what you call Shangri-la, Yuri," said Lynn Ann thoughtfully. "Even a super-industrialized Japan has a place like this. We also saw something very similar in the Chinese mountains. Their Shangri-la is a bit different, though."

"The Emperor, who in this tiny place had concocted a plan to build a Hall of the Great Buddha that would float like a mirage in the valley, must have been a nihilist," said Shōzō half to himself.

There's no way an emperor could survive as a nihilist, thought Yurie. A nihilist ruler would be overthrown even if it meant burning down a mountain. She tried to imagine the travel-weary Emperor Shōmu, hiding in this peaceful hamlet.

"Considering that Shōmu had the grand scheme of building the Hall of the Great Buddha," said Yurie, "he probably wanted a capital here, not a detached palace, but the locals complained that the area was too prone to arson. In a few years the area reverted to its former desolation."

"You mean, it became quiet and peaceful again," Henry responded, laughing.

Barely visible amid the young leaves was a long, seemingly interminable procession of laborers, their flickering ghostly forms dragging timber and huge stone blocks.

"You can look at it this way," murmured Yurie. "Something moved forward a little, some gained, and some abruptly lost. What's certain is that a great many people suffered because of what happened."

"You're right," said Henry. "A long time ago a king in India—I forget his name—had a palace built and demolished, and then started all over again. As long as I can provide jobs and feed my people, all's well, he supposedly said." It was hard to tell from Henry's tone whether he had meant to praise or mock the king.

## 13 ∽

SHIGERU'S SON TŌICHIRO WAS VISITING with Mizuki when Yurie brought back the bedding after the departure of Lynn Ann and Henry.

It was the first time Yurie saw Mizuki seated side by side with the young man who everyone believed was her cousin—and perhaps her stepbrother. The likeness of the two touched Yurie deeply. She gazed at them long and hard.

You would have no doubts if you were told that they were siblings. Their foreheads and finely sculpted cheekbones were distinct Sugano family characteristics.

The dark pupils in Mizuki's slightly puffy eyes danced in an enigmatic glow. Her eyes, set in single or possibly double folds, narrowed to slits just like Fū's. Yurie recalled that the slight overcrowding of her front teeth, just visible above a sensuous lower lip when she smiled, was a constant source of embarrassment for her. My mother had a set of teeth exactly like that, Yurie said to herself. Over the generations family resemblances crop up here and there like the dancing sparks of a bonfire.

Every foreigner's face looks peculiar to the uninitiated; because of that oddity one finds the natives of a country appear similar by virtue of being native. Americans often mistook Yurie for another Japanese when she was in the States, while she found sorting out Americans' faces much more difficult than making out a Japanese face.

"Dad's gone back to Tokyo with Mom after staying with us only a couple of days in Uji," began Tōichiro. "We could tell she wanted to stay behind to pack all the stuff she had collected during her stay, but Akiko and I insisted that we'd take care of everything. We practically had to drive them out of the house. Thank goodness, that's over. I think it was her idea to bring him to Uji to see his first grandchild.

"Dad says he wants to buy the Myōkō house back because it is the only thing remaining that belonged to the Sugano family. If you ever decide to sell it, he wants to know. But it looks like Mom wants to stay in the Kansai area," he continued, trying to sound out Yurie.

She could of course interpret Shigeru's offer as a show of concern that the upkeep on the often-vacant mountain cottage might have been a little too much for Yurie and Shōzō. In fact the timing of the offer could not have been better because she had begun to put serious thought to ridding herself of whatever small assets she owned. Not wanting to commit herself in one way or another, she smiled enigmatically, thinking to herself that Fukiko would not relish the idea of sharing a house infused with the scent of Fū.

The talk of the Myōkō house held little interest for Mizuki. Instead, she was recalling what had transpired during the recent telephone conversation she had had with Shigeru. He had told her that he wanted to make an overnight trip to Kyoto to see her. She would have kept the whole matter to herself if today's guest had been Fukiko, but she disliked the idea of keeping the visit secret from Tōichiro.

"Uncle Shigeru initiated the contact and invited us to a meeting, so we went ahead and briefly met him—the first time since my mother's death," said Mizuki mildly. "I thought it a good opportunity to introduce Karl."

She had unburdened herself to Karl in great detail and many times over about the thorny affair between her biological mother and Uncle Shigeru, which undoubtedly raised questions about her own birth. She was confident that he had made a careful observation of Shigeru at the Kyoto meeting.

She could have kept the story of Fū's affair to herself, but talking about it made her feel closer to Karl, whose mother, a collaborator with the Nazis during the War, had left her husband and abandoned the infant son to the care of his two older sisters. She had eventually escaped to the States with her Jewish lover.

But unlike his mother, Fū had stayed with her husband Seiichiro until his death. No matter how tongues wagged, and many did, Mizuki was the apple of her father's eye. It was only after his death that she decided to go along with Fū's idea of leaving Japan and going to the States.

Shigeru had said to Mizuki at their meeting. "I didn't give you anything for your wedding." As he wrote out a check on the spot, he casually suggested that she and her family take advantage of being in Japan to make a cross-country trip. The amount, two million yen, immediately compelled her to deal with the implications of accepting such a large sum. She imagined she saw the faces of her dead parents and Fukiko and felt she should decline the offer.

Ever since she was a little girl she had often heard her mother say, "Have Uncle do it for you." She found these words despicable.

"That's the way Papa is." By uttering these words in front of Seiichiro, Fū probably meant to belittle him. The words sank deep into a corner of Mizuki's mind, attaching themselves like barnacles.

"Why not ask Shigeru to do it for you?"

When she spoke those words as though nothing had happened, Fū's face would contort and split into two halves, one concealed, the other visible only to her husband. She seemed to be two entirely different people. It was like a female demon Nō mask depicting a woman torn into identical halves, one revealing fury, the other sorrow, and then spliced back together.

Whenever she said, "I'm crying out in anger because you won't," Seiichiro would gaze at her adoringly as if she was a goddess on a pedestal. The chain that bound them together would clank ominously as they tottered around. All Mizuki could do was cover her ears.

It appeared to her that they were silent accomplices, scheming against an easy prey, Shigeru. She even imagined that, although Fū's words sounded obscene to her, they might well have been music to Seiichiro's ears. In summoning up such memories, she was seized by a wave of incomprehensible sadness.

Seiichiro's affection, which had set no boundaries between Fū and her biological child, baffled the young daughter. But on occasion he would shower more affection on Mizuki, and the mother would become jealous of her own daughter, and everyone around her would feel the brunt of her resentment.

As long as Mizuki could remember, Seiichiro had never held a job. As a father he already looked very old—more like a venerable and trusted handyman. That really embarrassed Mizuki and she avoided inviting her friends over as much as possible. With a gift for theatrics and for smoothing things over, Fū would play the consummate wheeler-dealer wife in front of the occasional visitor, adopting the most appropriate style of speech as if Seiichiro was backing some major political or financial deal. "Papa's a real lucky guy. He's got no worries." She would sidle up to him, wiggling her shoulders seductively.

To outsiders he must have appeared as the typical wealthy husband who lets his wife do as she pleases. When the Sugano family was prosperous, the carefree air of the financially secure wife must have come naturally to Fū. Yet even when the family fortunes declined, she continued to maintain that façade to protect his reputation. Perhaps she had made him into what he had become. It could be said that the reverse was also true. He drove her to become what she had become. They could only survive in this pairing, and not as two separate individuals.

To this day, Mizuki was not sure whether Fū had been genuine or overly dramatic. It was probably impossible for her to convey anything truthfully without dramatizing it as one would on stage.

It was obvious that she was constantly on Seiichiro's mind even when he was preparing a meal for the family in his clumsy way.

"Fū's very fastidious, you know, about chopping onions," he would say. The sight of him serving a meal was at once comical and pathetic.

Complaining to Mizuki about something, he would usually say, "Fū'll be angry."

Seeing his daughter sit in front of a mirror, he would come right behind her and say, "Just like the *Tale of the Matsuyama Mirror*."

Overwhelmed, he would gaze at her reflection and begin to chuckle —"The same look!" His words always startled her, and the dread of them was enough to make her cringe.

When Fū had said, "Go to Shigeru—" for the umpteenth time, Mizuki glared at her, shouting, "I don't want Uncle to do anything for me!" and threw a wash cloth at her as she ran to her room, yelling, "We're acting like beggars!" She cried for an hour.

At that moment she had found her father's silence and imperturbability strange and incomprehensible even though she was absolutely certain that he loved her more than anything in the world. When Fū yelped about the family's disreputable past for all to hear, looming behind the outburst was the image of a gnarled colorless root, which had infiltrated itself deep into hardened clods of black soil inside Seiichiro. Trample on me if you must, bury me in the soil if you want, but I will grow back no matter what, Fū seemed to be crying out. You see, Mizuki, you are the living proof of that. You think you can uproot yourself. You can't. Look, you can't do a thing on your own. You're helpless. At least that was what Fū wanted her daughter to believe.

Mizuki had kept on crying, crying at the helplessness in which she found herself imprisoned.

ALL THESE MEMORIES FLOODED BACK as she stared at the two million yen check and the man who had written it.

"I'm sure my parents used all sorts of tricks to squeeze money out of you, but that's not my way," she said quietly to Shigeru.

She had no idea whether the amount was an extravagance or a pittance to him, but it was clear that he was not giving it to her just because she happened to be his niece. Confident that Seiichiro really loved her as a daughter, she longed to tell him that she had never regarded him as her father no matter what people whispered.

Karl's face bore an I-know-nothing look throughout the meeting. He really wants the money, thought Mizuki. Turning away from her, Shigeru faced Karl, addressing him directly. "Hey, Karl, don't you agree that you don't know a thing when you're young? Mizuki's father, my older brother, was an eccentric but always looked happy. How come that happy smile never made much sense to me? Mizuki's mother was a real egotistical *woman*, but at least she helped put that smile on his face. On top of that she provided him with this cute little lover Mizuki."

Using the word lover, instead of daughter, he cast a quick glance at her.

"Your uncle wants to give this gift, not to you, not to your parents, but to the children you're raising," he said emphatically.

But, as if taking it all back to confuse her further, he once again turned his attention to Karl. "It must be tough for you to have such a strong-willed wife," he said. "Men are really going through an ordeal nowadays. Take, for example, this female self-assertiveness that is like the ever-expanding molten rock under the earth's crust. Finally men just throw up their hands. We have a saying in the East, 'Women and dwarves are difficult to raise,' and we are resigned to that.

"Nowadays, I hear that the only thing a woman wants from a man is a test tube's worth of sperm; they're just fine without men. What's the world coming to? Women electricians climbing utility poles, male telephone operators and pre-school teachers.

"In Japan we had philosophers whose greatest wish was to sit in meditation and think thoughts of nothingness. So I decided to follow in their footsteps and eventually found myself sitting glassy-eyed on the floor of a Bulgarian monastery. What came floating to my mind's eye was that happy face of my older brother. In other words, I never attained enlightenment but I now know that a guy with a happy face is like a god."

The tension in Mizuki's jaw began to ease and for a brief moment she had the urge to make Shigeru happy.

"So that was what you were thinking," she said with compassion. "I've been feeling the same way lately. When I think about the smiling faces of people long gone, they seem happier, calmer, and I've come to the point in my life where I no longer need to drive myself mad just to live.

"To children, a rich uncle is like a king in a fairy tale. Once I wake from that dream, though, I'm worried that all that wealth might disappear in a gust of wind like the dried leaves of autumn."

It was as if Fū's guile had manifested itself in Mizuki's words as Fū, toying with those autumn leaves, would stick out a hand unabashedly for more money, the very same hand she had withdrawn earlier. Mizuki began to daydream: My family has fallen into poverty and here's a man who's doing everything he can to rescue us from financial ruin.

She remembered Yurie had told her that was exactly what Shigeru might have done to help her parents. In her mind's eye, the possibility haunted her like the shadows of black cows moving through a thick mist, and from deep inside the mist she thought she heard a baby crying—possibly herself or maybe Mary or Leonard. The baby was howling, its mouth forming a letter O as big as its face.

"Being younger than you, I still feel sorry for women," said Karl, referring back to Shigeru's comment on women. "And I find women who make outrageous remarks cute." Nodding his head, he looked toward Mizuki and added, "I won't let my wife climb a pole and work a utility line, though."

"Oh, my, you certainly don't mind watching me pick berries up in a gingko tree, do you."

"I just let you do it because you seem to enjoy it so much. I don't mind putting frozen fried chicken into the oven but that's as far as I would go."

"Even with prepared food in the fridge, if I've got to serve it myself, I'd eat out," Shigeru said dryly.

THE FACT THAT MIZUKI COULD NEVER BE equally open about Shigeru in her conversations with Tōichiro dampened her spirits. Through no fault of my own, I'm still paying for what my parents have done—I'm still sponging off Shigeru and if that makes me feel uncomfortable, if I'm disturbed by a man linked to Fukiko and Tōichiro, I shouldn't have accepted the two million yen in the first place. She felt disgusted.

On the other hand, without the check incident, she would never have found out about what was really troubling Shigeru. She felt she had awakened from a dream that was never meant to be.

"Mom says, Why should Dad hide away in the Myōkō house when nobody's pressuring him to retire?" said Tōichiro quietly, looking away from Mizuki and Yurie. "I think he wants to copy Shōzō. But Mom has made it crystal clear. 'I can't support you, I'm no Yurie,' she says. On the other hand, Dad says, 'I no longer want to work on big public projects and will instead stick to the residential business.' Well, it's his choice, but I think *he* is coming unhinged."

Tōichiro's unconventional use of the masculine personal pronoun, *kare*, to refer to his father conveyed something nostalgic to Yurie, like a word or phrase in an old favorite novel. As a very modest display of protest in her youth, she too had tried to distance herself from her parents and authorities or people senior to her, by referring to them in the impersonal, gender-neutral third-person *ano hito*. She found it extremely interesting to hear Tōichiro, ten years her junior, referring to his father as *kare*.

"What do you mean, unhinged?" asked Yurie.

"He has shown an abnormal interest in Akiko—I wonder what he's up to. He would clean his dentures with her toothbrush, for example. He pretends he'd just picked up the wrong one, and goes over his dentures as if he was carefully polishing the crown jewels. Disgusted, Akiko got a new one, but he does it again. When she couldn't take it anymore and finally told him firmly, 'Father, please, no more mistakes,' he stepped out into the garden without a word and began to chirp, chirp, like a *hototogisu*. What's he trying to do? Don't you think it's weird?"

Akiko was Tōichiro's wife. They had been living together for many years since college, but only when she began talking about having a baby and then became pregnant did they get a marriage license to enter her name in Tōichiro's family registry.

She had told him that there was no rush to make it official. "Let's wait and see how long it takes before your folks find out about us," she said, "because I don't want to get to know your mother or father as long as *I* can help it."

She had been more or less getting along with the in-laws right after the couple officially became man and wife. But now that a grandchild had come, things might not be going as smoothly as expected.

In her mind Yurie pictured the image of Shigeru imitating a *hototogisu*, the bird that lays an egg in a bush warbler's nest so that the unsuspecting mother hatches and raises the chick. However, she was unable to bring herself to mention it; she instead concentrated on reading Mizuki's reaction to Tōichiro's story.

If the rumors of Shigeru's actions forty years ago were true, he had indeed let his brother Seiichiro raise his chick. Was his recent strange behavior perhaps meant to confirm that fact?

"Dad's also put the idea into Akiko's head that Mom and I are having a *dubious* relationship. I call that harassment," said Tōichiro as if throwing up his hands in exasperation.

Fukiko's excessive attention to her son was something that used to alarm Yurie. When a woman's relationship with her husband fails, she almost invariably becomes fixated on her son.

"We appreciate the fact that Mom's crazy about our child, but Akiko has different ideas about bringing up a baby. Thank goodness, my parents have left Uji. I'm not so sure how they'll get along in Tokyo, though."

Tōichiro was really the spitting image of the young Shigeru. The shape of the back, the way he craned his neck ever so slightly forward, would cause anyone to mistake him for his father. Also, his voice after a word or two on the phone sounded so much like Shigeru's that one could not tell the difference.

He often stole glances at people, reading their reactions in stubborn silence, and then suddenly the skin around his chin would tighten and what he had decided he must say would burst out. The resemblance to his father was uncanny. Shigeru's effort, if he had indeed tried at making Fukiko say that their son was in fact Natsuyama's, could not be anything but utter nonsense.

"Yurie, was there something between you and Dad?" In a defiant tone Tōichiro asked with a sarcastic smile on his face and a quick glance at Mizuki, a glance that seemed to say, Let's get it all out in the open before witnesses.

"It was a case of unrequited love—I guess I was jilted," replied

Yurie, again fixing her gaze on him with a broad smile on her face. *Déjà vu.* Tōichiro's arrogant poses and speech were once Shigeru's, she thought. My, how I had tried to copy Shigeru when I was much younger than Tōichiro is now. What was I trying to do anyway? It was as though that young woman was not really me, but someone else. In the end Shigeru found himself trapped in a self-criticism of his own obsession about what he had done.

Screech, screech, screech, birds traversed the sky. Yurie loved the way the sweet little creatures flew up so close to lure you into their games but were so easily frightened away. Those flighty days of youth, filled with sadness, would also make you laugh—they were all so real again.

Shigeru was ever vigilant about not letting a woman ruin his life. That was him, Yurie recalled with affection. What is he now trying to prove to his daughter-in-law? In her mind's eye some black mass that was moving through the forest at night was entangled in the shadowy figures of Lynn Ann and Henry, who had come and gone like wisps in the wind.

"Shigeru's probably warning us to take a good look at the strange, spooky things that happen in the world," added Yurie. She thought she saw a faint smile creep across Mizuki's lips.

"Mom's imagining all sorts of things," said Tōichiro indignantly, fixing his eyes on Mizuki. "She doesn't like it if I see Mizuki, gets offended if I visit Yurie, so I want both of you to keep quiet about my coming here. The more suspicious she gets, though, the more I'm tempted to do exactly what she asks me not to do. I'll just play dumb and do what I damn well please. Incest isn't my style, so I'd rather woo Yurie and taste a little unrequited love."

Slowly turning away from Mizuki, he looked intently at Yurie and said what was clearly meant for his cousin, "In other words, Dad looks at Akiko the way I'm eyeing you. What does a woman feel when a guy does that?"

Sensing that he was just teasing her, Yurie tried to solicit her cousin's support, but Mizuki changed the subject and said rather dryly, "One of my American friends is married to someone who had a vasectomy. She said to Karl in front of her husband and me,

I want to have your baby, what do you say? She's quite a brilliant scholar. Her work on Japanese empresses during the Nara period has received very good reviews."

Mizuki was probably referring to Shigeru's comment about women who say all they need from a man is a tube of sperm.

"What's that got to do with what I said?" Tōichiro's attitude became defiant again.

"Oh, I just thought you sounded a little like that friend of mine," Mizuki said. The tone of her voice was as soothing as a balmy spring day.

I don't know what's what but everything is like everything else, thought Yurie, listening to the exchange as if basking in the warmth of a gentle spring sun. Nothing's unrelated in this world, but I guess some folks overdo it and talk their heads off about connections and relations, picking up on things that are the least connected.

She also began to think about the image of a pathetic woman in despair on seeing her own grey hair reflected in the mirror.

"This morning I heard a *hototogisu* for the first time this season," she said out of the blue. "Well—at least that's what I thought it was."

"It must have been a bush warbler, possibly a nightjar. Too early for a *hototogisu*," snapped Tōichiro.

"No, it was a *hototogisu*," insisted Yurie. "I could still see the pale white moon in the sky—'Only a hazy morning moon stayed with me'—the way it was described in that famous line of *waka* poetry."

"Well, Mizuki, how did Karl respond to the woman who wanted his baby?" asked Tōichiro, ignoring Yurie's interruption, and returning to the story of the vasectomy.

"He cast me a quick sidelong glance and replied, 'I don't believe in making babies.' But from the look on his face I don't think he found the proposition that objectionable because he added, If it's just for fun, I'll be happy to oblige provided of course your husband and my wife agree to it, or something to that effect," said Mizuki, giggling.

"What did the wife say to that?" Tōichiro was all ears.

"I think she said something like, 'I've got more than enough men to amuse myself.' She was so sure of herself, so certain all the men in the world wanted her."

"Well, I'm sure Karl thought he was being courted," said Tōichiro, rolling his eyes and grinning at Mizuki.

"Courtship rituals change with the times, don't they?" said Yurie.

However, something close to a feeling of desolation crept over Yurie who was unable to visualize the wasteland that must have been inside the head of this brilliant female scholar. The effect was a little like trying to draw something out of an object that was devoid of color and shape. She tried to superimpose the image of this superwoman upon Mizuki's glossy vermilion lips.

"Why in the world do women want babies anyway?" muttered Tōichiro to himself.

Yurie thought she had heard these same words uttered by Shigeru many years ago. Wasn't it when Fū had summoned him to the Myōkō house and told him that she was pregnant?

Shigeru's wife was the type of mother who would never suspect that her precious son would live with a woman out of wedlock for almost a decade yet would also be beside herself with joy at the news of a grandchild.

During those ten years he had lived at Akiko's apartment, Tōichiro used to go back once a week to his company's boarding house to tidy things up. When his mother came to visit, that was where he had taken her; she had no idea what was going on. In his dresser were the shirts and pants that she had bought for him, freshly pressed at the cleaners, giving her little reason to suspect anything untoward was happening. She believed him when he told her that he always worked late and came home from work just to sleep.

"My parents are really strange," he said, suppressing a chuckle. Yet, their strangeness was probably not something he had lost sleep over. It was entirely possible that he just wanted the like-minded Mizuki and Yurie to commiserate with him.

"I don't understand women, either. After all the spooky things Dad's done to her, Akiko still treats him well. She even plays games with him and says things like, 'You're what Tōichiro will be twenty years from now.'"

Yurie had heard from a friend, a nursing home employee, that most senile people behave like perverts. Talking animatedly to Yurie about an old woman who started making advances to her son because she mistook him for her dead husband, the friend also observed, "When it comes down to it, the only thing that will clear up an old person's senility is being around the opposite sex."

Many senile old men in nursing homes immediately start behaving normally once they find women they like.

Tōichiro responded carelessly, "In other words, both Mom and Dad should have affairs. Those two aren't sexy at all when they're in each other's company."

Yurie had never seen them together. In fact she had not seen Shigeru for a very long time. That made it difficult for her to size up their relationship, sexual or otherwise.

But they were not really exceptional; so many, if not most, couples were not sexual, let alone sensual with each other. However, Lynn Ann and Henry's relationship was different; it was well established and deeply rooted. Even in their absence, Yurie was still convinced it was so.

## 14 〜

FOR NO APPARENT REASON, Shōzō WANTED TO SEE Shigeru when the news came of his return from Bulgaria.

"It may be time to head back to Tokyo. Shigeru's there now," he said to Yurie.

Yurie came out of her reverie lying on the floor where she had remained motionless for hours. When Shōzō was still working, he had often left the house while she was still in bed only to return hours later to find her exactly in the same place. Except for trips to the kitchen or the bathroom, she always resumed her favorite position. To his surprise, he had observed that she was capable of maintaining absolute stillness for several hours without falling asleep as she let her mind drift. "Provided torture is not meted out to the inmates, nothing would make me happier than a prison stay," she had once told Shōzō. "That would really calm me down."

She slowly raised her body and scrutinized Shōzō from head to toe. "Flo-o-u-n-n-der!" she spat out with a rather contemptuous smile on her face. "Flat on your belly glued to the ocean floor, gazing up at the sky, you never miss a chance to gobble up any prey that happens by."

Her tone quickly became abusive. "That's the way you've always been. I've been swallowed up and can't even wiggle inside."

It's you, not me, who looks like a flounder, lying there motionless on the floor, Shōzō said to himself. He recalled in great detail the other unflattering descriptions she had used to mock him.

"Flo-o-u-n-n-der!" she shouted again, glaring at him, eyes bulging like a flat fish.

She had called him a raccoon some twenty years ago when he was rather portly. Later the raccoon metamorphosed into a fox. The adjective "sneaky" that came with her old standbys, raccoon and fox, was now being resurrected and attached to a flounder, as in a "sneaky flat fish."

When had she become so coarse and dropped the polite feminine style of speech? As a newlywed, she used to coo to him, "Would you rather do it this way, Honey?" or "Would you do it for me?" But now it was hard to tell whether she was a man or a woman. And then all of a sudden she would start babbling, which was in essence closer to a soliloquy. The trouble was that Shōzō intuitively knew what her state of mind was at that moment.

"So now you're taking an interest in what Shigeru may be thinking," she began relentlessly. "Bit by bit you've been helping yourself to things that rightly belong to me. When I was enjoying myself alone at home, you quit your job. Now you hang around me all the time, sticking your nose in everything. Why don't you get out once in a while and take some interest in something other than what I'm thinking?"

She just can't accept things as they are, thought Shōzō. In other words, she can't accept me as I am. He had swallowed up this inscrutable woman so deep down inside himself that he couldn't even feel her bones.

The country went to war and was defeated. There were too many things in my childhood that were beyond my power to change. I must have learned early on that the easiest thing to do would be to accept things as they are. Am I the result of that kind of thinking, accepting what my mother had said, what women have said? He continued to mull this over when suddenly Yurie erupted again.

"You've shackled me with a chain called freedom. Sneaky flat fish!"

"So now you've removed that chain to liberate me. Yup, I'm a happy flat fish."

Nothing she said made much sense to him but he somehow began to feel he really *was* a flounder. Once on a fishing trip in Alaska he had tried desperately to haul in a Pacific halibut, the largest species of flounder—probably weighing one hundred pounds—but couldn't because an approaching ferry in the inlet had produced such a large wake that he had to cut his line to keep from capsizing. Right—If I'm going to be a flat fish, I might as well be that gigantic halibut. And whenever she called him a fox or a raccoon, he had also begun to feel that he was indeed one of those creatures. She came up with such fantastic metaphors! He somehow felt fortunate being a fox or a raccoon.

Or perhaps Yurie was endowed with the insight; he secretly longed to be what she kept calling him. Serves you right, Shōzō said to himself. You're not even aware of the fact that you've been humoring me all this time. The thought put him in a very good mood.

"I've been conned and cooked into raccoon stew," she said firmly.

Wait a minute, wasn't that me? Their roles were suddenly reversed, launching her story in another illogical leap.

"I've been gutted, cooked, and devoured. I've been led to believe that I write novels just to get a fox's bag of fake money and do what I damn well please."

She continued to rant and rave, returning abruptly to the subject of Shigeru. "You're fond of him because he had paid no attention to me. That doesn't make any sense. What's so interesting about a guy who doesn't find your wife attractive? He's just chicken. He can't even make one woman happy. And if he can't bring himself to run away from a woman, he might as well accept it. What an idiot."

You may have a point there, thought Shōzō.

"All the men who've run away from me were idiots. That's why Peter never became a great writer. A man cursed by a woman inevitably falls apart. That's the way it's always been. A man gets lucky only through a woman."

I'm not so sure about Yurie, but that was certainly the case when Peter lost Monica, Shōzō said to himself.

It's true, the realistic is the rational. Fascinated, he watched

Yurie, a tangle of irrationality, who was puffing and sucking in air like a goldfish. I'm a bit slow, but wasn't it just a little while ago, he recalled, when she accused me of not being imaginative about Fukiko, Shigeru, and others? Here he was finally beginning to be more like she wanted, and she didn't care. He was amazed. If I pointed that out, she would say without batting an eye, That was what came to mind at that particular moment. Oh, never mind. All I've got to do is remain calm. Anyway, it's her battle. Her contradictions will eventually come home to roost.

"Can't you clean up your speech a little more? I'd just love to hear you warble like a canary."

If she wanted to, he knew her voice could be cloyingly sweet, as soft and calming as a gentle spring rain. But lately she had completely abandoned such soothing vocalizations.

Living creatures have the ability either to call forth or to forget something their distant ancestors once possessed. To Shōzō, the woman in front of him began to look like a Medusa, perhaps a dragon or a gigantic snake. The safest thing for me, he thought, would be to change into something inconspicuous, like an ant or a mouse.

The Medusa, the dragon, and the gigantic snake, which have all been exterminated by heroes, still live on in our imaginations. The very fact that heroes destroyed them has perpetuated these legends.

Shōzō recalled what the next door neighbor's wife had complained to him when he was living abroad in a little forested hamlet. Her husband would suddenly develop a headache or stomachache like a schoolboy who refuses to go to school. First pleading, then cajoling him in a reassuring voice, she would then call his company with some plausible story as to why he was not yet at work before she would finally succeed in getting him out of the house.

The same techniques are used to motivate recalcitrant children.

"A child who doesn't go to school grows ears as long as a donkey's and hoofs instead of feet."

The poor child stares intently at his toes.

"You see, your toes are already starting to look funny."

That will do the trick. The child finally gives in. Most probably that was the way the wife spoke to her husband. She would tell him how his actions would affect their children's futures while bringing up the subject of someone whose luck was far worse than his. All of this would be delivered in a voice as sweet as the warbling of a canary. But sometimes it would take on a sudden shrillness as her mouth would foam like a crab brandishing its pincers in the air until her exhortations fortified him into believing that at work he was as fearless as a Napoleon. His symptoms appeared with the regularity of a menstrual cycle but in the eyes of the public there was no question that he was a powerful executive of a large corporation.

Broad smiles on their faces, the same wife and husband had once thrown a Christmas party, passing around eggnog and bourbon.

In contrast, Shōzō could not help thinking about his own plight. With her daughter Chie, a contented Yurie had sprawled herself on the floor like a mother cat nursing her kitten, oblivious to the world around her but ready to devour her own offspring if she was not fed. The savage gleam in her eyes said as much. What else could be done but feed the beast in her? He was the same as the threatened husband who was afraid of turning into a donkey.

"Warble like a canary?" Yurie began on the offensive. "Don't you know Desdemona's frail voice has everything to do with having the jealous Othello about to wring her neck? Ophelia was what she was because of Hamlet and Polonius, and Cordelia because of King Lear and her wicked sisters."

Her voice began to crack as she spoke and she started to cry. She must have been overcome by sadness at her inability to transform Shōzō into an Othello, a Hamlet, or a King Lear.

His mind fumbled with the memory of how he used to lose his temper at her preoccupation with Shigeru, but time had dulled this recollection.

The way Yurie had dealt with men was similar to a rock breaking the calm surface of a body of water. It spreads a chain reaction of ripples in its wake as it disappears under the disturbed surface. Only after she had toyed with a rapid succession of men and the ripples of those affairs had safely dissipated was Shōzō able to take stock of things. Occasionally he would succumb to a fit of jealous rage, but observing the frightened look in Yurie's eyes, he had felt sorry for her. He also had a sense that she was angry with him for not letting on that he had noticed anything untoward.

If his indifference continued, she would pursue whoever caught her fancy openly and without hesitation, seemingly just to agitate the silent yet watchful Shōzō. In the middle of the night she would telephone a man repeatedly, aggressively challenging him. Her manner in these affairs lacked control or modesty—Shōzō could not help but feel sympathy for her male victims. Focused entirely on a man's internal, psychic world, her curiosity quickly died once she had absorbed as much as she wanted. You could say that she had a special gift for getting men to divulge their innermost secrets, but woe to those who refused to go along; derision was her parting gift. In the end she called them cowards to their faces.

Frightened by her obsessive hectoring, which was her preferred method of extracting information, the men eventually grew circumspect. That fact was obvious to Shōzō. Once in a while his pity shifted to Yurie. Convinced that no man was stupid enough to try to match her level of obsession, he was not as anxious as he might otherwise have been.

The trouble was that the men who caught her attention also interested him; her quests often became his. As a result, when a man got to know her beyond a certain point, the object of the man's concern shifted to Shōzō.

He failed to think of blaming the men on the assumption that she did the seducing. There was always the possibility that a relationship could turn serious and irreversible, but a man whose ego matched Yurie's was bound to reject her. If she sensed a man was half-hearted about the affair, she would withdraw. And vice versa.

In Shōzō's mind eye, an eternally young and mischievous imp flitted in and out of such affairs. It's a little like those long-drawn-out sex scenes in films and on television which leave the viewer bereft of all feeling, thought Shōzō.

If you think about it, today's young people may in fact have very little curiosity about anything sexual. When sex is easy, people lose interest in it; indeed they lose interest in anything that's too accessible.

Taboos produce boundless curiosity. If Shigeru, the violator of countless taboos, has lost the key to the locker in which he's imprisoned his curiosity. On second thought, that's unlikely. He must be carrying the key in his pocket all the time.

For some time Shigeru referred to women as if they were commodities. Appraising them as one might the coat of a show cat, he would out of the blue divulge his escapades to Shōzō, describing in very direct, graphic terms the women he had bought, as if the descriptions could somehow revive his flagging spirit. He seemed to be laughing at himself. Nowadays if men described women in those crude terms, they would be frowned upon. So they are resigned to chase fantasies—maybe it's not so much "resigned" as "forced" to chase.

What happens to people who are devoid of visions or dreams, and are left with only an ever-increasing hoard of gadgets to choose from? Frightened of having their sexual behavior put under the microscope of cold detachment, young people grow neurotic about it. The quality of a medieval castle towering behind them, the size of a feudal army, or the superior nature of a piece of armor, becomes easy fixations for the young sophisticates of today. Brand names sell well because the young have no confidence in their own taste—even though buying generic merchandise seems to be the latest thing for young snobs.

Shōzō's reflections returned to Shigeru, who one day stopped talking about women altogether. That probably coincided with the moment the listener inside him began to notice the ignorance of the speaker outside. But that was as far as his newfound sensitivity could go. Shōzō felt slightly disappointed by this transformation, but also experienced a sense of relief. Shigeru could not maintain the façade of the comical yet cuddly boy in the man who repeatedly exposes his own ignorance. You cannot dislike a man, Shōzō said to himself, for boring a listener with his sexual escapades because his amusing simplicity in the end compensates for the time wasted in the charade.

Shigeru also began to display signs of fear toward his brother Seiichiro, a result perhaps of a deep smoldering hatred bottled up within him that would never see the light of day.

Fū's bickering with Shigeru was also carefully veiled. In fact, she kept his hatred of Seiichiro in check by continually disparaging her husband.

"Fū can only speak truthfully when she's lying." Those were Shigeru's words.

Shōzō thought this was the only time when Shigeru really conveyed the image of a woman in flesh and blood. Well, he does know something about women after all. That was when Shōzō began to have some respect for him. But a gloomy silence ensued. Fū was never mentioned again.

He used to say of Fukiko, "She's stupid," or "She's got no imagination." But finally even the belittling remarks stopped. Shōzō also remembered his indirect references to Fukiko: "Having no imagination is the best way to go, you know," or "As long as you can talk yourself into it, everything's easy." He also admitted, "She doesn't do anything she doesn't want to."

She showed not the least hesitation in purchasing a box of condoms at a nearby drugstore to put in the suitcase she packed for Shigeru's extended business trips. Shōzō had heard from Yurie that Fukiko had once asked her, "I doubt he'd need that many. Do you think he would?" The question sounded deliberate.

"Chances are he'll dump the whole box on his way home still unopened," Shōzō had said with a chuckle.

A warm, quiet rain continued for several days. Yurie struck up a conversation with a good friend of Mizuki's on the way home, an old woman who often shopped at the nearby supermarket. Yurie suddenly paused under a magnificent loquat tree laden with gorgeous ripe fruit when the shrill cry of a bird pierced the air. Chasing the specter of the bird with her eyes, the old woman said:

"That's a *hototogisu*. How can it cry like that day and night? Legend has it that a young man killed his older brother during a dig for yams, suspecting that he had not been given the best of them. Because of his crime, it is said that the man was reincarnated as a *hototogisu* and cannot get his food unless he cries eight thousand and eight times a day.

"Day and night, he cries even in flight until his throat bursts and bleeds. Feeling pity for the *hototogisu*, woodpeckers leave him insects and lizards impaled on tree branches, they say."

Didn't I hear a *hototogisu* on the morning of Tōichiro's visit? Yurie wondered. Also, on the night Henry and Lynn Ann came she had heard a bird crying out as it darted across the backyard. Told that it was a bit too early for a *hototogisu*, Yurie thought it was a different bird, but it began to cry morning and night.

The old woman had told her about the legend of *hototogisu* because she happened to see a dried-up lizard impaled on a thorn of a Bengal quince.

"My late husband's favorite haiku was, 'With that shrill voice ... ,' which he often quoted. I wonder who composed it. Now that he's gone, all sorts of things about him are coming back. The fact that he's dead makes me more aware that he was once alive."

> With that shrill voice
> How could he devour a lizard?
> A *hototogisu*.

Hearing the haiku, Yurie immediately called to mind one of Bashō's famous verses:

> It devours snakes, I've heard,
> How frightening
> The shriek of a pheasant.

She also remembered seeing two pheasants flying through the groves at the Myōkō house, dipping their heads in unison as they prowled in the underbrush. The patchwork of her memory was then stitched together to form scenes of Fū sewing a piece of fabric with spool patterns for a *futon*. Shigeru rested on the floor, a newspaper draped over his face. "Why do women have babies?" Yurie recalled him mumbling to himself.

Now that they had heard the shrill, plaintive call of a *hototogisu*, Yurie and Shōzō decided to head back to Tokyo with the image of the Hiei mountain range, layer upon layer of mountains dissolving into the brume, vividly etched in their minds.

AMONG THE HEAPS OF MAIL AWAITING their return was a letter from Fumiko Yamashiro, posted from Paris. Her exquisite calligraphy had always seemed rather anachronistic in today's Japan.

Dear Yuri,

During my trip to China I ran into a couple of your friends from your Alaska days—Mr. and Mrs. Coleridge. I think they had just visited you in Japan. What a small world. I met them in a museum in Shanghai.

I was sipping a cup of tea in the museum café when a couple came to sit at the table right next to me, and we chatted, asking the typical travelers' question, "Where are you from?" And then the thread of our conversation led me to discover that they had lived in the same Alaskan town as you did, and they in turn learned that I was Japanese.

I always thought that the things we had experienced in those bygone days in small towns, where everyone knew everyone else, were lost forever, but there it was.

Before I came to Paris, I stopped over in Japan and tried to telephone you, but you were not home. I also missed you three years ago when I returned to Japan because you were in the United States. We're always passing each other by. It looks like I'm going to live in the States for a long time. Yet who knows, I may change my mind and go back to Japan when I'm old and gray. I guess I should take things one day at a time.

So, as I'm still in the here and now, I have a small favor to ask. I would like to get a copy of *A Study on Bronzes of the Yin-Zhou Period* by Inao Hayashi published by Yoshikawa Kōbunkan Press. I think it is quite an expensive edition, and

I would appreciate it if you would let me know how much it costs, with postage, and how long it might take you to get it. I've thought of ordering it through the museum where I work, but considering the fact that it's a limited edition and that I will be traveling through Europe and won't be back in the States for a while, I feel I'd better not dawdle about getting it. I'm really concerned about the availability of this book, and I would be most grateful if you would get a copy on my behalf.

Would you let me know to which bank I should transfer money? I am having Ms. Fuha in Paris take care of my belongings and plan to visit with Ms. Sawada in Vienna and Ms. Chida in London.

When I roomed with you in the dorm at Musashino, I used to find the comings and goings of friends like Sawada and Chida a real nuisance, but now I feel they are the real treasures I took away from those days.

You must know that Sawada has divorced her diplomat husband. She is living in Vienna with a flutist, someone studying Korean music. I saw him three years ago when he performed in Seattle.

Did you hear the gossip that was going around college that you would be the first to be married and divorced? But you are still with the same man—something Fuha finds quite surprising. We are like a bunch of sparrows huddled here together, letting our imaginations go wild. What is he like? Fuha's ex-husband is the branch manager of a Japanese bank in Paris, quite a prominent figure in the local Japanese Club.

I would appreciate it if you would send Fuha the account number for the transfer—I'll be in Paris until the fifth of May. The other day we were discussing our dorm life thirty years ago. We decided that our poverty-stricken life in postwar Japan was something like the hippie communes that sprang up in the 1960s in the States and spread all over the world. Where the American hippie movement rebelled against a lifestyle that created as much poverty as it did wealth, we took up our "hippie" lifestyle almost unconsciously—there really was nothing to rebel against because an external force, the war, had annihilated everything. When you're in a tough situation, you feel an animal strength that you'd never dream you had. It's like the person who can haul out something extremely heavy from a raging inferno or musters enough courage to jump off a cliff in hot pursuit of something. Back then it was just like that; our slumbering spirits were awakened by this inner fire and we lived like flowers and insects in a paradise of poverty that was shared by everyone. Then the world turned rigid in the blink of an eye. We have created moats around ourselves, choosing a solitary path through life as if we had nothing to share with each other. Our commune has disappeared, with each of us taking our own path, at times longing for something, yet doubting everything. Sawada the Princess who slept in a tattered futon may have decided to get a divorce because she could not forget the paradise we had once lived in. Her present boyfriend seems quite young.

May the fifth is the Boy's Festival. So many things remind me of the festival: carp banners, *kashiwamochi* sweetmeats wrapped in oak leaves, and irises in bloom.

Speaking of banners and the Boy's Festival, I remember there was a family who had lost a son in the war. They used to make banners for a living. Nobody does anything like that anymore in Japan, do they?

Someday I'll let you know what we said about you in our conversations back then. Thanks again for taking care of the book order.

Fumiko

Putting the letter aside, Yurie asked herself, A son who died in the war? Who is Fumiko referring to? The man she had wanted to marry went to war, but after he returned from a Siberian POW camp, her five years of waiting patiently was conveniently forgotten because he chose not to go to the altar with her. The woman who had beaten Fumiko out in the marriage competition had tied the knot with someone else during the war. But as soon as the woman learned of the POW's return, she got a divorce and moved in with him. Left to her own devices and resolved never to depend on any man, Fumiko earned enough academic credits for admission to college during the postwar higher education reforms. Totally immersed in her studies and already much older than the rest of her fellow students, she was slightly unapproachable, which seemed her way of declaring to us, I can no longer rely on a man like you do.

If she was still single, it probably had something to do with what happened between her and her first boyfriend. However, no matter how many times Yurie re-read the letter, the words "the man who died in the war" jumped out at her. She did not think the story she had heard about Fumiko was a fabrication. It was possible that Fumiko had changed things around to suit her present feelings thirty years later.

I vaguely remember something about this family who made banners. Irises were Fumiko's favorite flowers, Yurie said to herself.

May the fifth had come and gone. Yurie and Fumiko had again passed each other by. Yurie immediately contacted Yoshikawa Kōbunkan, and when she learned that the book was still in stock, she ordered it. Fumiko might have misinterpreted her silence and placed it herself. If that were the case, she would just keep the copy.

# 15 ～

CHIE DROPPED BY IN THE EARLY EVENING to let her parents know what had happened during their absence. She usually brought her husband Takashi along on visits with her parents and this occasion was no exception. Yurie wished she could be alone with her daughter once in a while, but apparently Chie felt vulnerable unless he was around.

Look who's talking, thought Yurie with a wry smile. People have begun to call Shōzō and me the tag-along goldfish turds because we're always together. Engrossed in a baseball game on television, Shōzō and Takashi seemed oblivious to the womenfolk, so Yurie decided to invite Chie to go shopping with her in Shibuya.

Chie had eventually learned to enjoy watching baseball with Takashi, even to the point where she could carry on an intelligent conversation about the Tokyo Giants or the Chūnichi Dragons, whereas thirty years with Shōzō had done little for Yurie. She still could not get it through her head that the batter and the catcher were on opposing teams. She found the pitcher's hurried scanning of the field highly suspicious, assuming that it was nothing more than an attempt to relieve boredom. To make matters worse, the pace of the game was too slow, the results too inconclusive. If she watched a game absentmindedly, it was mainly because the ball-players' physiques reminded her of panthers on a cliff scanning a valley. However, that image and the game failed to connect with each other in her mind.

To her ears, the sportscaster's play-by-play, riddled with its incomprehensible jargon, sounded like a Swahili dance chant. If she were alone with him she would usually ask Shōzō to use the earphones, but with Takashi around, that was out of the question. Not quite in the mood to return to her writing, she felt like having a quiet chat with Chie.

Why did she still find baseball so utterly boring after having lived thirty years with someone who loved it? Was she autistic, or was it just a matter of different tastes, like preferring bread to rice, or vice versa?

Chie was staring at her.

"A suede jacket in this heat? Summer, winter, it doesn't seem to make any difference to you," she said reproachfully.

Yurie must have gotten into the habit of wearing the jacket all year around as a response to the Alaskan cold. After twenty years of constant use, its pockets were unraveling and her hands would go right through them. Too lazy to fix the holes, she decided that the torn pockets made perfect mittens in the winter. But Chie's remark made her self-conscious. When she was about to remove it, Chie interjected resignedly.

"Don't. You look a bit like an artist in it, anyway."

You have no idea how comfortable I feel in this old jacket, Yurie said to herself, yet she was still a little hesitant.

Chie was more or less teasing her whenever she made a remark about her looking like an artist. That always irritated her. She quickly changed into a cool, gauzy, blouse in bright green.

"Like the costume of a has-been stage actress, pulled out of an old cedar chest. Looks pretty good, though. It has a certain charm as long as I sit several rows behind you," commented Chie.

Yurie was clearly being told that her daughter would not be seen anywhere near her.

"You just don't know anything about color coordination," retorted Yurie.

With a sulky look on her face, she ambled over to a nearby mirror and saw a green rhino about to charge. Crushed, she immediately pulled off the blouse.

In the end it was back to the suede jacket. Chie was right. She was sweltering in it but knowing that Chie would comment on her pudgy arms as soon as she removed it, she decided to put up with the discomfort.

Once they were on the bus Chie began to talk about a strange telephone call from a foreigner as if it had just slipped her mind and now she was remembering to tell her mother about it.

During Yurie and Shōzō's absence, Chie had agreed to check their mail, air the rooms and water the plants in the condo a couple of times a week. The telephone call had come during one of her visits.

"As soon as the caller heard my voice, he said, 'Oh, Yuri, you're still alive.' He took me completely by surprise. So I said, 'I'm not Yurie. This is Shōzō and Yurie's house. I'm their daughter.' He turned very formal with me then and said, 'I thought your English was too good.'"

She cast a quick glance at Yurie, thinking to herself, Why's her English so poor after all those years abroad? She never ceases to amaze me. I think she's just too stubborn. She reminds me of someone who's never been able to drop a country drawl even after years in Tokyo. Well, with her it's probably more like not wanting to copy someone else's style.

"He went on to say, 'You sound just like her, though. Are you an American?' I said, 'No. I'm Shōzō and Yurie's daughter, so I'm Japanese, but I was born in the United States and spent much of my childhood there.' He was persistent, and kept asking where I was born."

At this point she peered carefully into her mother's face. It was hard to tell whether Yurie was listening. As usual she was staring absentmindedly out the window.

"When I told him I was born in Seattle, can you guess what he asked next? It wasn't 'How old are you?' It was, 'Are you married?' 'Well, yes,' I said, and since he sounded like he wanted to know when I was born, I told him. In 1956, in Seattle. To my question, 'May I ask who's calling?' he answered, 'Peter, Monica's Peter—Shōzō and Yuri will know.' When I told him you were away, he just said, 'Monica sends greetings to Shōzō, likewise Peter to Yuri.'

Wh-o-o was tha-a-a-t? German? He had such a thick accent."

"An old friend of mine from Stockholm days."

"Really? When you were younger than me? I think he said he was calling from Narita on a stopover to Bali. Apparently he got your telephone number and address from someone teaching Japanese Literature at a university in New Haven, Connecticut. He said he had broken up with Monica, and his present wife is Parisian. She works for some television network and that was why they were going to Bali.

"He went on and on about Monica. 'She's married to some painter you know. He's the one who draws creepy pictures, and young people seem to like him a lot.' He gave me his name, but I don't remember it.

"If you want to get in touch with Yuri, I said, I've got her number at Mount Hiei, but he just said, 'No, it's okay, talking with you is just fine.' I think he did take down the number, though. Did he contact you?"

Yurie was often out with Shōzō in Kyoto. He might have tried to call, but she was almost sure that he had not.

She was mulling over what he said about getting her telephone number from someone in New Haven. It was six months ago that Henry had seen him at San Francisco Airport and had given him the number. Maybe the whole thing had been made up. Well, there were some people in New Haven who would know Yurie. That much was true.

At least in her experience, the average Westerner seemed to be much more adept at telling tall tales than Asians. In the West it is taken for granted that the world of imagination is to be enjoyed and shared by everyone.

Now that Henry and Lynn Ann have gone home, there's no way to confirm Peter's version of the story. Besides, even if I did, it wouldn't do any good. It doesn't matter, Yurie said to herself. It just goes to show you that every story has some truth to it—maybe half—the rest is imagination.

"The same caller asked me, 'Do you look like your father or mother?' I told him that people tell me that I look like Dad. His response was, 'Really? It's too bad I can't meet you—when your mother was younger than you, we used to fight a lot.'

"Now I remember something else. He began to sing in good Japanese, 'Now in bloom, In full bloom, What flowers are in bloom? Lotus flowers, In full bloom they are, Open they are, But closing before your eyes.'

"And then he said, 'You see, what I've been telling you about Yuri and me is true. I learned the song from her.' Then he translated the verse into English and said, 'She also taught me the English version.' Anyway, he said he was going to Bali to see the lotus flowers. I probably shouldn't have, but at that point I couldn't help teasing him a bit. You mean you want to see the petals close right before your eyes?"

By casually relating the whole story to her when Shōzō was not around, Chie had proven herself to be quite a match for her mother. Yurie's face broke into a big grin.

"Although the conversation was weird, he was a very interesting guy, He may have been a bit tipsy."

"Yes. A drink or two under his belt always put him in good humor," Yurie said.

"Mom, did you teach him Japanese?"

"Well, you could say that. I taught Japanese to lots of people back then."

A glimmer of the past was slowly coming back to her.

"Often the first thing people wanted to learn was, *I love you*. We don't really have the equivalent, do we?"

"I don't think so."

"Japanese probably think expressing that feeling is an impossibility. It's not something that two people, you and I, could get away with declaring. There's an uncertainty, a mixture of arrogance and humility in that expression, they would say."

Our shopping today, for instance, Yurie reflected. It's not so much that I'm doing this with my daughter as that a certain situation has been thrust upon me. If I met someone now and he asked what I was doing, I'd simply say, Just shopping, without using the pronoun "I."

"I wonder if 'I love you' means, please chain me down," mumbled Yurie. Chie was stunned.

Do some people find those words too self-evident and frightening to express? Or do others refrain from saying them because they can't be true?

"Peter said that he'll drop a line from Bali."

"He did?"

Yurie didn't think there would be any letters forthcoming. If someone remembered me in some distant corner of the world without too much ill feeling, she said to herself, nodding, that would be a great comfort.

> Now in bloom
> In full bloom
> What flowers are in full bloom?
> Lotus flowers
> In full bloom they are
> Open they are
> Before you know it,
> Closed they are.

Yurie hummed the tune as they got off the bus. Children at play would open and close a circle with linked hands to the melody. As they were swept along with the throngs of shoppers, she noticed for the first time that very few children were out on the crowded streets, and remembered that in the old days she always saw hordes of them playing in all the vacant lots.

On the rare occasions that she ventured out, she was invariably overwhelmed by the sight of merchandise piled high in every store window. People who had to have it all were probably still left unfulfilled.

Chie was asking her, "One of Takashi's former teachers suddenly passed away but he has to present a paper at a conference on that day. Should I attend the funeral in his place?"

"I think so. You don't have the right clothes, though, do you?" said Yurie. "Your Grandma provided me with whatever a bride could possibly need but I haven't done anything for you. Back when everyone was so poor, my neighbors were jealous of what she did for her granddaughter."

Yurie seemed to be defending herself for having neglected Chie.

"Grandma's family lost a fortune when she was very young. She must have felt utterly miserable at the family's loss of their former social standing. I think that was why she lavished things on me in such a big way," she went on mumbling.

Chie sensed a vulnerability lurking behind these words.

"I'll get you a mourning dress."

They stepped inside the Tōkyū Department Store. As usual, Chie didn't find anything she liked.

"How about a suit?" suggested Yurie hopefully, but Chie countered that she would not look good in it.

"I really don't need anything. I'll pick something black out of my wardrobe."

She had been about to walk out of the store when she caught sight of a two-piece suit, which she immediately decided she had to have.

This happened whenever they shopped together; after a casual inspection of an entire collection, she would quickly move on to another designer unless something caught her fancy, always throwing a contemptuous look at her mother as if to repel her impatience and eagerness to pick out something for her daughter.

She detected a whiff of provocation in the way her daughter would quickly refuse to consider anything that was not to her liking, even when it came in the form of a flattering suggestion. In those moments she felt that a daughter who could not bring herself to ask a favor of her parents revealed not so much modesty as arrogance.

If she didn't like it, you couldn't give it to her. And if she did accept it she didn't seem to appreciate what you had bought for her. Before long, Yurie stopped buying her presents. She interpreted her daughter's rejection to mean: Don't expect gratitude for such trivialities. Or perhaps she was declaring to her mother: I've got my own tastes. Brought up in the States, she showed a strong desire early on to become financially independent and demanded very little compared to other children. But Yurie saw a nasty little girl in a daughter who would never humor her parents just to please them. If she had been so inclined, Yurie could have called attention to this arrogance that refused to recognize vulnerability, sadness, patience, or self-sacrifice in the act of pleasing someone, or being humored by someone. But in the end she thought better of it. Chie would have to learn these things herself.

Yurie knew better than anyone else that those lessons on life, full of solemn pronouncements given by grownups in her own childhood had often driven her to rebel. People now long dead mumbled those lessons to themselves, shaking their heads and bemoaning the behavior of the younger generation. And those same words would come back to haunt later generations. She almost felt compelled to share her thoughts with Chie, yet usually held herself back. And every time she kept her silence, that same silence, which people had maintained in her youth, seemed to grow in her heart, nearly suffocating her. Only the repetition of penance seemed constant.

"The less you desire, the easier life gets," said Chie suddenly.

Her tone seemed to taunt Yurie. Her daughter's generation had grown up watching their parents with cold calculation, carefully listening to the grownups express their desires, thought Yurie. Perhaps Chie also meant: I wonder if we're happier just because you've given us what you always wanted. Yurie could not help feeling more than a little sad that a generation that had never known starvation lacked the imagination to give voice to their own desires.

She recalled how Chie had talked about the anxiety of living abroad as children who were brought up by foreign nationals—in her case, Japanese parents living in the States, parents who were often ignorant of the host country's sensibilities.

She had once said, quietly reminiscing about her childhood twenty years ago. "We were usually among the smartest kids in school. Without that edge, we felt we'd be bullied to death."

Her smile perhaps indicated that she pitied herself for being such a smart kid.

A child knows when he can't wheedle things out of his parents. Yurie herself had yearned to have one of those tunnel-visioned mothers whose sole preoccupation in life would be her daughter. Since the family had a cook, Yurie never had the exquisite pleasure of eating a school lunch prepared by her own mother. She desperately envied those less fortunate children who still had the luxury of eating a lunch prepared with the greatest loving care by their mothers. She knew that she could never coax a lunch from her mother, a woman who was totally preoccupied with her avocation—painting or reading and laughing over some humorous novel. That was the way she was. What could a child do about it? Like mother, like daughter. All Yurie could do was immerse herself in what she wanted to do as totally and obsessively as her mother.

Chie's got it worse because I'm hardly the average mother. I write novels. That was probably what was on her mind when she recounted her days in the States.

That was why this child was so uninhibited about demonstrating her iron will. It was like peering into a bottomless pit. Yurie stared into it—the source of her daughter's bullheaded decisiveness—as she selected her own clothes, ignoring her mother's helpful suggestions.

"I wonder if I should have a child," Chie said abruptly.

"Oh, my, how nice."

Yurie had begun to worry that her daughter had shown no interest in starting a family.

Why, just a few days ago she was saying she was not so sure that children could survive in the twenty-first century. Yurie would rather fret about the problems of the here and now, one day at a time; in the past she had made herself too unhappy worrying about the future.

"Do you know ants love onions?"

Chie changed the subject again.

"Really? They do?"

Yurie felt seduced by the sound of the word "child," which took her completely by surprise. I never liked kids in the old days, she said to herself. How strange.

"Yes, they do. Half an onion lying around will be swarmed with ants in no time. I think it's the sweetness of the juice. Those shiny black creatures would come back day after day to feast on it. I was squirting insecticide on them when I began to feel that I was one of them myself. That depressed me.

"Seeing them suck up the sweet juice in the brilliant light of the sun, I decided to let them have what was left by throwing it into the garden. That was when I thought about having a baby. It was like a beam of sunlight penetrating deep into my belly. I don't know any other way to put it, but I began to feel that as long as I exist, I occupy a tiny part, even a dot, of the universe."

In Yurie's mind images of mothers, one who would fix school lunches with tender loving care, another who would rather read and paint than cook, collided and merged like layers of shiny black ants swarming on an anthill. Women who resist having babies are not out of the ordinary, she said to herself. Paradoxes seemed to pile one atop the other.

"Why not? The world's made up of dots, anyway," said Yurie. "As long as we do our best, we'll be linked together for eternity."

Chie was carrying a shopping bag that contained her newly purchased black suit in a box.

"With a bright scarf," she said modestly, "I can wear the two-piece on ordinary occasions as well."

And here she was, thinking about having a baby.

Yurie fell silent at the memory of her mother, who had had a mourning outfit made up for her daughter, insisting that it would be bad luck not to have the proper clothing for every occasion. Yurie had worn that very outfit for her funeral procession. The crystal prayer beads she had held in her hands, she was told, had been handed down from grandmother to mother.

The crystals shimmered like water reflecting the young parsley leaves in the melted snow of a mountain stream. She could almost hear the trickling of the water.

She tried to remember the time of day Chie was born but she couldn't. Like Momotarō the peach boy of folklore, who was enclosed in a peach floating down a stream, Chie came right out of the fruit. Nor could Yurie recall the name of the hospital. But she remembered bragging to her mother in a letter about the way Americans handled new mothers, how during a short convalescence they would rouse the poor tired mothers out of bed to take a shower. However, nowadays it seemed Japanese maternity wards were run in the same way.

"I wonder why I forget everything," said Yurie.

"He certainly remembered you."

"Who?"

"Peter."

"Oh—I have fond memories of him because we were once very close. I can't remember the painter who married Monica, though," she said quickly instead of what she really wanted to say. I was trying to remember the time of your birth.

Monica's second husband may well have been one of her classmates at the Arts School in Stockholm, she thought.

When Chie was growing inside her, Yurie had learned the absolute physical difference between men and women. For women a fetus ripening in the womb is purely physical, but what convinces men about the growing fetus is the pure mental aspect of the pregnancy.

Nevertheless men forget this crucial difference when they want to make love to women.

Peter had no idea about a life forming inside Yurie in 1956, but wasn't Shōzō already ruminating about its significance?

At that very instant Chie turned to look at her. Yurie thought she saw her baby face floating before her. Shōzō had taken care of the newborn baby far better than its mother. Whenever the infant lifted her head, she had always looked not for "Mama" but "Papa."

These things had been borne out of the past. Yurie took a careful look at Chie, pondering the cruelties of life that await the growing newborn.

"You had no eyebrows when you came, except the shape of the bare base that was just like your father's," said Yurie somberly.

"That's why I got his wooly-worm eyebrows."

She also smiled just the way Shōzō did.

"I have a lot to work with, so I can shape them any way I want."
She shaved her thick eyebrows, leaving well-shaped arcs intact.

This funny baby who had hardly a strand of hair to begin with was now subduing her thick eyebrows and a luxuriant shock of hair.

As usual, she was wearing a black sweater. Black was showy but looked very becoming on her.

## 16 ❧

"Shigeru called while you were out," said Shōzō. "He sounded like he wanted to see the Myōkō house, so I told him, Why don't all of us go for a visit?"

Really? I wonder if he really wants to buy the house back, Yurie said to herself. She assumed Fukiko would not accept the invitation, but she herself telephoned that same evening. This time it was Yurie who picked up the phone.

"I understand that you'll be taking us to Myōkō. I'm sorry to put you to so much trouble."

"Not at all. We're delighted. After all, that's where Shigeru was born and we thought you might like to see it. It's been a while since anything has been done, so it may be in bad shape. We were just saying that we need to go back there. You might end up helping us clean the house. Would you mind?"

When they were living abroad, Yurie and Shōzō had purchased the house on the strength of an excellent exchange rate. They were careful not to bring up Fū's name in Fukiko's presence knowing that it was the house where her husband and Fū had carried on their liaison. Although mention of the house must have evoked many unpleasant thoughts in her, it might also have provoked her to want to see the place for herself. A rather eerie picture suddenly sprang into Yurie's mind: a perfectly tranquil Fukiko in Fū's kimono seated in front of her.

"Well, why not leave just before the summer vacation? If we brave the rainy season, we'll be able to avoid the onslaught of tourists."

So things began to take shape, and Shigeru agreed to take a few weekdays off in June. They headed for Myōkō by train, planning to rent a car once they reached the city.

Aboard the train, the two couples were able to sit across from each other. Fukiko was in the same splashed *kasuri* pattern of subdued brown that she had worn on her last visit with Mizuki at Mount Hiei. Yurie could not fathom why she had chosen, after so many years, to wear the same kimono that day and on this occasion.

The white-haired Shigeru, a man in whom Yurie had never seen much of Seiichiro's likeness, was beginning to look more like him. Yurie and Shōzō were abroad when Seiichiro passed away in his forties. It was rather uncanny to see so much of him in this younger brother now in his sixties. Tōichiro also had the high cheekbones of the Sugano family, and the stubborn set of his jaw might have been inherited not so much from his father but his uncle. Family resemblances are a jumble, yet no matter how these shared attributes are assembled and reassembled, identical faces are rare. Different elements have been subtly added for new patterns to emerge.

A little apprehensive about seeing Shigeru again after so many years, and about a creeping senility with his decidedly strange behavior toward his daughter-in-law, Yurie was relieved to find him calm and dignified, concentrating on the scenery outside as the bullet train sped through Nagano Prefecture toward Myōkō. The same kind of wrinkled skin around his jaw line had been passed on to Tōiichiro, who pronounced that his father had gone senile.

Because of his above-average height, he had a tendency to crane his neck, stooping forward slightly as he had marched straight to the train. The plump Fukiko at first trotted after her long-legged husband to match his stride, but soon gave up and slowed her pace. Yet in no time she reappeared right next to him. It seemed her efforts did not go entirely unnoticed, but he still ignored her, refusing to curb his gait. In those brief moments of solitude he might have been reaffirming his own existence.

Pongee is a rather coarsely spun fabric, and did not fit the soft contours of Fukiko's plump body. Prim and proper with hands crossed on her lap, she was not so much sidling up to her husband as maneuvering to focus her attention on Shōzō and Yurie, who were seated across from her.

A tacit agreement between Shigeru and Fukiko not to invade each other's space seemed to be in play. It appeared that neither of them was making any effort to get the other's attention, yet they were not ignoring each other's presence; each hovered in the other's murky consciousness with such certainty.

Does he know the history behind that kimono? Yurie wondered. It was in that same kimono with the infant Mizuki in her arms that Fū had sought to intimidate the young student Fukiko, who was engaged to marry Shigeru.

I wonder how the kimono was passed on to Fukiko after Fū's death? Mizuki had given away all her mother's personal effects to anyone who would have them, and by this route quite a few things fell into Yurie's hands, but she had not heard that anything was passed down to Fukiko. That would probably be the last thing she wanted and it would also be beneath her dignity even to touch them.

Shōzō did not have so much as a passing interest in kimono. All his attention was focused on who was wrapped inside the garment. When Yurie stood before him in a new kimono or some other new outfit, a typical exchange would go like this:

"What do you think?"

"Still some years left."

If she had tried on something that had been abandoned for twenty years in the closet, his typical response would be:

"When did you get that?"

Shigeru at first assumed that the brown kimono originally belonged to his mother, but when he actually saw it on his wife, he was not so sure.

Fū had sent it to him with several items of Seiichiro's wardrobe after his death. "She's to be commended," he said when he saw the kimono in the shipment. "She's even enclosed something that belonged to Mom."

Fukiko had been startled by the sight of the familiar garment but refrained from telling Shigeru about it. Instead, she had tried in her own way to express the significance of the gift by wearing it when she had paid a visit to Mizuki at Mount Hiei. Fū had sent the garment to her deceased husband's younger brother, thought Fukiko, to remind him of their liaison. Relatives had spread the rumor that Fū had become what she was because her cruel dead mother-in-law had taken possession of her. What did they mean by that? It would be more accurate to say that Shigeru had been captivated by the specter of his own mother, whose spirit had possessed Fū.

With a touch of nostalgia, Fukiko had remarked casually during her visit at Mount Hiei. "In the old days women in their twenties often looked gorgeous even in muted colors. Fū's radiant beauty was overwhelming." It was her way of expressing a sense of superiority that she felt toward Yurie, who was unlikely to attach any particular signicance to her words.

Pretending not to notice the kimono on Fukiko, which he assumed was his mother's, Shigeru still had no idea what was being withheld from him.

From the fit of the kimono on Fukiko's petite, plump body it was difficult to picture the tall Fū; Yurie had never seen her in that particular kimono. All she knew was what Fukiko had told her. I didn't know Fū preferred pongee, she said to herself. In her own way she began to picture Fū in a dull brown kimono with an obi the color of persimmons, no, rather the color of a dark oppressive wintry sky.

Even if the colors and patterns were showy, Fū always wore clothing that was soft to the touch, letting it hang loosely on her body. Unlike Fukiko, she disliked quiet pastels.

Fukiko never wore a kimono the way Fū did. Every fold was perfectly in place, the way a professional teaches you to put on a formal kimono. Typical of her generation, Fukiko was unaccustomed to wearing the traditional garment.

She opened her handbag and, suddenly remembering something important, extracted a white envelope. She spread in her hands nearly a dozen snapshots of Tōichiro's baby boy. When Americans showed off their family photos, Shōzō and Yurie always exchanged a quick look that said, There they go again. But in this case the two politely obliged, glancing at the snapshots in Fukiko's hands.

"He looks just like Shigeru in his baby pictures. Well, I wanted a girl, you know," Fukiko said. "The older a child gets, the more I wish it were a girl. They say boys are nice to their mothers, but it doesn't stop there; they're nice to all women. You realize that for the first time when they marry. That's when foolish mothers go into hysterics," she said with a laugh.

Back in Tokyo with Shigeru, she had shed most of her lilting *Kansai* dialect, but some traces were still discernible in her slow, unhurried speech.

"The other day at a class reunion I met someone who's got a boy and a girl. Y-e-e-s, both children are married. She said, 'When I help around the kitchen at my daughter's house, I can just about guess the cabinets where she keeps the soy sauce, vinegar, and so on, and sure enough, there they are. The same is true for plates and chopsticks. But that's not the case at my son's house. I don't have the foggiest idea where things are. Where's the soy sauce and vinegar? I ask. My daughter-in-law keeps them in the most unexpected places. Besides, I feel constrained about opening cabinets without asking her. To tell you the truth,' the friend continued, 'I feel more affectionate toward my daughter's child than my son's.'" Fukiko had completely reverted to her *Kansai* dialect toward the end of the story.

"You're lucky, Yuri. You've got a daughter. A boy replaces his mother with his wife, and that's the end of it."

Yurie was not so sure.

"A girl's really merciless to her mother," she said.

She was trying to comfort Fukiko.

CREAMY WHITE *ENJU* FLOWERS FROM JAPANESE pagoda trees adorned the Shinshū valley in June, and a thick mist of tiny butterflies coursed through the valley.

Like knights mounted ramrod straight on white horses, the tall pale clusters of tiny *tochi* blossoms popped in and out of the mist.

Given the Western air about it amidst the surrounding village community, the Myōkō summer resort area had been in obscurity in prewar Japan. But its very Western-ness had helped it in the postwar economic boom, unleashing the suppressed energy that lent legitimacy to the area, transforming its main street into a middle-class neighborhood lined with American-style drive-ins and stores. No longer the sleepy village it once was, Myōkō pulsated with the kinetic energy born of an industrialized nation.

In the old days, the owners of the summer villas were a minority who were bound together with a certain class consciousness despite their extremely individualistic lifestyle. Among Yurie's most vivid childhood memories of being brought to the place by Fū was the oppressive social tension she had felt when passing villagers on the country road.

Nowadays, all the passersby had a touch of loneliness about them, a loneliness mixed with the irresponsible impatience of city dwellers who would never dream of prying into other people's business. Several factories had been invited to the region and so you could hardly call the area an agricultural village. People from the cities who filled the train station were mere bystanders milling to and fro on the platform.

"The *tochi* isn't the same as what is called *marronnier*, a chestnut tree," pointed out Shigeru at the lovely sight of the cone-shaped clusters of white blossoms as the car Shōzō had rented sped down the highway to Myōkō.

"I saw the *marronniers* in full bloom in Bulgaria. Every day tourists from abroad overran the monasteries' gardens. Rather like the temples in Kyoto during cherry blossom season. When it comes to viewing something that makes a lasting impression, foreign tourists and Bulgarians are all alike."

Devoid of historical buildings, Myōkō was a place of leisure rather than a tourist attraction.

"Why in the world did he build a house in the sticks? People criticized Dad for that," said Shigeru. "Apparently he did it because Mom's parents lived nearby. She returned home often when my brother and I were young. I was born here in the middle of August. They told me that morning sickness and the sweltering summer heat took so much out of her that she stayed on half a year after she gave birth to me."

Shigeru's memories spawned further memories for Yurie, and especially for Shōzō. He had met her for the first time when Shigeru brought him to the Myōkō house where she was staying with Fū for the summer. She was still in grade school, and Shōzō a young man of seventeen.

I think I heard the same story about Shigeru's mother, he thought. Out of the blue, Shigeru, the upperclassman, had begged Shōzō to accompany him to the country just before the end of the semester, and together they sneaked out of the dorm.

Shōzō and Yurie had looked in on the Myōkō house only occasionally over the past ten years, and while their memories of earlier times were foggy at best, Shigeru seemed only to remember events that happened long ago. Seeing the Myōkō Heights Station from the car window, he remarked that no such station existed when he was a boy.

"Buying groceries wasn't easy, and to get produce you had to make friends with neighboring farmers," he explained.

He wanted to take a walk through the white birch grove near the house. Shōzō stopped the car, dropping off Shigeru and Fukiko, and drove on.

THE WHITE BIRCH GROVE THAT THRIVED in Shigeru's memory was nowhere to be seen. All that remained were half a dozen trees, spared, it would seem, for decorative effect.

Breaks in the mist also failed to reveal the row of straw-thatched roofs in the old village of his memory. He dawdled, seemingly rooted to the spot by the sight of rows upon rows of vacation homes visible through the tears in the misty curtain.

"I should have known this would happen. After all, I went all the way to Bulgaria to build a resort hotel," he said to Fukiko wryly.

Confronted with evidence of what he too had been doing for forty years, he felt dizzy as if someone had smacked him in the head.

"The Bulgarians always brag to foreigners about their nuclear power plants," he continued. "Whenever they complimented me on the hotel I designed, they never failed to mention their power plants, which is what they really wanted to talk about. They sometimes mixed up building projects and praised me for designing a music hall or something done by another foreign architect whom I'd never met.

"Bulgarians love classic styles of clothing. A little like the old days, when almost every young Japanese mother attended her children's entrance and graduation ceremonies in very formal black-crested *haori* half-coats and kimonos. I saw you in the same outfit when you returned from Tōichiro's high school entrance convocation," he said, turning to his wife. "That was what came to mind watching the Bulgarians who stayed at the hotel where I was lodging."

Fukiko was confused, and after several months of separation she did not know what to make of the subtle change that was taking place in Shigeru and their relationship. The change was awkward, sudden, and hard to describe. She had never heard him go into such detail about a trip abroad. At a loss for words, she wondered, Has he ever paid attention to what I have to say or do? It was indeed an interesting revelation.

She found his newfound obsession rather sinister as it inexorably surged toward her. She was the type who accepted things as they were; a human being was as immovable as a mountain.

All she could do was climb or descend the mountain, or rest in its shadow once in a while; it never occurred to her that she might somehow move it by force. Shigeru was the opposite. He demanded your attention no matter what, and if he took a dislike to you, he was ready to pick your personality apart and remake it to suit himself. Or so it seemed, she thought. Even if that's the case, he's never succeeded in bringing me around. That was why she had never even imagined she could ever win over other people. *Do what you like.* When something totally unexpected sprang from his lips, she just made sure she looked appropriately impressed or surprised.

She had decided early on that if he agreed to accept her as she was, there was no other choice but to accept him as he was. That was how she had been living her life. But still, he had always held some crazy ideas, things that had never, ever, occurred to her, and tried to force them on her with a persistence that utterly bewildered her. The only possible explanation for his cantankerous behavior in the face of her refusal may have been that he just wanted to offend her. All she did was watch, dumbfounded, but she neither resisted nor cooperated with him. I am what I am. If he really doesn't like our relationship, he'll think of a way out. How about starting an affair, or even divorcing me? If something like that really happened, what would there be for me to do? Go along to get along. That's my philosophy. But then, what he has to say or do sounds interesting. When he goes to extremes, all I have to do is say, You can't do that, and ignore him. He's helped bring up my baby, that's enough for me. No matter how much you're pressured to do something, if you're not interested, you just can't do it. This was the way she always dealt with him. In other words, she was the type who never expected anything extraordinary out of life; instead she liked to watch things happen from the sidelines.

Once you deem your husband an overgrown baby, he ceases to be an equal. So nothing he does should bother you. And sons—those selfish creatures—what more need I say? She said silently to herself.

But why, why doesn't he just leave me? Why didn't I try to leave, no, why don't I even think about leaving him? I may have been fantasizing that someday he'd lose interest in me. He may have the same fantasy, which may be the glue that has bound us together for forty years: Why doesn't she leave? I wonder when he'll leave me? This bizarre relationship keeps us on pins and needles, each waiting for the other's next move. It's so strange that he still hangs around.

After fleeing Fū, he seemed to try to mold me into her image. Did he really think he'd succeed?

I haven't turned into her because he isn't a Seiichiro, because the conditions that created her didn't exist for me. Here we are under the illusion that we've done what we please. I feel like laughing when I recall all the outrageous experiments that he's tried on me. What can I say? Come to think of it, the fact that he's got so many fantasies also makes me feel alive.

People say that he's talented, or that he's a world-famous architect, but I honestly don't know how to judge him. He is what he is because good things just happened for him. Hard work or no hard work, it was just his destiny. It appeared that Fukiko had learned this line of reasoning as an adolescent during the war. The war was something a little girl was powerless to affect. If a bomb dropped on your head, there was nothing you could do about it.

When she met a very talented and accomplished person, she simply saw him as nothing more than fortunate, and, what's more, she could never understand why he might be convinced of his own power. What's the use of bragging about the fact that you were born a human, not an ape?

That was why she often neglected to join in when someone praised her husband. She wasn't displeased but the compliments were a little like clouds changing their shapes before her eyes. Who knew what shapes they would next assume? If misfortune befell her, the only thing she could do was accept it.

Her indifference to life never sat well with Shigeru early in their relationship. But this uneasiness gradually metamorphosed in his mind until it turned into fear. She did not unnerve him, yet he had the feeling that the soles of his feet were being pulled toward the center of the earth. At the same time his upper body was left floating free. And all he could hear was the sound of the whispering wind in the distance. Whenever he came into contact with women who would raise a fuss about something, or the kind for whom payment was required, he was startled by the same distant whispering wind.

When Fukiko was not around he often daydreamed about breaking up with her, wishing instead for a woman who would twist him around her little finger. But when he happened upon that type the sigh of the wind in his head unsettled him. Once he was back with Fukiko, if her detached attitude became so annoying that he actually said, "Get out," she would simply say, "Okay, if that's what you want," and she would leave. That would be enough to utterly deflate his ego.

So even when he tried to distract himself with mindless chatterboxes, an uneasy feeling would overtake him and he found himself back with his indifferent wife. She was always there, an immovable mountain. Thoughts of his accomplishments, the praise, regrets, satisfaction, as well as the emptiness of his life, ebbed and flowed in his head when he sat quietly in his room at the monastery in Bulgaria. Yet nothing had a life of its own to excite him. The only reality was the quiet sound of the distant wind, which grew inaudible every now and then. That made him anxious.

On the pretext of conducting some architectural research he had secured a place to stay from the monks at a monastery. He was neither Christian nor Buddhist, so images of Christ, Mary, Buddha, or Kannon never insinuated themselves into any part of his consciousness. Examining architectural treasures with the eye of a specialist was the furthest thing from his mind. It was simply that while he sat absentmindedly in his monastery room the same familiar sound of the wind echoed in his ears.

In Shigeru's daydreams, a grinning Seiichiro stood there, a ragged beggar watching Fū yap like a frustrated dog beside him. He heard the faint, faraway sound of the wind as the image of Fukiko quickly superseded that scene. Why did Fū stay with my brother until the end? I guess yelping like a dog was all she wanted to do, just as Seiichiro only wanted to watch her do it.

NEGOTIATING A HILL NEAR THE MYŌKŌ HOUSE, Shigeru searched in vain in the nearby grassland for the tiny gentians he had seen as a boy.

The mist moved in again, blotting out everything except for a spider's silky thread, which shimmered in the grass. Then miraculously the mist cleared. Shigeru saw a spider hop onto a tiny branch where it began to weave its magical web swaying in a gentle breeze.

When he was a boy, Shigeru had dreamed of spanning a bridge into the sky as he studied the cobweb of a breeze-blown spider, or of building a temple as he inspected the interior of a beehive. He was moved by the perfect harmony of the web's slightly irregular lengths of thread, and by the minutely differing sizes of the tiny beehive chambers. The infinite irregularity of the linkages touched him.

"You have no idea what's on my mind, do you?" He broke the silence.

"I don't, that's why I can go on. You haven't a clue about what I'm thinking, either, do you?" asked Fukiko, chuckling. "Weather forecasts rarely hit the mark, but we still try to predict the weather no matter what. Funny, isn't it?"

"Gambling will never go away. It doesn't make any difference how much we lose, we keep on doing it."

The *kakkō* bird began to sing, and after a lengthy pause resumed its melody.

Everything shrouded in mist once again, Shigeru stood lost in its timelessness. When it cleared abruptly, they were staring into a large magnolia growing on one side of a ravine.

"What's this?" Fukiko cried out in alarm.

She froze, startled by the enormous blossom that had made its sudden appearance. It was just starting to open, heavy with yellow stamens that were packed inside the fat waxen petals.

"What a creepy flower." She looked away. It reminded her of the nape of a woman's neck—a woman in her prime.

Shigeru stared at the flower for a long time and suddenly thrust out his hand, pulling toward him a branch with a waxy white bud right next to the half-open flower. He pressed the bud against her neck.

"Please don't—"

She tottered, waving her hands as if to brush away the mist.

"What a smell. I hate it," she said in disgust, ducking her head to evade the bud.

Shigeru executed an abrupt about-face and climbed back up the slope, panting heavily. The mist-borne sound of his breathing echoed in her ears, but his retreating figure suggested irritation, as though to shake off something. When he had bent the branch, she had noticed it was entangled with a cluster of discolored flowers like a heap of crumpled paper in a wastebasket.

WHEN FUKIKO PAUSED IN FRONT OF THE HOUSE that Shigeru had just marched into as if it were his own, she heard Shōzō's voice. Once inside she saw a dirt floor, and beyond it a raised wooden platform at the center of which a hearth was cut out in the classic village style. Built into a wall close by was a fireplace, an addition that Shōzō and Yurie had probably installed. A few wooden chairs circled the fireplace. An old clock on the wall had stopped.

A clattering noise filtered in from the back of the house—Yurie was trying to open the shutters.

Shigeru's eyes gravitated from the hearth to the fireplace and back again. "Charcoal is hard to get nowadays, so we've added the fireplace," said Shōzō. "There's enough firewood from fallen branches in the yard for our rare visits. The tall chimney also helps heat the house more efficiently. We can't do things like this in Tokyo anymore, so we enjoy it. We've spent most of our time at Hiei and haven't been here for quite awhile. You might have noticed it's a bit musty in here."

A kitchen was visible in an open space beyond the dirt floor.

"Remember Fujino, the young woman who grilled fish kebabs for us over the charcoal?" said Yurie as she came in with *saké* and tea on a tray.

Fū had once told her that transportation was so poor back then that fresh fish from the Sea of Japan was not available locally, and people instead learned to enjoy freshwater fish from nearby lakes and rivers. Everything she knew about this house was connected with her, making it difficult to continue her story in Fukiko's presence.

"Mom had me here because she suffered from the heat and didn't want to leave," said Shigeru.

It might have sounded to Fukiko that he had said, She gave birth to Mizuki. Yurie was a little concerned about Fukiko.

"Mom had a little sister. I mean my aunt Yoriko, who was born after my older brother. So that means the nephew is older than his aunt. Mothers and daughters often had babies at the same time in the old days."

Unexpectedly, he turned to Yurie and said, "That young aunt of mine was only five or six years older than me, but much younger than my older brother. I called her my big sister Yoriko, and we played together like brother and sister."

Uh-huh, Yurie said to herself. The woman who came to bad-mouth Fū—that was Yoriko. How her visits always put my mother out of sorts.

Even before Shigeru's mother died, Yoriko had taken on the role of representing the Sugano family. She often came to visit Yurie's mother, who was more or less Fū's surrogate mother, to bitterly complain about Fū. As someone who had tried to lord it over her nephews—whom she considered as brothers—Yoriko evidently could not tolerate an outsider. On the other hand, from Fū's perspective, it was this bossy, impostor of a sister-in-law who had driven her to outdo the two brothers.

"She's doing fine," said Fukiko. "She's the only aunt Shigeru-san has, and they're so close in age that he still calls her his big sister. Without her, I wouldn't know a thing about his family."

It seemed that, as far as Fukiko was concerned, Yoriko was not an unpleasant individual by virtue of the fact that she disliked Fū.

"She often talks about this house, you know. I've wanted to see it at least once."

"I seem to remember that I met her a couple of times when I was a kid," said Yurie, almost adding, She must be the same age as Fū, but quickly bit her tongue.

"Grandma on my Mom's side was a very old-fashioned woman," said Shigeru. "She never came around to see us unless she was invited by Mom's in-laws to a wedding or a funeral. But this place here wasn't the main house for any of the family, which allowed Grandma to indulge us and occasionally visit when we stayed here. Mom really looked forward to being here, because it was like coming home. She let her little sister come and stay with her, and I was asked to play house with her.

"Dad's relatives weren't pleased at all. Whose villa is it anyway? they said. Their typical sarcastic remark was that he built it for the exclusive use of his wife. Japan's prewar family institution may have appeared patriarchal, but I wonder if it wasn't actually run by a matriarchy."

True, a house is fated to be used by a woman and her relatives, thought Shōzō. Who suffered more within that family institution, or tried the most to destroy it—men or women? It was all very confusing.

Just as the mother of the two brothers summoned her own mother and sister to this house, Fū, who became Seiichiro's wife, had brought Yurie, her own blood relative. That was how she had rid herself of the specter of her female predecessors.

Now, who did Yurie bring along this time? What has been driven out seems inevitably drawn back to its place of origin. There stood Fukiko quietly in that subdued, splashed brown kimono.

"Now when I think about it, Grandma gave birth to Mom at the age of seventeen. Mom was in her thirties when I was born. So the Grandma, who was barely fifty, said she felt embarrassed chaperoning Yoriko the daughter and me the grandson, who were almost the same age," mumbled Shigeru to no one in particular. Yurie handed him an *otedama* beanbag. Tiny beans were on the verge of spilling out of a hole that a bug had eaten in the silken bag.

"Looks like this has been here for ages," she said. "Maybe you played the game of *otedama* with Yoriko."

There was enough old bedding in the closet for a few overnight guests. Probably Yoriko, Shigeru's mother, and his grandmother had slept in them. Yurie had sent Mizuki anything that was even slightly redolent of Fū's presence. What remained in the house belonged to a time before Fū.

While the women laid the bedding out in the sun and cleaned the house, the men surveyed the environs.

For supper, Shigeru insisted on having steak at the Akakura Kankō Hotel.

"So you want beef steak," repeated Shōzō, with a look that said, He still likes that heavy stuff.

"I want one that oozes blood when you cut into it," said Shigeru. Shōzō knew restaurants in Japan would never serve a bloody, rare steak.

Yurie recalled that when Fū had stayed overnight at this same hotel with the Myōkō house only a stone's throw away, Seiichiro had created quite a scene in the lobby. Her mind superimposed that memory on the image of a slice of beef oozing blood.

When she stood up to get some ice from the refrigerator, Fukiko followed, whispering into her ear. "Don't you think Shigeru-san is acting a bit strange?"

"What do you mean?"

"He was like that with Tōichiro as well."

"Too young for senility, though."

Tōichiro had mentioned something about strange behavior and asked her not to say anything, but it slipped out.

"Pardon?"

Fukiko braced herself and started again.

"Just a while ago—"

She meant to tell Yurie about the magnolia incident, but the words froze on her tongue and would not come out.

"He's saying he wants to quit his job."

In response to Fukiko's hesitancy, Yurie simply said, "I'm sure he gets worn out from time to time. You know how men are."

I pity him—that was what she had started to say, but checking herself, she said instead, "Men don't like to be pitied. They tend to overdo things and exhaust themselves."

The early evening was cooling down considerably. As Yurie was looking up at the threatening sky and debating in front of the glass doors about whether to put up the shutters before leaving for the hotel, she sensed the presence of someone behind her. She swung around to find herself staring right into Shigeru's face.

She was again startled when he suddenly thrust a hand over her head to pull out a desiccated praying mantis stuck in the wire mesh of the screen door. The last time Yurie had stayed at the house in the early afternoon of a hot summer day before heading for Mount Hiei, two praying mantises had locked themselves in a coital knot at the same spot.

The insects had remained in the same position almost half a day.

With a shake of his swollen body, the male finally took wing, sheltering himself from the heat in the vines of the *yūgao* "evening faces" that grew next to the veranda.

The female, unrepentant, remained utterly still as though nothing had happened. It was only the next morning that Yurie learned the female had disappeared to lay her eggs elsewhere.

Shōzō, who had kept vigil the whole time, could not get over the fact that the female had not eaten the male on the spot and had to check this unusual behavior in an entomology book.

"Fabre says here that one female praying mantis ate seven males. According to him, in that stage of the reproductive cycle what a female sees is not a mate but a source of food. Probably this particular female and the seven males were trapped in a cage and none of the males could escape."

What Shigeru had picked off the screen was an entirely intact winged-insect—a slender brown male.

Which summer evening had it been when Shigeru, wanting to be left alone, waved off Yurie—the black swallow-tailed butterfly?

# 17 ∽

BACK FROM DINNER, SHIGERU STARTED DRINKING where he had left off at the hotel. As a social drinker, Yurie usually held her liquor well but this time she had gone a little overboard.

Would he really buy back this house? Expectation lurked somewhere in the corner of her mind. *Well, considering the remote mountain location, all I could get is barely ten million yen. How long could I live off that?* She began to mull over her daily life, a life that afforded little financial stability.

The house that Seiichiro had inherited stood on a two-and-a-half-acre lot with a hillock in the back that was covered with white birch trees. Most of the land except a tiny strip skirting the house was already sold, as necessitated by his family's decision to move to Tokyo after the war. "I want to sell whatever's left to further finance a business venture," he had written in a letter to Shōzō, who was living abroad at the time. "But the house is full of fond memories and I don't want it to go to a stranger. Would you consider buying it?"

Seiichiro's proposal confused Yurie. As a child she always assumed that his family was a cut above her parents' despite the declining Sugano fortunes. Back when Shōzō was faced with a sudden transfer to the States, the penniless Yurie had turned to Seiichiro for cash, asking him to sell her trousseau to some foreigners to defray the moving costs. Because of this and past favors, rejecting his offer was not an option, and as a result they had bent over backward to secure the money for the purchase.

If we had acquired a sizable piece of land in the suburbs of postwar Tokyo instead of this house deep in the mountains, we would have made a small fortune by now, thought Yurie wryly. What it comes down to is that we just don't have what it takes to make a buck. Yurie was amazed at her own lack of entrepreneurship. How-ever, land speculation and refinancing schemes to gain a profit failed to capture her imagination.

Then what in life caught her fancy? Watching the face of someone she just happened to meet, or listening to the mumbling of a total stranger and then finding herself mesmerized by the melodious sound that reverberated in her head. When she came to her senses, she found herself writing down all those unforgettable things she had heard and witnessed. Apparently that was what always happened.

Be that as it may, Yurie said to herself, her mind going back to the Myōkō house, if Shigeru—a man who had had an affair with Fū in that house—were really serious about buying it back, one would have to call that a sentimental obsession. It had nothing to do with investing in real estate.

MOST OF THE BIRCH GROVE HAD BEEN subdivided into residential lots. Villas that had been built a decade ago stood close by. Now hemmed in by the villas and factory dorms that had sprung up during Japan's high-growth period, the Myōkō house had stood forlorn for over sixty years. It looked like the weather-beaten travelers' roadside stone guardian called *kōshinzuka*. In fact, Yurie and Shōzō called the place the haunted house.

"Let's keep vigil for the *kōshinzuka* spirit tonight. If we fall asleep, three worms will creep out of our bellies and tell the gods about our misdeeds. So, let's keep awake to outsmart them," said Yurie.

"Really? We might as well confess before someone squeals on us," said Shigeru, laughing.

She felt strangely relaxed in this haunted house. The next door neighbor was apparently enjoying the kind of affluence that would always be out of her reach. Ordinarily, if your neighbor senses that you're a little better off than he is, that could be sufficient to invite his resentment, and resulting in an increased stress level. On the other hand, you could sit back and relax with a neighbor who considered you less fortunate, less accomplished, and therefore no threat.

Japanese had experienced the same sense of liberation sojourning in America while their native country was suffering postwar privation. Now that Japan was a wealthy nation, Japanese had to be careful what they said when abroad. And if they worked like busy little bees—as Japanese are wont to do—they were subject to severe criticism. Working hard is sometimes seen as edifying, sometimes offensive. Why is that? Yurie's mind began to make its way through Shigeru's personal and professional life. His accomplishments in the business world seemed to have highlighted the powerful influence and beauty of Japanese architecture for the entire world to see. Nonetheless, she had no idea how to properly assess his work as an architect.

The only thing she could say with absolute certainty was that women with all their contradictions were more than he could handle—what she had seen and heard about him in her childhood attested to that. Ironically, these contradictions had taken a physical form in the buildings he designed. She wondered what the man she knew had to do with the creations she had seen in his architectural portfolios.

In general, his designs removed decisively any excess spatial energy that would have the potential to explode and collapse his overall exterior plan. His buildings merged unobtrusively into the surrounding landscape, projecting a sense of calm and security. The interiors, which were probably not his forte, displayed a glaringly mechanistic rationality.

"Shigeru was so soured on Fū that he apparently has decided never to treat anyone else's wife as a woman," Fukiko had once told Yurie.

Remembering her words, Yurie said to herself, Here she is someone else's wife, and she is revealing things about her own husband to another woman, the wife of another man. I feel strangely

light-headed, someone's playing with my mind. Yurie stared intently into her face.

Yurie could not quite tell whether she was suspicious and wanted to make sure that nothing indiscreet would occur between Yurie
and Shigeru, or she was simply leaving things alone. But surely she
must have been imagining something entirely different.

Shigeru seemed to have opted for the life of an average male
out of anger at any woman who refused to treat him as a man—to
prove, as it were, the kind of influence he wielded, forcing his wife
to say what she had to say about him. He was also the type of man
who could only assert his manhood by purchasing the services of
women.

Why is Fukiko beating around the bush? Why not come out
and say, I'll stab any woman who steals my husband. I'm sure he's
the type of guy who wants to be threatened rather than ignored by
a wife who stoically accepts his practice of buying women. He probably wanted to hear her say, If you get into trouble with another
woman, I'll stab you to death.

Yurie cast her memory back to those men who had come and
gone over the past thirty years of her life. Time and again she had
witnessed how a man would completely transform himself into
someone brave and purposeful if a woman put her heart and soul
into him, but, if she reneged even a little, he would fall apart and
wither away. She found this predictable pattern both endearing and
frightening.

Even in a chance encounter Yurie was quick to detect, with the
exchange of only a few words or a look, a man's general disposition
from the sexual aura he exuded. A man who rejected Yurie must
have rejected other women as well, and a man whom she found
quite attractive must also have attracted other women. If you ex-
plored a man's life in terms of how it was nurtured, it would be
inconceivable not to factor in the presence of a woman.

The sight of a pitifully browbeaten man always filled Yurie with
indignation, as her novelist's imagination churned out possible
variants of his life story. It was because he had not been fortunate
enough to meet a woman who would shield him, or even if he had

been so lucky, perhaps he had not taken her seriously. Or else a good-for-nothing woman had most probably ruined him.

Up to this point in generating scenarios, her creative powers seemed to have an impetus and a logic all their own. But then her mind would come to a screeching halt and she would fly into a rage, cursing all men for everything and nothing in particular. There was no telling whether she felt she had to save all the unfortunate men of the world, or she had got it into her head that it was solely up to her to draw out men's strength. Or maybe in a swift gender reversal she just resented those men who had snubbed her, blaming them for every misfortune that had befallen her.

The focus of her scorn and fault-finding would eventually narrow down to several specific men, finally leading to the realization that Shigeru had paid no attention to her. If you had enough sense, she formed the words silently to Shigeru, if you had listened to what I had to say, you could have had the best guardian angel imaginable and erected the masterpiece of the century. Reverie would then quickly turn into delusion. It was me who was behind your lyricism, yielding, fading into the undulations of the roof tiles, in the irregular continuity of shape in one of your buildings I had once seen in a photo essay. You lack the imagination to transform your design into a mysterious bird swooping down on the surrounding streets, mountains, valleys, and plains—it's all because you ignored me.

Mysterious birds were perhaps not to Shigeru's liking. And he was probably trying to distance himself from Yurie to escape from the terrifying wings of her fantasy. The way he handled me was simply awful, so cold and matter of fact, she said to herself. She was again in control, safe in the confines of her own ego. I was there to help you, to draw the best out of you. She consoled herself with the thought that he was just a fool, likening their several innocent past interactions to a comical mating dance in the wild.

Before mysterious birds began to soar into the sky of her imagination, when the innocence of a union of two young virgins was only a dream, she had imagined herself to be as precious as the delicate new shoot of a tree, swaying imperceptibly in the mist of an early spring day.

Probably the young Fukiko was the delicate bud of a silver willow, Yurie the tiny pink shoot of a cherry tree.

In Yurie's mind Fukiko had grown into a gigantic willow firmly rooted in the ground, thick branches outstretched confidently reaching for the sky with utmost ease, while Yurie, gazing at the willow, was no longer a tiny cherry sapling.

But the memory of Fukiko's warnings about Shigeru unnerved Yurie. She felt like screaming at her. Oh, why didn't I make another pass at him? Your husband didn't seem to care whether a woman was married or not—it was written all over his face that he wanted her to seduce him. I remember I felt guilty myself for not seducing him. That would be a crime for him. I knew it. You were too sexually insensitive to give yourself over to the temptation of a seducing man.

I wonder if there are women around who take a man at his word? Instead, women turn peevish when a man doesn't make a grab for them even if they say no. The vindictive Yurie, who never set a limit on how long she would carry a grudge, gave Fukiko a contemptuous glare. Obviously an advocate of public order and morals, Fukiko slowly raised a hand as if removing a mask from her face, smiling sheepishly like the monkey carved on a *kōshinzuka* stone marker.

"You're a novelist," she said, "I should think having fantasy for a steady companion must be so much fun, yet so sad."

The comment startled Yurie. She was very well aware of her own rather self-centered personality, and while she would have absolutely no memory of what she had said to someone, she could always count on never forgetting what was said to her. But this time she made some effort to recollect what she should have remembered. To be more precise, in wishing to match the energy of her listener, she automatically expected the same from the other party. Yet this time, oddly enough, she found herself respecting Fukiko—someone who was decidedly different in her interactions with people.

"One of my friends had a nervous breakdown worrying that her husband might be turning into a sexual pervert," continued Fukiko.

Suspecting the friend to be Fukiko herself, Yurie said, "If the wife cares for him that much, chances are it would never happen."

Giving a sigh of relief at her timely escape from the world of fantasy, she realized how comfortable she felt with Fukiko.

Fukiko's carefree manner was something a working woman like her could ill afford. The image of a writer in a constant rush to put pen to paper—and to call the repetitive task of filling blank pages day in and day out a profession—had somehow lost its luster in Fukiko's presence.

Chasing after all those countless words, words rich and suggestive in their meanings that would otherwise have been buried and forgotten, may not be much of a profession, she thought.

"Oh, my, I miss those days when I was a housewife just like you. I could just let my mind wander where it willed," she said, letting out a deep sigh.

She reminisced about those days scribbling down something that had little chance of being published and accepting as her own what Shōzō had brought home. They now seemed precious, but would never return.

"The other day I met a best-selling novelist from a socialist country at an international writers' conference," she said, thoughtfully. "His suit was a bit too baggy, yet he was a very attractive man with beautiful clear eyes. I wanted to tease him, so I said, 'While we've got the time, let's do an experiment. Write down everything we can't say openly in public.' He didn't say a word, but squeezed my hand tightly."

She remembered that his eyes had darted to the ceiling as if in anger, full of an expression that could be interpreted either as a smile, self-restraint, or perhaps the beginning of a cramp. The memory sent her back into a sad yet joyful reverie.

A dream is a dream, from which you always wake up, she was saying to herself when Shigeru suddenly spoke up.

"Being alive is just a dream within a dream, you know."

"Ahem, you mean you lie only in dreams."

"A lie can also be the truth. If you say, That's a lie, it's understood there's something about it that isn't."

Incredulous that Shōzō could not tolerate liquor, Shigeru wagged his chin at Yurie, and looked Shōzō in the eye. "You think you're having fun with something that's more intoxicating than liquor. You've got to have guts to invest in a living thing. All living things die, you know."

Yurie had no recollection of Shigeru ever humoring her, but this time she felt she was being provoked. My, my, what's made him say that? She was completely mystified.

"Your life depends on meeting someone who'll play up to you," he said, quickly glancing from Shōzō to Yurie. "You could say a happy face is the face of someone being hypnotized." Was he trying to hypnotize the two or was he merely lost in a daydream?

"Doesn't she look like the only thing that would interest her is the core of the earth?" he said, this time his eyes on Fukiko. "Nothing else exists, everything in life is self-evident. She doesn't show the slightest interest in imitating others."

A hint of provocation aimed at the three listeners crept into his voice.

Shōzō listened, grinning. Yurie was relieved. He isn't senile. He's very lucid, she said to herself. He's trying to excite himself. Or maybe he's already figured out what's what, she corrected herself. He might have reached the conclusion that if you can't move a rock, you might as well enjoy it as a rock garden. Well, nobody would touch a rock that happens to be a wayside *kōshinzuka* shrine even if it could be moved.

The people in front of her were grinning like three stone monkeys.

"You've always loved to take chances," said Shigeru, turning to Shōzō. "We talk about the three vices—drinking, playing mahjong, and betting on the horses. But you see life itself as a high stakes gamble."

His words reminded Shōzō of what Yurie had called him—"A sneaky flatfish." He suddenly felt he had swallowed a very large needle that he could not spit out. My stomach acids aren't strong enough to dissolve it. Could it be that my stomach lining's wrapped around it and turned it into a tumor?

"Speaking of horses, suppose it broke a leg," said Shigeru, raising his head, glaring at his audience like a wild horse about to neigh, its mane streaming in the wind. "With a broken leg it'd be shot, no, poisoned, I think," he added, staring vaguely into the distance.

"Is anyone gutsy enough to shoot a horse he's trained himself?" he asked rhetorically. "Have you heard this folktale? There was a man who wished for a wife who wouldn't eat. One day, a woman appeared and said, I am what you want. He liked what she said and married her not knowing she was a monster in disguise.

"True, she never touched a grain of rice when he was around. What's more, she worked like a busy little mouse from dawn until dusk. She slaved away in total silence with the gentle eyes of a tiny mouse. However, their supply of rice kept running out. Suspicious, the man woke up one day in the middle of the night and hid himself in a closet. There she was sitting in the corner of the kitchen. She quickly parted the thick black thatch of hair atop her head, revealing a gaping hole in the center. His heart almost stopped. She grabbed a handful of cooked rice and threw it into the hole. Her red lips broke into a sweet smile. Impatient for more, she lifted the container, and, turning it upside down, dumped the remaining rice into the hole. She made sure not a grain was left in the container, and with perfect composure shook the heavy mop of hair forward to seal the hole. Then she calmly washed and rinsed the empty pot. The dark shadow of this silent woman scurrying around the kitchen revealed a broad-winged monster that could only have come out of the bowels of the earth.

"Ha, ha, ha, imagine that huge gaping hole in the parted hair on top of her head. Ha, ha, ha. I should say that what was thrown into the hole was not cooked rice, but a man, who melts inside that dark hole like those tiny rice grains. Ha, ha, ha. She dumps in the rice, turning the pot upside down. It's enough to send chills down a man's spine. All men can do is create rules and rituals. Cooked rice is to be served in a small bowl. The rice must be eaten with chopsticks delicately, and then chewed well for the taste, or things like that."

"When he's got to eat to survive, it's ridiculous to wish for a wife who won't eat," retorted Yurie quickly.

"It's a fantasy, just a fantasy. What we're really afraid of is that gaping hole."

"Who'd shoot a horse with a broken leg, without looking at the poor creature?" asked Yurie.

In response Shigeru raised his head and neighed at her.

"Who could it be?" he said mockingly. "Hey, Yuri-chan, are you really a female? Horses have mares and stallions, you know. You and I should take care that we don't get shot. When you're writhing in pain, that's the moment they'll pull the trigger. Ha, ha, ha," he guffawed.

"What frightens me these days is the thought of Shōzō on my back dangling a carrot on a stick in front of me, cracking a whip," she said, laughing.

Her hearty laughter echoed Shigeru's. Ha, ha, ha. Fukiko looked confused; Shōzō slowly moved his head from side to side, a gesture that meant he was either irritated or in good humor.

"To be honest, I feel bad about pressing this unruly mare on you. Go ahead and frighten her to your heart's content," Shigeru confided.

At those words, Shōzō stole a quick glance at Yurie.

Shigeru felt a twinge of envy for a man who could show dread before his own wife. What nerve! He's not shy about it either. Was it a sense of responsibility that held me back when she followed me around? He mulled this over. He now regretted his reluctance but found it rather amusing that the spark was no longer there to arouse him.

When Shōzō displayed that look of fear in front of other people, Yurie felt embarrassed, but then his face would swiftly take on the presumptuousness of a stone monkey. That also irritated her.

Fukiko found the whole thing absurd. Why did these self-absorbed artist types exaggerate so much? Shōzō began to doze off. It was past two in the morning before the couples withdrew to their rooms.

Awakened by a noise at daybreak, Shōzō shook Yurie. She was shivering in the early morning chill. His usual complaint that she had pilfered all the blankets during the night never came. Instead of pulling them back, he was straining to hear something. The sound went on for a while, and then everything became quiet again. After a while they heard Fukiko's muffled voice.

"Something's wrong with Shigeru-san. Where's the phone?"

She was squatting in the corridor, panting heavily in a night-gown that exposed the pale whiteness of her shin.

Shigeru was dead by the time a doctor rushed to the house. A short while later the ambulance they had requested arrived, but there was nothing the paramedics could do but return to the hospital.

Her mind in a daze, Fukiko said not a word.

"It seems he had a weak heart," said the doctor.

She simply shook her head as if she had lost her voice. From what they could gather, he had already lost consciousness by the time she sensed something was wrong and tried to wake him. Yurie wondered about the ensuing silence after the initial noise.

The man who had chatted with them over *saké* several hours earlier was now lying dead, as quiet as a poisoned horse. Why had he ever come to this house?

Fukiko's face looked like the pale *yūgao* "evening face" blossom, which closes its petals when touched by the light of the early dawn.

"He'd just returned from abroad," explained Shōzō on her behalf. "We didn't know anything about his heart condition." She was obviously too traumatized to speak to anyone.

"He had a very busy schedule upon his return and was feeling relaxed for the first time on this vacation. But this had to happen," added Yurie. "Isn't that right, Fukiko?" Again there was no response.

Shigeru had eaten a steak the night before, complaining of the poor quality of the meat, Shōzō explained to the doctor. "He may also have drunk a little too much. He was a bit excited but there was nothing to indicate anything was wrong. All four of us continued our conversation after we returned from dinner at a hotel." Again, the two main things about Shigeru last night were that he was excited and talkative.

The doctor, while listening intently to what Shōzō had to say, scarcely glanced at Fukiko.

"You must be shocked," he said quietly. "So sudden. Life is often unfathomable. He had waited to die until his return to Japan and his wife. He was very fortunate. I can see no signs that he suffered."

In other words, the old doctor was probably trying to say that Shigeru had died a peaceful death. He looked only at Shōzō and continued. "In a nation known the world over for longevity, some say living too long is a curse. I hope I'll be lucky enough to die as he did."

Remembering something, the doctor cocked his head and said that he had been in this house. He then glanced from Fukiko to Yurie and said,

"That little girl, is she here?"

He quickly surveyed the room. He had mistaken the dead man for Seiichiro. Told that the deceased was his younger brother, he appeared to remember Fū but mumbled in confusion, "Oh, the younger brother of that beautiful wife?"

"He was born in this house," said Yurie, choosing not to correct him. She did not know how familiar he was with the Suganos, but he did seem to remember the family who had lived here for several years before and after the war.

"Is that right? You're a cousin of that wife."

He gazed at her.

"How's that little girl doing?" he asked about Mizuki again.

This was the first time anyone had referred to Fū or Mizuki since the four arrived at this house. Could it be that Fū had been with them all along?

Yurie expected Fukiko to start crying at the doctor's query, but she seemed to have disappeared. In her place was Fū, smiling. Despite her vacant stare, Fukiko looked just like Fū—tall, sensuous, and unrepentant.

# 18 ～

A HELPLESS IDIOCY SEEMED TO SETTLE OVER Fukiko. Shōzō picked up the phone at once and informed Tōichiro of his father's death. But even if he had left immediately for Myōkō, he would not arrive until the afternoon, Shōzō said to himself. It was out of the question for anyone to head back to Tokyo that day.

It was quickly decided to hold a private wake at the house; Shōzō had not consulted Fukiko when he telephoned Mizuki, who after all was her only niece.

For other urgent calls, the distracted Fukiko took over from Shōzō, lifting the phone from the cradle in slow motion as if picking up a stray thread from the floor. She first began to dial Shigeru's colleagues, then her own relatives. Both of her parents were dead; her sister lived in Tokyo, and her brother in the Kansai region.

The gist of the several brief calls was: I'm not at the Tokyo house. We were just visiting here. We'll have the funeral in Tokyo. She was heard telling her sister that there was no need to come to the Myōkō house, but that she should join her in Tokyo. Her brother was on business in the States but was expected to return in a couple of days. In the meantime, several mourners rushed to the house to extend their condolences. It was not until late that night when the family was able to hold the private wake.

Among the nearest kin at the wake was Shigeru's only living aunt, Yoriko, a sprightly, white-haired elderly lady.

The minute Yurie greeted her at the front door she had said, I tell you, it must be karma that he died at this Myōkō house."

Mizuki and her family were already there. Yoriko scrutinized Leonard and Mary, glancing from Karl back to the children. She then lowered her eyes.

Sitting in a corner of the room with his long legs folded beneath him, Karl flashed a diplomatic smile at her.

"Why don't you sit on a chair?" suggested Yurie. He dragged his stiff legs toward a chair, hands outstretched as though clinging to an invisible pillar for support.

Leonard and Mary approached the coffin with perfect composure and as if on cue began to recite verses from the Bible. Then they rejoined their father, whispering into his ear something about the shape of the coffin.

After a short while, Karl returned to their hotel with the children and Mizuki stayed behind. The two children took their leave with a proper bow and a "Good night" in perfect Japanese.

As soon as they were gone, Yoriko asked Yurie in a stage whisper, "Will the foreign guests be at the funeral in Tokyo?"

"No, I'll be the only one," said Mizuki tersely.

Once callers began to arrive, Fukiko had been a new person, confidently fielding questions with the utmost efficiency.

"Shigeru-san would be pleased if your whole family attended," she declared with her head held high.

"Too bad there won't be any chairs," interjected Yoriko.

"I shall arrange that."

"I'm sure foreigners would find a Japanese funeral an interesting learning experience," said Yoriko disdainfully.

Tōichiro's baby boy was fussing; Akiko gathered up the exhausted infant to put him to bed in a back room. Yurie went with her to help with the bedding.

Besides making a number of calls and checking train schedules for the following day, Tōichiro leafed through Shigeru's address book, pausing at this or that entry to ask his mother. Who are these people? I guess I've got to call his company to find out.

In the meantime Yoriko seemed reluctant to accept the fact that the house belonged to Shōzō and Yurie.

"I shall sleep in the detached room," she insisted, insinuating that she knew every nook and cranny of the house.

"This is the Mamas' house, Aunt Yoriko," Tōichiro reminded her emphatically. "A room has been reserved for you at the same hotel where Mizuki and her family are staying."

She countered the thoughtful offer with a vigorous shake of her white head, protesting at length that she was frightened of hotels and that she had once heard about a young woman who was attacked by a stranger in a hotel room.

"There's nothing to be scared of at the hotel," he said curtly. "It's no Tokyo skyscraper, and you're not a young woman. Your room is right next to Mizuki's family and they can keep you company if you like."

His candid but implacable reasoning still failed to win her over.

There was not enough bedding to go around if she stayed. "We'll take the hotel room," said Shōzō resignedly, and left with Mizuki and Yurie at dawn.

"I'm sorry. I've got such a stubborn aunt," said Mizuki, feeling guilty for what Shōzō and Yurie had to endure. However, they actually welcomed the improvisation that had freed them from the trouble possibly brewing at the Myōkō house.

Yurie was frightened at the strange calm that had overtaken her in the aftermath of Shigeru's sudden death. She had had that same feeling on the day the war ended.

Time is never in stasis; it floats, weaving to and fro.

Fukiko had come out to the foyer to see Shōzō, Yurie, and Mizuki off when she suddenly began to wail and collapsed on the floor, almost hitting her head on a pillar. The three rushed back inside to consult Tōichiro, who in turn told them calmly that he knew what to do, so they shouldn't worry.

"Now that Aunt Yoriko's decided to hold court, we're all in her capable hands," he added matter-of-factly.

So they finally got into the car and made their exit.

A rain shower had come and gone by then, and a lone bird cried out its song once, and then again, to which several birds twittered in antiphony.

When they reached the hotel, they heard a *kakkō* sing in the thick morning mist that coursed down the valley, blanketing everything in its path. The *kakkō* warbled a very different tune from that of the *hototogisu* of Mount Hiei; it sounded almost like an answering echo to its Hiei cousin.

WHILE YURIE HAD BEEN PUTTING UP bedding to make room for the delivery of the coffin and the mourners' arrival, she happened to see a copy of a well-known collection of classical Japanese poetry near Shigeru's pillow. When she casually picked it up, the book fell open to a dog-eared page on which several poems had been circled in pencil:

> While still in this world,
> I would set down this request,
> I beg you, *hototogisu*,
> on the mountain path we take
> to death, please be my guide.

> Envoy

> Oh, *hototogisu*
> you cry and cry,
> yes, I will promise
> to meet you if you *are* waylaid
> on the mountain path we take to death.

The *kakkō*'s song she had just heard resonated with the first stanza; it was probably written by a woman. On the same page another poem was circled:

> How sad and desolate
> it must be, in the evening twilight
> that journey
> taken all alone
> suspended in midair.

As she passed by Shigeru's body, her mind dwelt on the man who had now fallen into an eternal slumber, his soul just setting off on its solitary journey.

"WHAT A GREAT WAY TO DIE," said Shōzō at the wheel, breaking the silence in the hope of lightening things up for the two suddenly mute passengers. "Lucky guy. I agree with that old doctor. I want to go like that, too."

There's neither rhyme nor reason to the way humans react to something that happens so unexpectedly, he reflected. He was taking extra care at the wheel as he drove through the arid expanse of misty fields that seemed suspended in midair, stretching to infinity.

In the dawn light, he saw a faint smile on a stranger's face staring back at him from the rear view mirror.

Mizuki sat absentmindedly in the back seat revisiting memories of some funny incidents from her past. One such scene was stuck in her mind, of a ridiculous date with an old man—certainly he looked very old to a twenty-something—but possibly younger than her uncle who had died around daybreak the day before. So many things had happened at the Myōkō house, and now the profile of the old man reappeared, stuck in the interstices of her mind, as one might say, like an insect wing fluttering in the wind, trapped in a wire mesh.

The old man, who was young at heart, had stirred in Mizuki a desire to explore a world only he knew. It was a chance encounter that prompted him to ask her out, and she felt a tiny spark of interest igniting, but it died quickly at the first sound of strained breathing as he whispered in her ear. She stopped seeing him. The gasping had laid bare a life near its final ebb, signaling a sense of danger that was absent in the men of a younger generation. She was seized by a sudden grip of fear and her imagination ran amok. If she had shared intimacy with him, she could one day have been awakened to find him dead beside her. What would I say to his wife? She feigned indifference to his continued overtures, as is typical of such a young woman, and giggled her way out of awkward moments by changing the subject quickly. The encounter was simply like a flicker of light then, the shadow of a mysterious black bird passing over her briefly.

However, the shadow had taken on a life of its own and tenaciously attached itself to her. If an accident happened, I'd start bawling and call Karl immediately, even before contacting the police or a doctor.

Later on she had half-jokingly mentioned this fear to Karl. He nodded thoughtfully, his face assuming the guise of an all-knowing protector, and said, "Suppose, let's just suppose, if that happened, or whatever happened—you shouldn't even think of doing anything rash when you're alone and confused. I would contact his wife myself." Mizuki burst out laughing.

She had decided at that very moment to marry him, and as chance would have it, he had reached the same conclusion.

While Mizuki was reminiscing, Yurie snuggled up to Shōzō at the wheel, and said sweetly, "When I'm dead, scatter my ashes and bones to the four winds, won't you? No funeral, no grave. Listen to me. Promise me you'll do that?"

She then turned around abruptly and said to Mizuki in the back seat, "You're my witness. Be sure it gets done. Promise?"

"Well, it's illegal in Japan to do what you've just asked," replied Shōzō with a grin. "It has to be somewhere in international waters."

"I often dream about the sea," said Yurie. "In those dreams I'm at that place in Alaska where we went salmon fishing. I don't know exactly where, some hidden island offshore. I see a rocky sea bottom, black-tailed gulls and cormorants swarming everywhere, a sure sign that there are salmon nearby, chasing a school of smaller fish.

"The dream comes to me in the early morning on chilly days. And in the dream I'm saying, Oh, dear, the same dream again. I wonder what that means. Then, I see Chie with a jar full of bones against her chest, leaning way over the side of a boat, dropping the bones one by one into the choppy water.

"The man steering the boat is one of our fishing buddies, but I can't remember his name. From time to time I see him turn around with a big grin on his face.

"In my dream Japan lies beyond Alaska, beyond the ocean. A

stranded blue glass ball, not a crack or scratch on it, caught in a tangled mass of black seaweed on a rocky beach, is swaying in the breeze. One of those glass balls Japanese fishermen used as buoys for their nets in the old days."

Yurie was about to say, You remember that, don't you? when she noticed the intent look on Shōzō's face in the soft dawn light, as if he were watching his fishing line in the water. She could almost hear the lap, lap, lapping of the waves caressing the seashore.

The car sped through a mountain pass with the gleaming Sea of Japan visible just beyond.

"By the way, Mizuki, the doctor who attended Shigeru had apparently taken care of you when you were little," said Shōzō, quickly changing the subject.

Mizuki's mind worked furiously, but failed to remember the faces of the people in the mountain valley, people she must have met as a toddler. The only memories she had from those days were of someone on top of a mountain, pointing out the glimmer of the ocean, of herself standing on a hill covered with lotus flowers as far as the eye could see—well, maybe it was just a rice field—and later making a wreath out of the blossoms.

Something else: a vague memory of her parents arguing over whether one could hear the rumbling of the sea in the distance. That rumbling was probably the sound she had continued to hear throughout her long stay abroad.

Shigeru had returned to his birthplace to die. She could not help thinking that his death, which came without the slightest warning, had been preordained.

This "road we all must take"—wasn't that what he was meditating about when he hid himself in that foreign monastery? she said to herself.

Remembering Yurie's story about Mizuki's dying mother who had recited one of Ariwara no Narihira's poems from the final chapter of *Tales of Ise*, she had re-read the verses just before leaving for Myōkō at the news of his sudden death. She mumbled the line, "A man, sick and dying." Yurie nodded, reciting the rest of the poem silently to herself.

I've always heard
this is the road we all must travel at last
But I've never dreamed
it would come so soon.

"Speaking of the poem, I found this book in the room where Shigeru and Fukiko were sleeping," she said. "I'd seen the same edition before, so I quickly leafed through it and read some of the poems that were marked—Saigyō's collection of poetry, *Sankashū*. You may want to take a look at them later. I'm sure that either Fū or Seiichiro marked them.

"Last night Shigeru chatted with us into the wee hours of the morning. I don't think he would have had the time to read every page even if he had noticed the book. Yet the book was right next to his pillow; you can't discount the possibility that either Shigeru or Fukiko picked it up. It'd be nice to find out from her if he actually read the poems before going to bed. I don't think people are that different from each other—I mean—don't they think and act in similar ways under similar circumstances? He might have done the same thing I did on impulse: pick it up and leaf through it."

"Which poems are they?"

"Well, take a look at the book when you have time. There's something about it, well … something almost nostalgic. A short while ago I heard a *kakkō* cry, not a *hototogisu*. The two marked poems are all about the *hototogisu*. The first was sent by a woman and the second was a man's response. You might call them love poems … "

Yurie repeated a line in her head:

While still in this world,
I would set down this request,
I beg you, *hototogisu*.
on the mountain path we take
to death, please be my guide.

Her mind was now going over the conversations of the previous day in the early morning hours. Someday she would probably find the occasion to tell Mizuki what they had talked about.

"Well, I think … Shigeru decided he had to see you," she said hesitantly. "And something told you to look over those classic poems your mother and mine used to recite … Eventually all the things we're saying to ourselves will be forgotten. But then one day out of the blue, we will remember them all over again. The same was true for Narihira and Saigyō, and all those women who tried to respond to them in poetry exchanges. Compelled by some mysterious inner force, they repeated what their predecessors had muttered to themselves—just the way someone had probably been compelled to mark the poems in the book. These poems belonged to no one in particular, but they are recited by everyone. Otherwise, why should they have such an impact on us now?

"But, we didn't talk about anything as sentimental as that last night. No mention of Fū, either, except we didn't refrain from talking about Yoriko. I've always thought of her as something of a dinosaur. Was I ever surprised when she actually showed up! She insists on putting in her two cents worth about everything, but there's no need for you to take her seriously, Mizuki. Mom often said she was the 'queen' of the last word."

"It's a wonder that Fukiko had decided to come to this house at all," said Mizuki, avoiding the topic of her aunt. "That's probably what you would call a premonition. They say a creature in the wild hides away when it is approaching death. Nowadays we hear stories of senile people walking out of their homes on the spur of the moment, and their bodies are found later in the mountains. I think it is instinct. They know their end is near. That's the most natural, the most proper way to die, they would say. I don't think they're senile at all."

"There's nothing for anyone to fuss about," agreed Yurie. "Just accept death as a beautiful finale. At the end of his life Shigeru was showing signs of growing reclusive. He was also talking about buying the Myōkō house. You know, Mizuki, maybe it is only at the moment you feel you're dying that you realize you're really alive. So if you ever find yourself wanting to hide and disappear, that's when you really begin to live. That's the moment you are freed from your obsessions; you are totally unencumbered—there's no beginning and no end. The barrier between life and death seems to break down and vanish.

"Have you reached the turning point in your life, Mizuki, where you can see both ends of the journey a little more clearly—the road you've taken so far and the road beyond that's been hidden from you? Or else, I wonder if you may just want to remain where you are for a while longer? You might not want to let go just for the sake of seeing what lies beyond. There's always the temptation, as they say, to leave the road and taste the pure water in the valley below."

"When I met Shigeru in Kyoto, his face was a puffy, yellowish blue just like my father's on his deathbed. That really concerned me," said Mizuki.

When she said "my father," she knew with certainty where she stood in relation to Shigeru. If he had scooped up the pure mountain water, the thick vapor now enveloping the valley might well be his soul.

She felt the presence of something elusive that had slipped through her grasp in the mist—a man who had died avoiding a meaningful dialogue, as her eyes followed the racing mist.

She had missed the chance to say what was on her mind. When she had finally sat face to face with him, she felt the overbearing presence of Fū that wedged itself between them. She found herself looking away.

At his suggestion, Mizuki and her family had already started a cross-country trip with the money he had given her in Kyoto. They had been planning a more extended tour during the children's summer vacation when news came of his sudden death.

Mizuki felt no regrets for the fact that the children had seen his face in death. Aunt Yoriko can be as sarcastic as she wants, I don't care, Mizuki said silently, shrugging her shoulders.

"I saw the face of a dead person for the first time," Leonard had told her. She found herself in agreement with Yurie's sentiment about people not ever dying—no—when they're dying, they finally know they're alive.

Why didn't I tell Shigeru what Fū had said to me? Mizuki willfully summoned up the vivid memory of that defiant voice, "Papa's like that, so Mama's decided to keep it that way for your sake." That was just before Mizuki left for the States. What was she driving at?

Fū's words were almost on the tip of her tongue when she debated whether to tell Shigeru. But in the end she was unable to bring herself to repeat them.

"Your uncle also likes it that way. It was better that way for you, too, so I did it for everyone," Fū had also said.

What did she mean by, "I decided to keep it that way, so I did it …"? Her eyes had been gleaming with malice when she spoke. How would Shigeru have interpreted that? She had used Mizuki's departure to the States as a pretext to egg Seiichiro on to wheedle more money out of his younger brother. A violent altercation had then erupted between mother and daughter. Mizuki had said to herself, I will never come back to Japan.

"I was always the one to humor everyone around me," Fū had said. "I've done everything I possibly could for everyone's sake. Listen carefully. I know you're saying to yourself that you'll never come back to Japan."

She had spoken with an I-know-what-you're-thinking tone of voice—like a *yamamba* mountain witch, who knew how to turn things against her victims, ready to devour them.

"Do whatever you damn well please. Who cares? Do exactly what you want. I've done what I damn well please, so you do the same. But remember, when you think you're doing what you want to do, you're only doing what you've been told to do. That's all. You say you've got your own ideas? Nothing like that exists in this world.

"But don't forget this. A man never likes a woman who can be twisted around his little finger. The kind of woman a man dislikes the most is the type who believes everything a man says, who is easily duped. A man mouths off the most plausible stories because he's been told to. What's so attractive about a woman who hangs on every word a man spews out and accepts things a man has been told to say? If a woman is so easily misled, the man might as well deceive her to his heart's content. I can't help siding with the man on that score.

"It works the other way around, too," she had said scornfully, the anger in her voice rising in pitch yet still subdued, enkindling a fresh flame of malice in her eyes. "The kind of men women dislike the most are the ones who are easily duped by women. If you think your papa and uncle are being duped, you can hate those poor darlings all you want," she grinned, adding, "They are not deceived. They're having fun. Let them. They lie big time. And we lie about the small stuff."

By using the word "we," Fū had declared that the middle schooler Mizuki was her equal. At the same time she seemed to be praising those men and not cursing them.

Why didn't I tell that to Shigeru? It might have been Fū's final testament.

Why didn't I? Because I knew somehow he had known it all along—that's why, she thought.

# 19 ∿

YURIE RETURNED TO TOKYO STILL IN A DAZE from what had happened over the last few days. It was as if she had finally made it back home from a very long journey that had taken her to the ends of the universe, a voyage she had embarked upon long before she was born. Suddenly she felt that she was Yoriko at the Myōkō house. Shigeru's mother, whom she had never met, appeared and she became her as well. She was now Fū, then Fukiko. In rapid succession she also became Shigeru, Shōzō, Seiichiro, Tōichiro, and his bawling infant son.

Shigeru had died at Myōkō, but death could have befallen any of us, including myself, reflected Yurie. Is it even true that he died? No, not really. I'm convinced that he had been living where I could neither go nor see—so why should anything change at all?

The lives of those people around her were dictated by some higher power, each living and dying in accordance with the goals assigned them. If that was true, the same power was at work within her as the world continued to revolve and stay its course. The very fact she existed meant that she had been an infinitesimal part of an amorphous, entangled mass of countless lives and deaths. She was not at all cut off from those who had left the world, or those who would outlive her. That was how she felt after all that had transpired.

It is the same thing, one might say, as a plant yields itself to the direction of the sun, or your footsteps fall unbidden, or your eyelids grow heavy at night as you fall asleep.

She was taken aback by Shōzō's calm demeanor and the lack of tension in his face during the train ride back to Tokyo. Since then, there had been no obvious signs of boredom or discontent to disturb the leisure of his early retirement. Sorting out various papers, he would admire a page or two he had picked out from a stack and mutter to himself as he consulted a reference work,"That's what it says, but I wonder if it's true."

The image of Shōzō as a white-collar worker toiling away for over thirty years seemed as unreal to Yurie as the faraway Himalayas. When such a life had been their only reality, they more or less accepted it as it was, yet they knew it had been a life devoid of wonderment.

The image of the faraway mountain range came back to her, and this time it metamorphosed into an incomprehensible speck of life: an insect foraging for food, or bubbles under a microscope effervescing in the pale green sap of a cross section of a plant stalk.

Some arboreal species are said to live thousands of years. The core of such ancients is often hollow but the outer sheaths are teeming with life. Countless leaves have fallen only to become fertile soil, repeating the process year after year. Some trees remain standing even after all their branches are shorn off by gusts of wind or incinerated by lightning.

When was it that Shōzō started complaining of dizziness, palpitations, and numbness in his legs? Wasn't it around the time she began to publish her work? That must have been like a nail hammered into his heart.

Eventually his complaint seemed to taper off. It was entirely possible that he began to see that the nail was being hammered not into his heart, but into whatever he was trying to make Yurie do. A man who wants his woman to hate the same thing he does knows how to take precautions when the tables are turned.

Men usually do not join women in badmouthing mothers; nor do they avert their eyes from an attractive woman. A man never thinks twice about staring at the type of woman other women loathe. A different frame of mind is at work here; a man gets caught up with things that a woman finds pathetic.

If that is true, there is nothing out of the ordinary about some women being obsessed with things men consider preposterous or ogling the type of men most men sneer at. Yurie often observed such scenes as if they were the sap oozing out of a tree. In short, I've got to spit out what's in my head; I'm a weird bug. Study this bug all you want and if you don't like what you see, just toss it. Do whatever you want with it. Yurie felt much better once her mind was made up.

Accustomed to hearing the music of the tales she had spun, Shōzō became dispirited once the tunes stopped.

It seemed that he wanted to make his dreams hers by letting her spin tales that he wanted to hear. He would bang on the instrument complaining about the quality of the sound or re-string it to make sure it played a tune to his liking.

Nowadays, however, he often lost his temper like a nagging housekeeper when Yurie spilled things at the table or failed to appreciate what he had served. How was it possible that he had so quickly adopted the air of a supervisor riding roughshod over her? Suddenly she understood the fear and grief of a husband who could only confirm his sense of self through the domineering, relentless presence of his wife.

A triumphant look on his face said, That serves you right. Now you know the pain men go through, men who say what they damn well please in front of their wives and children. All the aches and pains that he had only occasionally complained about migrated swiftly from one spot to another in his body, and they in turn appeared to have taken up residence in Yurie's body.

Since he had quit his job, he looked as calm and contented as a flatfish lying in the muck on the ocean floor on a balmy spring day. She felt angry and sad at the same time.

ONCE AT HOME, FATIGUE HAD CAUGHT UP with her, tripping her on the steps inside the front door. Since childhood she had the habit of bumping into things and people on the street; that she repeated this bumbling about even in her own home baffled Shōzō. But then again, that might have been precisely what had kept him at her side.

"When I was very small, I used to go out to gather *tsukushi* horsetail plants on the river bank," said Yurie, half-crying and half-laughing as she clutched the pillar in the foyer. "Although no one was around, I still expected someone to lend me a hand climbing the steep bank. I squatted down with my face buried in a dandelion field, my arms outstretched, crying for a long time. I began to believe the sound of my own sobbing was a song someone was serenading me with—"

I must have dreamed that someone would be waiting there for me with open arms, she thought ruefully. Or, did I believe at that moment that my arms had become wings, and if I flapped them hard enough I would be able to take to the air? I still dream a lot about flying.

Birds are perfect navigators. When they take off, they seem to know exactly where they are headed. They must also know the right wind direction and cloud formations for their long journey.

As Yurie walked down the hallway, she suddenly had a flashback about a flock of birds that would congregate at exactly the same time every morning to fish at exactly the same spot. She had seen them just before Chie's birth in a house nestled in the woods by a lake in Stockholm, and again much later after Chie was born, in a lakeside house in a wooded suburb of Seattle. And this morning she had absentmindedly watched birds hop from branch to branch in a *deutzia* bush at the Myōkō house.

I may not be able to fly or have a sense of direction like a bird, she said to herself, but surely I must own something authentically human that would substitute for all that. She had definitely recovered her self-confidence.

Her own cocksure self once again, Yurie stood up and walked straight toward the dining table with the precision of a bird in flight and began to thumb through the mail. And then a memory of what Fukiko had said on the train to Myōkō flashed through her mind; a mother has a fairly good idea of what her daughter keeps in each of the kitchen cabinets.

Chie had piled up on the dining table all the mail she had collected during Yurie's absence. The bulk of it was printed material that she would have to slog through, its sheer mass a reminder of the long restless hours of reading that loomed before her.

Checking for things that might need her immediate attention, she quickly flipped through the pile, and was about to open a letter posted from abroad, the only one that had a handwritten address. She stopped short. The almost illegible addressees were Yurie and Shōzō Mama, and the addresser was a Coleridge, not Lynn Ann or Henry, but Annabelle.

Lynn Ann had written only once since they went their separate ways in Kyoto. Their relationship did not have the intimacy of friends who exchange letters on a regular basis. Their long silence did not alarm her, considering the fact that the pair had come to Kyoto to barge in on their idyllic country life with hardly an advance notice.

Mystified by Annabelle's name on the envelope, she quickly opened it. The content of the letter was also handwritten. She made out the word "deceased …" Startled, Yurie read the rest.

> …
>
> I found your address in a notebook that belonged to one of the deceased. I'm sorry it has taken me this long to inform you that Henry and Lynn Ann Coleridge died in an automobile accident on the twenty-ninth of last month.
>
> You may know this already, but my father Henry suffered from cirrhosis, yet it did not seem to deter him from enjoying life to the fullest. He was indeed fortunate in his later years to have Lynn Ann as a companion and they had a good life together.
>
> She had evidently overcorrected for a winding stretch of the road along a lake near the Columbia River and the car drove over a cliff. They died instantly.
>
> After they had returned from Japan I spent a night with them in April, listening to their stories about you. That was the last time I saw them alive.
>
> I meant to start off my letter telling you that I re-

member you very well. We met on Yolka Island and played ping-pong together in our backyard. You left a book, a children's story, on a tree stump and I took the liberty of keeping it without telling you.

I really liked the story about an Eskimo woman with lots of illustrations in it. Some of them show men hunting in the snow fields, building igloos while on the hunt, and women giving birth; some pictures showed girls wearing clothes made out of leather which their mothers stretched, dried, and chewed until soft. The girls play with leather dolls, leather balls, and eventually become mothers themselves. There's a picture of a group of Eskimos blanket-tossing a man.

They build igloos, and tents out of animal hides, and use dried whale intestines for windows and sails for boats.

In this snow country everyone lives wherever they like. The inhabitants enjoy the visit of the occasional stranger and the event calls for dancing and singing to amuse the visitor; but on the whole, contact with people they hardly know makes them uneasy. In fact if someone overstays their welcome, he becomes a monster, a monster so frightening that the host must flee.

The husband of the woman in the story hunts whales, polar bears, seals, and reindeer with a bow and arrow and from time to time supplements his kills with the geese and snow grouse he catches with a net. It's quite easy to catch molting geese like that at the North Pole.

But other women become jealous of the hunter's wife because she's always wearing a lovely coat made from the fine skins of the animals her husband catches. It is said that a truly frightening monster with magical power kills anyone who becomes jealous. The author says that she has never seen this monster yet she knows exactly how to draw it. That makes me an artist, she writes in the preface. How can she draw this monster when she's never seen it flying in the sky, or swimming in the ocean, or running in the snow? She thinks she will actually see it when she dies.

And life goes on. The girl becomes a mother and grows old. One day during a journey she gets off a sled and disappears into the vast expanse of snow. "My grandmother walked into the snow just like that when I was a little girl, and never came back. That was what they did long, long ago." I think those were the last sentences of the story.

Between the pages of the book were some dried flowers—"black lilies" and "shooting stars." You must remember them. Lynn Ann was the author of the book, and the illustrator was an Eskimo painter; I learned later that Lynn Ann had given you the copy.

When I first met her, she wore a shooting star in her hair. (Yurie did remember a peony-red *shōjibakaba* flower in Lynn Ann's hair when she returned from a stroll to the Ikenotani Jizō wayside shrine, on Mount Hiei.) A peony-red shooting star, not a black lily, was just the thing to highlight her glossy light brown hair. A black lily looks like the wings of a black butterfly perched on a dead person's lips. Once in a dream I clutched a black lily to my chest. I was lying in a coffin on a grassy knoll near a beach. Black lilies were in bloom everywhere.

The petals of a shooting star spring out from the center of the flower like rabbit ears, like a shooting star streaking across the sky. I'm sure that's the origin of the name.

I have kept the book you had left behind and the dried flowers inserted in it all these years. And I put them in Lynn Ann's coffin. Please forgive me for not returning them to you.

I am grateful for your kindness to my father Henry and his wife Lynn Ann while they were alive.

Annabelle Coleridge

ANNABELLE HAD NOT EVEN ONCE referred to Lynn Ann as her mother or stepmother. Pushing the letter toward Shōzō, she felt a light going out in her head. She threw herself on the floor, rolling over on her back.

He took his time with the letter, carefully going over it several times. After a while he joined her on the floor, and the two lay side by side staring at the ceiling.

She thought she saw the shadow of a bird dart across the ceiling.

"So, that was a *hototogisu* after all. Remember that night on Mount Hiei when Lynn Ann and Henry came. A bird had flown out of the darkness crying in mid-flight."

The words of a poem in the *Sankashū* came to her again and merged with what Lynn Ann had said under the blossoms of a cherry tree at Gion about scary flower spirits.

> On the branch tips
> of the cherry trees we see in full bloom—
> the *hototogisu*
> he is practicing up his first song
> in this village deep in the mountains.

Separated from its flock, a bird arriving much too early from the mountain of the dead, sang the first song of the year at the top of its lungs, the first of its eight thousand and eight, as it came to take Lynn Ann and Henry away.

"Henry was gazing at the *hototogisu* in the dark," said Yurie. The coincidence moved her profoundly. The cry of a *hototogisu* merged with the death of two people who had traveled a great distance to talk their hearts out.

One by one the people who visited Yurie and Shōzō had flown away. Were they like shooting stars, disappearing into the void of space? No, they were still present as lovely peony-red shooting stars, blooming in the fields of her mind's eye.

She had completely forgotten about the book she had left on the beach at Yolka.

"I know there was a ping-pong table right next to where those two boys were making a coffin," said Shōzō quietly. "A guy held a racket in a hand-shake grip and stood far from the table, never missing the ball. That was Henry, and hitting back at scattered balls was a blonde, Annabelle, who held a racket like a baby spooning her food."

"I just can't believe—" Yurie was thinking out loud.

Lynn Ann had been such a good defensive driver, not someone who would lose control of the car on a steep hill or a winding road. Besides, she was still young, with at least twenty years of life ahead of her. Her beautiful Dietrich legs still set men to fantasizing. There was no way a monster could have jumped out of the Columbia River to snatch their lives away.

Henry's liver was always on her mind. "We live life with a little something extra," she had said. Did she mean that they had already seen the monster?

"It may have been a suicide. No, a double suicide—" Shōzō muttered to himself after re-reading Annabelle's letter once again.

It was time to go to Shigeru's funeral. They quickly changed into mourning clothes. While dressing, Yurie's mind went over again and again what Annabelle had said in the letter. Why do things like this happen one after the other?

The rational side of her brain tried very hard to accept that Lynn Ann, Henry, and Shigeru were dead, mere organic matter now, but she was having a very difficult time of it.

What existed before does not simply disappear. It just turns into something else. What that something is cannot be known, but it exists anyway.

Lynn Ann, who had canoed with her first husband on the Columbia River, had plunged into that same river with her second husband. Shigeru had returned to his birthplace to die. What about us? How are we going to die? However we die, we will probably pass on to our close friends what has been preying on our minds.

SIGHTING AN UNACCOMPANIED MIZUKI—neither Karl nor the children were to be seen—Yoriko, who had behaved like a VIP throughout the funeral ceremony, casually whispered into Yurie's ear: "I dare say a relative with a foreign husband and children would have looked too conspicuous. It would also be such a bother to have to explain things to the rest of the guests."

Yurie stared straight ahead, pretending not to hear. "All the condolence speeches were first-rate. Even a cabinet minister has joined us," Yoriko ran on contentedly.

Yurie hardly ever watched television, so she had no idea what the cabinet minister looked like or to which ministry he belonged. Yoriko's face started to take on a self-satisfied glow of invincibility, and enthralled by every gesture or word spoken by the minister, she was taking mental note of all the fine points of the lavish funeral to take home and share with her country relatives.

Although she was much older than Shigeru, her face was extraordinarily smooth, a sure sign of a long life ahead. Was this overweening creature so omniscient, Yurie wondered, that she could pick out a cabinet minister in any crowd, or declare that it showed good judgment on the part of the niece to refrain from bringing her foreign husband and family to a Japanese funeral? She had dressed herself in black kimono so picture-perfect that you would think she was a model in a funeral advertisement.

There was no indication of any rumor circulating among the mourners about Shigeru's sudden death. Even Yoriko failed to show the slightest curiosity as to how he had died.

Instead the guests were busy searching for familiar faces among the crowd, bowing away and wondering to themselves if they would ever run into a familiar face for a little reunion somewhere after the funeral.

Yurie had never seen Mizuki in a kimono. She found her likeness to Fū striking. The elegant line of her neck and shoulder were especially captivating. The bright lipstick and rouge she wore made her look much younger than her years. She was definitely attracting a lot of male attention.

What Yurie saw among the mourners was the specter of a man who had vanished from the world before they had time to shun him.

One of the messages of condolence that was read to the mourners proclaimed: "He died soaring into the sky." Another testified: "He erected palaces in the sky."

People felt reassured by Shigeru's glorification in death. Some of the bereaved looked anxious and unfocused, but for the rest death meant no immediate loss; instead it foreshadowed something entirely different. One even sensed the air of something ready to spring forth, something secreted away until the perfect moment for its emergence.

The funeral procession crept along, swaying like the blossoms on the Japanese pagoda trees that adorned the valley near Myōkō, and bowing like the shooting stars on the beach at Yolka. And Fukiko's pale face loomed in the mist like a magnolia blossom.

BACK FROM THE FUNERAL, YURIE FOUND CHIE waiting for her. She wore a black skirt, which was part of the mourning outfit that Yurie had bought it for her, and a fully pleated blouse with a peony-red flower pattern on the sleeves. For a moment Yurie thought she had glimpsed shooting stars again.

The fact that she bought Chie the mourning outfit had become significant in her mind as if this coincidence somehow brought about the deaths of so many people. She looked away from the black skirt. Who's next?

"What did you think of the funeral?" asked Chie. The tone of her voice sounded as if she were asking, Did you find the play interesting?

"The sutra chorus was nice," she added.

You would think she was referring to a concert. Yurie had no recollection of ever being enchanted by sutra readings when she was a girl. Instead the chant triggered something akin to panic in a nauseous envelope of incense. For Chie, however, who had been raised abroad, sutras were like the meditation music of some exotic country, a secret door that piqued her curiosity.

"Chie, when I die, scatter my ashes in the ocean. Then I'll turn into bubbles in the sea."

"Well, if you say so," said Chie with a grin. "If it's at all possible, I want you two to die at the same time," she added. "If one of you is left behind, you've got to find a mate real quick. I wouldn't know what to do with a single parent."

"My goodness, very few kids would talk like that, especially if a parent has lots of money."

"Well, you have no financial resources to speak of."

"Without money, I wouldn't find a mate, either."

"Then you two have got to hang in there as long as you can," said Chie somberly. "We're living at a time when there are more parents than children. It's tough on us. You talk constantly about the Pacific War, but those of us who've only heard about it from our parents, who've never experienced a war, can't tough it out the way you did, the way you survived. There's no Darwinian selection process for us. It's scary."

"Indulgent parents often forget to tell their children what they need to be told," said Yurie. "Children, on the other hand, become resentful. Why didn't they tell us beforehand? Did they intentionally hold back, or was it just a momentary forgetfulness? Which was it? Once I started raising questions like that as a young woman, the resentment I had toward my parents finally melted away."

At that moment the image of a struggling parent unable to kill his child loomed in her mind. A parent usually dies first, so even if a child talks shamelessly about patricide, he is easily forgiven.

"We once visited the tombs of the royal family in the Soviet Union. I forget which cathedral it was," continued Yurie casually. "Pointing to the most magnificent tomb of all, the interpreter for the tour group said, 'This resplendent imperial tomb enshrines a crown prince killed by his own father.' I wonder if he had comissioned it to cover up the murder."

Chie stared at her mother. The twinkle in her eyes was now gone.

"Well, whether you choose to be hard-nosed or easygoing about life," said Yurie, gazing at the peony-red shooting stars on Chie's blouse, "I hope you'll live a long one, long enough to catch on to why parents decide it's useless to tell their kids what to do."

"The pair who visited you in Kyoto—are they dead?"

Chie had apparently read the letter from Annabelle that was lying open on the table.

"I have a feeling they died on their own."

"What do you mean, died on their own?"

"A suicide, I mean."

"Why?"

"Because Henry had an incurable disease."

"Hmm, he was traveling in that condition?"

"It appears to have been a suicide—I just have that feeling."

Chie was silent.

"I've just got that feeling."

With that remark, Yurie started shedding her mourning clothes. She was about to grab a bathrobe lying on the floor but changed her mind. Instead she put on a black skirt and a black sweater.

"Mom."

"Hmm?"

"It looks like I'm going to be a mother."

Chie was smiling among the shooting stars.

Mizuki and Karl dropped by with their children. They said that they had travelled all over the Tōhoku region and Hokkaido in their rental car, staying at country bed-and-breakfasts along the way. Karl showed off some of the snapshots they had taken. After a visit with Shōzō's friends in Sapporo, the capital of Hokkaido Prefecture, they toured the famous lakes Akan and Mashūko. Their cross-country trip had resumed right after the funeral and they had just returned a couple of days ago.

Among the snapshots was one of Leonard and Mary playing among the anglers on a sandy beach at the mouth of the Ishikari River in Hokkaido. Yurie peered at the picture. We were there a long time ago, she thought.

Mizuki's family had planned to stay in a hotel upon their arrival in Tokyo, but Fukiko was so lonely that she had begged them to stay with her. They eventually acquiesced to the request. Such an arrangement would have been inconceivable just a month before. Death changes things. That's what it does to us humans, Yurie said to herself.

"Fukiko wouldn't stop talking about my mother. I wonder

what's come over her," said Mizuki ruefully.

"I guess she's finally been freed from her obsession," said Yurie with feeling.

"She also complained that Aunt Yoriko was already telling her what to do for the forty-ninth-day memorial service."

The relationship between Yoriko and Fukiko in the aftermath of Shigeru's death was already undergoing a subtle transformation.

According to Mizuki, Yoriko told Fukiko in no uncertain terms that she would make a special trip to Tokyo to attend the memorial service. She also declared that since there were no decent sweetmeats for memorial services available in Tokyo, they should be ordered from a specialty shop in Kanazawa that Shigeru's mother had patronized. To this, Fukiko simply told her, Please do as you see fit.

"I'm sure Yoriko wouldn't like having us around at the time of the service, so we're thinking of moving to a hotel," said Mizuki.

She also reported on Tōichiro's unexpected discovery. Shigeru had life insurance policies but almost no cash. Why? Tōichiro had protested vociferously. How could they, the perfect couple in everyone's eyes, have been so ill prepared? His every waking moment was now being devoted to raising enough money to pay for the funeral.

"Should I return the two million yen?" Mizuki fretted aloud.

"Don't. If you bring up his pocket money now, it'll just create more trouble," Yurie said impassively.

If he was that broke, she said to herself, he would not have been in a position to buy our Myōkō house. No, a successful architect of his caliber with lots of major projects should have been able to afford it. I guess living from one contract to another was his way of doing things. Was Mizuki trying to show some sympathy for him—and herself—by glossing over the tattered financial affairs of someone who had passed on? We might as well make the place our retirement home, she thought resignedly.

Akiko had also questioned Fukiko sharply. How did my father-in-law spend all his money? How about you, Mother, how did you manage the finances? Don't tell me you have debts that we're not aware of. She even looked as if the taboo subject of Shigeru's womanizing was on the tip of her tongue, which infuriated Fukiko.

"My daughter-in-law even insinuated that I may have stashed away some money." Her complaint continued, increasing in its vehemence. "Taking care of the Tokyo residence was all I could handle. I received only a fixed amount for living expenses. Shigeru was not the type who would hand over everything he had earned for his wife to manage. From day one he was vigilant about protecting his own space, to which I had no claim. Of course, that was in our pre-nuptial agreement. In return, he never interfered with how I spent the money he had given me."

An uneasy balance of compassion and resentment was evident in the way she had spoken, the two warring emotions that she felt for a man who had refused to relate to his wife.

"I think what she really wanted to say was that Shigeru had carefully kept his secrets to himself, and always had a large sum of money at his disposal," said Mizuki, continuing her account of Fukiko's complaint. "Or, did she want to say that Shigeru's secretive behavior was what formed his personality later on?"

Mizuki unwittingly began to refer to her father's younger brother by his first name—not Uncle Shigeru, as Japanese custom would require for a man who could be either her uncle or her father.

Fukiko had also said, with a touch of bitterness that might also have been meant as an apology to Mizuki. "The way my own son feels about me now, I should have demanded as much cash as I could from Shigeru-san and stashed it away."

"She even told me that she'd give me part of the insurance money," said Mizuki, looking quite concerned. "Of course, I've no intention of accepting it. I'm not a member of his immediate family. I don't even mind returning the two million yen, either. When things are settled, I hope there's at least enough left for her to live on."

"She'll be fine. Her house is prime Tokyo real estate, one third of an acre," said Shōzō, decidedly sympathetic to Mizuki. "Shigeru gave you much less than what it's worth. Besides, she has a son. If she says she wants you to have some of the insurance money, take it."

Shōzō could be counted on to keep quiet about any woman's flaws, speaking out only when he wanted to show her some sympathy. The same could not be said when it came to men. His silence must mean that he was critical of their failings.

Already worried that they wouldn't be able to pay the inheritance tax, Akiko had suggested that the Tokyo house be demolished and a condo built on the lot so the mother-in-law could live off some of the rental income.

This is what you'd call managerial acumen, and this from a woman who had watched with cold detachment her late father-in-law use her toothbrush every morning.

"They say the taxes and costs of upkeep on a house with a good lot in Tokyo are so outrageous that Fukiko could never keep her house without a full-time job," continued Mizuki.

Oh, dear, thought Yurie. She had never given a thought to the financial worries that come with a piece of prime real estate.

"Akiko doesn't know it," resumed Mizuki, "but Fukiko has been consulting Karl since his specialization is in comparative economics and he knows a lot about European as well as Japanese and American tax and inheritance laws. The fact still remains that he can't read and decode documents written in legal Japanese. I know that giving advice is always risky, and she might tell him things he doesn't want to know. And I don't like Tōichiro suspecting anything untoward. So it's not a good idea for us to wear out our welcome." It appeared that she wanted to avoid making waves and hoped to return to the States as soon as possible.

Yurie and Shōzō had to vacate the Hiei house as their lease was soon to expire. That meant they would to have to make one more trip to Kyoto before the end of the month.

"We've been only roughing it in our sleeping bags for half a year at the cottage but we've accumulated so much junk that we've got to go back there and clean up the place. Why not stay here at the condo while we're gone?" suggested Yurie.

Mizuki and Karl exchanged a glance that said, What do you think?

Why do people set off on a journey? Why do they want to change abodes? Isn't it because they want to wash away some of the accumulated grime of the years and take a really good look at their true selves? They believe that there is something different out there, something they haven't recognized in themselves before. That discovery will catch them by surprise in their encounters with new people and mysterious surroundings.

Life's peregrination for Yurie and Shōzō, Mizuki and Karl, Lynn Ann and Henry, and Shigeru was like running into old friends. Or, it was like finding favorite garments they had discarded long ago, which they would carefully try on in the hopes of resurrecting what the clothing had once meant to them.

Their world would slowly merge with the strangers' inside the dark enclosures of their favorite garments as one continuous, indistinguisable expanse. What is it that has been resurrected in the pale light of this murkiness?

Chie took out her old Scrabble board for Mary and Leonard. The children were immediately caught up in the game.

"Yuri, do you have an English dictionary?" asked Mizuki. "Use it so that you won't make spelling mistakes," she said to the children, handing them the dictionary.

"A parent can be so arbitrary. Sometimes I say, Learn Japanese. Other times, Don't forget your English. That's tough on the kids. Their Japanese has improved dramatically after a year at school and by now it's probably better than mine. But, as a parent, I worry that they might forget their English, so I've given them books in English to read during our cross-country trip. We'll be heading back to the States at the end of August."

Mary knew exactly how to use the Webster's College Dictionary. "Well done. What grade are you in?" asked Shōzō. "I'll be in the fourth grade in September back in the States," she replied proudly. To demonstrate her competence, she quickly found a word with a strange Latin root, one that neither Shōzō nor Yurie had ever heard of, to fit in the space on the board. She went on to explain the word's meaning to Leonard. The look of parental pride on Karl's face seemed to proclaim, Look at my girl, she's a genius.

"Fukiko suggested, 'Why not leave the kids here in a school,'" said Karl. "But we've decided against it. I don't think it's a good idea to leave them behind."

His Japanese had improved a great deal since the last time Yurie and Shōzō had spoken with him. It was still a bit stiff but polite.

"You know, Yuri, I think it's my children, not me, who'll take up the translation of your work," said Mizuki softly in a rather dreamy voice. "So, I'll bring them up to speak English."

When it came to translating her work, Yurie felt rather detached from the whole matter. She wrote in her native language and the process of translating what she had written into another language was somebody else's job. Just as different players perform the same piece of music differently, so a translator would bring out something the author had not even been aware of. A translation should be done by someone who really wants to do it; it's not something with which the author should get involved.

"Mary may be a poet. I think she gets it from her mother," said Mizuki with pride. "But maybe it takes more than genes to produce a good poet. They say the Wolf Boy couldn't learn the human language when he returned from the wild."

The conversation then shifted to the story of a boy in India who was brought up by wolves, then to the tale of a young male descendant of feuding European royalty who had been raised in the family cellar.

Once the talk at the table veered to such complicated subjects, Karl's Japanese was not up to par, and inevitably the four switched to English. However, Shōzō and Yurie's English was shaky at best, and while Karl and Mizuki carried on in English, the foursome mixed both languages—with Mizuki interpreting from time to time.

The discussion boiled down to the fact that neither the Wolf Boy nor the Cellar Prince had been able to free himself from his childhood trauma, and when they returned to their respective societies, they failed to appreciate the culture.

"I think translating Japanese into English means that one has to develop a good grasp of what's behind the culture, feeling it from within," said Mizuki. "The translator must feel with his own skin what the native reader feels resonating in the words. Correlating what lay beneath two entirely different languages is as tough as what the Wolf Boy experienced. If wolves had a language of their own, I wonder if they could ever convey the deeper meanings of their language to humans? I think it's a daunting task to master two languages equally well. Besides, speaking the wolf language would be far more difficult than hearing it.

"I've decided to bring up my children in an English-speaking world. Once they grow up, I'll be able to do things together with my children in the same language. That will give me a chance to see a different Japan from abroad. I'll also find myself figuring out what's behind the appearances of reality in the States and in his country," she said, jerking her head toward Karl. "When I'm on this side of the Pacific Ocean, I catch a glimpse of something very different about the States, things I don't notice when I live there."

Something like that is also taking place in me, Yurie reflected, trying to visualize the state of her own moss-covered cellar. She was having a mental struggle with how to explain the invisible moss.

"I hear Chie's going to have a baby. You must be overjoyed," said Mizuki, changing the subject.

"Thank you," Yurie replied in confusion, bowing self-consciously, as if someone were forcing her to do it.

"How does a man feel about a baby, which is, after all, part of him?" asked Mizuki, turning to Shōzō to sound out what had possibly gone on in the minds of Seiichiro and Shigeru at the time of her birth.

"Well, how can I put it?" he said slowly. "I should say it signals a kind of closure for a man as a living creature. Or, perhaps he feels compelled to set out on a different course of action. Watching your kid grow is a bit like you're being mocked by a part of you that had walked away, which is in turn confronted by your own self."

"I shouldn't have refused her so I could experience what you've just described," Karl said in Japanese, casting an envious look at Shōzō. He now regretted turning down the offer to father a child with his former girl friend whose husband had gotten a vasectomy.

"On second thought, it really makes no difference because a man doesn't give birth," resumed Shōzō. "He'll never identify with the baby the way a woman does. Even if he's told it's his—a newborn as pretty as a young rosebud—it seems to have no relevance for him, except that it has something to do with a long-forgotten thought and action that is simply to be admired. It should be the same for you, Karl."

"Just imagine that you created Leonard and Mary in a dream," said Mizuki, turning to Karl. "That's much more humane. I've been hounded by the image of a woman whose hair is flying helter-skelter, bound hand and foot by the excessive attachment to her child, the father, and herself. So I've opted to assimilate my imagination into my own flesh. You know, Karl, I'm glad that you're my equal when it comes to raising our children. Women have the average man over a barrel when it comes to that. What I'm trying to say is that if there is a battle to be fought between men and women, let it be over masculine and feminine imaginations."

While listening to her, Yurie thought it strange that children, who live by instinct rather than intellect, yearn for their mother's wings even long after they are needed, and yet at the same time do everything in their power to reject them. Mizuki had fantasized time and again that she could still seek shelter in those smothering wings that she had willingly severed. Although physically capable of it, she refused to conceive a child and instead tried to convince herself that she had given birth when she had not. What bizarre, complicated creatures human beings are. Yurie was impressed by Mizuki's imaginative act, which she had called "humane."

"Speaking of dreams—" said Shōzō with a sly smile. "I had a really weird one for the first time in ages."

"So did I on the same night," said Yurie with a suggestive smile.

Provoked by their exchange of smiles, Karl leaned toward Shōzō and said in Japanese, "Sounds interesting. *Is it?*"

"Two women appeared from nowhere," continued Shōzō.

"My, my, quite a situation," said Karl, laughing heartily.

"But it was pathetic. One of them walked away with a contemptuous look that said, You won't do."

"The other one?"

"She took pity on me. Poor thing, she seemed to say. It was a bit like getting a handout. As usual, I woke up at that point and it was all over. Ahaha," Shōzō chuckled to himself.

"How about you, Yuri?" asked Karl with a snicker.

"Stranger than that, but similar."

"How so?" Mizuki urged her on, rolling her eyes.

"Also women. Two of them. I said to myself, That won't be fun. Then I woke up. They had huge late-Renoir hips."

"Uh-huh, that's what they call the disease of civilization," said Karl, his demeanor suddenly becoming very serious. "I once read an article by a biologist who wrote that homosexuality also exists in some animal species. According to him, the kind of people one sex finds attractive won't get a second glance from the opposite sex, and that's how homosexuality happens."

In the meantime Yurie's mind was going over the letter she had received from Fumiko Yamashiro the day before. Yurie had written to her that a copy of *A Study of Yin-Zhou Dynasty Bronzes* had been purchased. But since so much time had elapsed between Fumiko's first letter and the arrival of the book, she might have already placed an order herself, and if that was the case Yurie would like to keep the book. In response, Fumiko wrote back saying that if it was not too much of a bother, please keep it. She also wrote with a whiff of disapproval that Yōko Fuha, who had decided to accompany her to the States from Paris, was still hanging around her house.

… Yōko said she wanted to see America, and I had always meant to return the kindness she and her husband had shown me during my long stay in Paris.

I remember her tastes had struck me as peculiar even back in our college days. Barely a few days after she came to stay with me, she took up with an American woman in her forties who runs a small bookshop that specializes in literature. Now she says she's going to be her partner and wants to try to make a living in this country. If things are getting too much for me, she says she'll move in with her lover. That's what the lover wants, too. So, she's hardly home nowadays. What shall I do? What should I tell her husband in Paris?

When I tried to reason with her, she told me in total seriousness that I should marry him. She guarantees his goodness and honesty as a citizen and a husband. What upsets me the most is that she is prepared to put this proposal to him in writing. She said to me, "I'm sick and tired of those inattentive men who ignore you. I just can't think of any other word but insensitive to describe them. Well, I'm sure the feeling is mutual and some may think I'm insensitive, so I don't mean to blame only men. Well, I'm not getting any younger and since I don't have much time left, I at least want to live with someone who's on the same wavelength as me. You've been observing men much more objectively than I have for more than half a century. You might be able to draw them out whereas I've never had the knack for it. He (she meant her husband) seems to respect you, and I should say he's fairly understanding. I know it will work." And that is how Ms. Fuha's bizarre argument goes.

What should I do? I don't know whether to laugh or cry. Now that her children are all grown up, there's not much for her to do. I'm sure that's why her mind is churning out these funny ideas …

Yurie's memory called up the image of the nunnish Fumiko in their college dorm. Why not try out one of your fantasies, Yurie said to herself, wishing she could egg her into action.

"I've just read a letter from one of my classmates, who, I think, is something of a lesbian," Yurie broke in. "Probably that's why I had a dream about two women. I don't know where Shōzō's dream came from, but in mine I felt like a man being trampled by a cow."

She then began to talk about Fumiko, Lynn Ann, and Henry,

because it was their chance meeting in Shanghai that had prompted the couple to visit Kyoto.

"Henry had cirrhosis and didn't have much time to live. I think Lynn Ann decided she'd die with him," she said sadly.

Going over the story of their fatal accident overwhelmed her; tears suddenly gushed out. The recent deaths of three people and everything that had ever happened to her seemed to have abruptly joined forces in her mind like water bursting through a dam.

Neither Mizuki nor Karl had heard about the accident.

"They're dead, gone. Lynn Ann drove the car into the Columbia River and they died. That was where she and her first husband went canoeing together. Henry's daughter Annabelle wrote me. There's no mention of suicide, but Lynn Ann was tough—she'd done all the driving across thousands of miles of North and South America. And she had such extraordinary reflexes. There's no way she could have hit the accelerator by mistake."

Her voice broke under a surge of emotion. The decision to step on the gas wouldn't have occurred to her until the last minute, thought Yurie. Nor did it occur to Henry because, although he may not have been a churchgoer, he seemed to hold the Judeo-Christian belief that even though his disease was incurable, he'd wait until God took him.

This was probably what Henry had said to her: "What beautiful scenery! Too bad you're driving and can't see it."

"No, I can see it perfectly, Henry. It's really lovely." The hazel-eyed Lynn Ann must have replied with a warm smile.

Rock steady at the steering wheel, she then stepped on the gas with one of her beautiful Dietrich legs.

Yurie did not know how Chinese felt about death but was certain that they did not share the Western view. Death could happen, Lynn Ann would say in her dignified voice, whether aided by a tornado, flood, or volcanic eruption. Someone may even want to jump into a river, thought Yurie. In her mind's eye she saw Lynn Ann nodding in agreement.

"No matter how you die, it's a kind of natural death—just like being born into this world," said Shōzō quietly, almost to himself.

"You're going to kill me one of these days. That would also be a natural death, wouldn't it?" said Yurie, sobbing.

She had a premonition that what just slipped out of her mouth would actually come to pass, and it was imperative that Mizuki and Karl take her seriously. She shouted through the convulsive sobs that were racking her: "That's right. If I'm to die, murder is the best way to go."

She then realized that such an outburst following on the heels of her romantic rendition of the accident might give them the idea that Yurie and Shōzō would follow suit in the near future in a double suicide. Her sobbing gradually dissolved into hysterical laughter.

Karl extracted a handkerchief from his pocket but quickly withdrew it, noticing that it had already been used, and handed her tissue paper instead.

Shōzō rose, darting quick, sidelong glances at the overwrought Yurie, and began to water the plants. He did this whenever he wanted to dodge a nettlesome situation.

"My goodness. Those people we had met at Hiei—" said Mizuki thoughtfully. She was so used to Yurie's hysterics by now that she had no trouble maintaining composure while reminiscing about her visit with Lynn Ann and Henry. I also met Shigeru in Kyoto, she said to herself, but I couldn't shed tears like that, even for a man who might have been my father. What's the meaning of all the tears welling up in Yurie's eyes? Does death mean that all these people had been alive? Her eyes blurred as she looked out the window at the sky.

Karl kept vigil for whatever might be stirring beneath Mizuki's calm exterior. His penetrating gaze shifted to the other two and then to all three, allotting equal time and scrutiny to each. Worn out from dealing with two languages, English and Japanese, during the whole conversation, he said to himself, Well, English isn't my native tongue, either. He felt irritated yet also overwhelmed by an indescribable yearning for German, yet when he opened his mouth to speak, his voice sounded casual.

"I hear the suicide rate among people forty and above is very high. Shōzō hasn't killed himself yet because Yurie's here. However, statistically speaking, it is a well-known fact that a woman's life span is longer than a man's."

"What you really want to say is that I owe it to Shōzō that I haven't committed suicide," said Yurie, her manner turning frosty. "No matter. To keep each other alive means that one of us is being killed, and that's not a particularly unfortunate thing, either. By the way, wasn't your dissertation about the inability of computers to predict the fluctuation of the stock market?"

"Right, right, you're absolutely right," said Karl, grinning serenely. "Mizuki's uncle died beside his wife, and Mizuki's father beside her mother. Let's say that Yurie dies before Shōzō and I collect data for an analysis that says her death was linked to her smoking and overindulgence. No matter what research data I'd put together, what it would boil down to, though, is that computers cannot help me predict my own death. Well, isn't that why you write novels?"

Watering the potted plants that had just begun showing signs of neglect because of his frequent absences, Shōzō thought to himself: Watering alone isn't doing much good anymore. It's time to repot. The wilting plants reminded him of the research on tree seedlings that he had done long ago. I've lived my life totally disconnected from the implications of that research. Now here I am without a clue, stuck in the midst of an impenetrable forest of unpredictable humans.

Finished with the plants, Shōzō felt sorry for Karl, the innocent victim who was having difficulty handling Yurie and was getting doused with a splash of cold water intended for him. He slowly returned to the table.

"That is how she picks on me, out of the blue and for no good reason either. I want you to keep an eye on who gets killed first, me or Yuri, because you'll be outliving us," he said.

As his eyes met Karl's, he added with a laugh, "A male may have to die to let his mate and child survive."

Saying this, he thought to himself that what he had been doing for Yurie over the past forty years—she was once a smart-alecky little kid—seemed rather heroic.

All he wanted was to let her live. She'd die if he wouldn't let her say what was on her mind. He had convinced himself of that. What is it that makes a parent take care of a squalling baby?

How many times, he thought ruefully, have I gotten a full breakfast since I married her? She lived by fantasizing things, spewing them out on paper, and then rewriting them. Because of the endless rounds of sleepless nights, the laughing and crying at the made-up stories that kept sprouting in her head, she was madness incarnate to strangers, but for him a creature to protect, whose sleep came with great difficulty and had to remain uninterrupted since to do otherwise meant death for her. That was why he had risen quietly in the morning for years, taking care not to wake her, reading the newspaper alone and leaving for work after a breakfast of milk and toast, locking the door behind him.

Men who didn't care to do what I did were extremely critical of me, shooting me a dirty look that said, What a pain in the ass, he's making trouble for us with that wife of his, letting her do what she damn well pleases. The simple breakfast of *miso* soup, grilled fish, eggs, and fresh green tea that they surely took for granted every morning was not there for me until I began to take over the cooking myself and when Yurie finally switched to getting up early in the morning to write.

He had a vivid memory of Yurie with tears flowing like rivers down her cheeks before the howling Chie, when she had muttered to herself absentmindedly over and over again. "This baby will be the death of me!"

A bawling newborn has no tears to shed; it's the parents who cry out with tears running down their cheeks. Yurie crumpled up the tissues wet from her tears and began to pitch them into the nearby wastebasket.

Mizuki looked from Yurie to Shōzō, thinking to herself, Sooner or later one of them will be the first to go. After the funeral is over, I wonder what kind of stories the lone survivor will tell, and to whom.

❧

# Glossary

**Ariwara no Narihira (825–880) and** *Tales of Ise* One of the most celebrated Japanese *waka* poets of the Heian period (797–1190), Narihira is said to be the model for the central character in *The Tales of Ise* (903?). *The Tales of Ise* is not organized in the traditional Western narrative form, but is loosely ordered as a collection of poetry in 125 sections in which various scenes introduce the context for the poems.

**Asuka Period (575–599)** An early era of Japanese history known for its significant artistic, social, and political transformations, all of which were heavily influenced by the introduction of Buddhism from Korea.

**Bashō (1644–1694)** The most famous haiku poet of the Edo period (1603–1868), who is well known for masterpiece of prose and haiku.

*bunraku* Also known as *Ningyō jōruri*, it is a form of traditional Japanese puppet theater involving chanters and players of the *shamisen* (a three-stringed musical instrument played with a plectrum). *Bunraku* theater originated in the merchant town of Osaka in the late seventeenth century. Each puppet is manipulated by three puppeteers who have undergone decades of training.

**Emperor Shōmu (701–756)** The 45th Emperor of Japan according to the traditional order of succession. His reign spanned the years 724 through 749. In 741 he established a system of provincial temples (*kokubunji*) in each province, with the famous Tôdaiji Temple housing the Great Buddha image in Nara at its head. He is also known as the first emperor whose consort Kōmyō was not born into the imperial household.

**Ginkakuji (Temple of the Silver Pavilion)** A Zen temple in Kyoto, bequeathed by Ashikaga Yoshimasa (1435–1490) who had initially planned it as a retirement villa with gardens. The temple is famous for its two-storied *Kannon-den* (Kannon Hall) and its innovative dry garden. It is known as the "the Temple of the Silver Pavilion" because of the initial plans to cover its exterior in silver foil.

*hototogisu* The Lesser Cuckoo (*Cuculus poliocephalus*). Native to Japan, the bird is a common motif in classical Japanese poetry, where it is associated with summer and the underworld.

**Jizō** A roadside stone stature of the deity Bodhisattva, seen in modern Japan as a protector of children, travelers and women.

*kabuki* A popular form of Japanese dance-drama from the Edo period (1603-1868), known for its flamboyant style of acting and elaborate costumes.

**Kamo River (Kamogawa)** A river in Kyoto. The pathways along its banks are a popular location for walks by residents and tourists. In summer, restaurants open balconies looking out onto the river.

**Kinkakuji (Temple of the Golden Pavilion)** One of the most celebrated Zen Buddhist temples in Kyoto, founded by the shogun Ashikaga Yoshimitsu (1368–1394).

**Lake Biwa** The largest freshwater lake in Japan, located in Kyoto's neighboring prefecture, Shiga. Because of its proximity to the ancient capital, references to Lake Biwa appear frequently in Japanese literature, particularly in classical poetry and in historical accounts of battles.

**Mount Hiei (Hiei-zan)** A famous mountain to the northeast of Kyoto, bordering between the ancient capitol of Kyoto and Shiga Prefecture. The mountain is historically associated with the Enryakuji Temple located at its top, which was the center of Tendai Buddhism in Japan.

**Myōkō** Once designated as a village, Myōkō City in the Niigata prefecture was created in 2005 with the annexation of two other towns, Myōkōkōgen and Arai. The city's name is derived from a nearby mountain.

**Nanzenji Temple** A Zen Buddhist temple in Kyoto that was established in 1291 as one of the "Five Mountain" (*gozan*) temples patronized by the Ashikaga shoguns.

**Niigata Prefecture** One of forty-seven prefectures of Japan located on the main island of Honshū on the coast of the Sea of Japan (Nihon Kai). Literally meaning "new lagoon," the city of Niigata is also the prefecture's capital. It was the first port on the Sea of Japan to be opened to foreign trade by the gunboat diplomacy of Commodore Matthew Perry, who arrived in Japan in 1852.

**Oda Nobunaga** (1534–1582) The initiator of the unification of Japan in the late sixteenth century, he helped to establish the political preeminence of the samurai, which ended only with the opening of Japan to the West in 1868. Nobunaga devoted his life to military campaigns and by the time of his death had gathered a third of Japan's feudal lords under his control.

*The Record of Ancient Matters* (**Kojiki**) The oldest extant chronicle in Japan, dating from the early 8th century. It is a collection of myths that attempt to explain the origin of the islands of Japan. Consisting of various songs, poems, and historical records, the *Kojiki* is commonly divided into three parts: the preface describing a creation myth and an age of the gods; the story of the first Emperor, Jimmu who descended from Heaven to rule over Japan; and a reign-by-reign record of mortal emperors who succeeded him.

**Saigyō Hōshi (1118–1190)** A famous Japanese Buddhist priest-poet of the late Heian and early Kamakura Period and one of the greatest masters of classical Japanese poetry. His poems reflect the turbulent times in which he lived and focus not just on sorrow for the ephemerality of things (*awaré*) but also on loneliness (*sabi*) and sadness (*kanashi*). He traveled all over Japan, living as a hermit in the mountains. His most famous work, *Sankashū (Mountain Hut Anthology or Poetry of a Mountain Home)*, contains poems on love, the seasons, and various miscellaneous topics.

**setsubun** Literally means the change of seasons. In today's Japan, a *setsubun* festival is celebrated in spring with roasted beans, which are scattered to the chant of "devils out, fortunes in."

*shakuhachi* A Japanese flute, traditionally made of bamboo, with a soulful and plaintive sound. It was originally a musical instrument favored by Zen Buddhist monks.

**Shigaraki** The location of the Imperial capital for a few months in 745 until a forest fire destroyed the palace.

**The Shinshū Valley** Shinshū refers to the Nagano prefecture, where the 1998 Winter Olympics was held. The region is famous for its natural beauty. The name, Shinshū, derives from the old province designation. The Nagano prefecture adjoins the Niigata prefecture where Myōkō is located. The train ride through Nagano provides Yurie, Shōzō, Fukiko and Shigeru, fabulous views of the Shinshū Valley.

**Shōwa** The designation of Emperor Hirohito's reign, 1926–1989. The early Shōwa was the time of military expansion that led to the Pacific War.

**Toyotomi Hideyoshi** (1536–1598) A loyal supporter of Oda Nobunaga who went on to become the first feudal lord to conquer all of Japan after it had been fragmented by more than a century of civil war. In addition to bringing political unity, establishing a new system of taxation, and defining the samurai as a distinct social class, he was also the first ruler to ban Christianity in Japan. Hideyoshi is regarded as Japan's second "great unifier" followed by the third and final one, Tokugawa Ieyasu (1543–1616).

**The White Hare of Inaba** This refers to the tale of a deceitful hare in *The Record of Ancient Matters* (Kojiki), which talks "sea crocodiles" (sharks) into lining up to form a bridge so the hare can cross the sea. When the hare is about to step off the last shark on to the land, he makes the mistake of ridiculing the shark for its gullibility at which point the shark attacks the hare, ripping off its fur. However, a traveling deity comes to his rescue, and the hare's fur is restored.

# CORNELL EAST ASIA SERIES

CORNELL East Asia Series

www.einaudi.cornell.edu/eastasia/publications

CPSIA information can be obtained
at www.ICGtesting.com
Printed in the USA
LVHW111857181119
637717LV00007B/18/P

9 781933 947600